Soul Eater

'the third of the consistently superb *Chronicles of Ancient Darkness* novels, is meticulously realised'

Amanda Craig, *The Times*

'crackles with atmosphere'   Julia Eccleshare, *Guardian*

'an original and beguiling series. Her characterisation is so complete that . . . her narrative never feels anything other than completely authentic.'   *Publishing News*

'exceptional storytelling abilities . . . utterly relevant and convincing.   *The Bookseller*

'a marvellous book . . . a living, breathing, world of a story, perfectly realised and never missing a beat.'

www.thebookbag.co.uk

'This is a wonderfully imagined adventure.'

Times Educational Supplement

'The relationship between the three protagonists is expertly played . . . Wolf's view of the world, firmly based in real animal behaviour, is entirely convincing . . . a triumph of the imagination.'   *Books for Keeps*

'Strange and thrilling'   *The Book Magazine*

Chronicles
of Ancient
Darkness

Soul Eater

MICHELLE PAVER

Illustrated by Geoff Taylor

Orion
Children's Books

First published in Great Britain in 2006
by Orion Children's Books
This paperback edition published in Great Britain in 2007
by Orion Children's Books
Reissued 2011 by Orion Children's Books
a division of the Orion Publishing Group Ltd
Orion House
5 Upper St Martin's Lane
London WC2H 9EA
An Hachette UK Company

1 3 5 7 9 10 8 6 4 2

A catalogue record for this book is available from the British Library

Printed in Great Britain by Clays Ltd, St Ives plc

ISBN 978 1 84255 114 1

ᛒ

www.orionbooks.co.uk

SOUL EATER

ONE

Torak didn't want it to be an omen.

He didn't want it to be anything more than an owl feather lying in the snow. So he ignored it. That was his first mistake.

Quietly, he went back to the tracks they'd been following since dawn. They looked fresh. He slipped off his mitten and felt them. No ice in the bottom. Yes, fresh.

Turning to Renn, further uphill, he tapped his sleeve and raised his forefinger, then pointed down into the beech wood. *One reindeer, heading south.*

Renn gave a nod, whipped an arrow from her quiver, and nocked it to her bow. Like Torak, she was hard to see in a pale reindeer-hide parka and leggings, with wood-ash smeared on her face to mask her scent. Like him, she was hungry, having eaten nothing since a slip of dried boar meat for daymeal.

Unlike him, she hadn't seen the owl feather.

So don't tell her, he thought.

That was his second mistake.

A few paces below him, Wolf was sniffing at a patch where the reindeer had scraped away the snow to get at the lichen. His ears were pricked, his silver fur fluffed up with excitement. If he sensed Torak's unease, he didn't show it. Another sniff, then he raised his muzzle to catch the scent-laden breeze, and his amber gaze grazed Torak's. *Smells bad.*

Torak tilted his head. *What do you mean?* he asked in wolf talk.

Wolf twitched his whiskers. *Bad muzzle.*

Torak went to examine what he'd found, and spotted a tiny bead of yellow pus on the bare earth. Wolf was telling him that the reindeer was old, its teeth rotten after many winters of munching gritty lichen.

Torak wrinkled his nose in a brief wolf smile. *Thank you, pack-brother.* Then he glanced at Renn, and headed downhill as silently as his beaver-hide boots would allow.

Not silently enough for Wolf, who flicked a reproachful ear as he moved over the snow as soundlessly as smoke.

Together they crept between the sleeping trees. Black oaks and silvery beeches glittered with frost. Here and there, Torak saw the crimson blaze of holly berries; the deep green of a wakeful spruce standing guard over its slumbering sisters. The Forest was hushed. The rivers were frozen. Most of the birds had flown south.

Except for that owl, thought Torak.

He'd known it was an owl's feather as soon as he'd seen its furry upper side, which muffled the sound of flight when the owl was hunting. If it had been the dusky grey of a forest owl, he wouldn't have worried, he'd simply have given it to Renn, who used them to fletch her arrows. But this feather was barred with black and tawny; shadow and

2

flame. That told Torak it belonged to the greatest, the fiercest of owls: the eagle owl. And to find one of those – that was bad.

Wolf's black nose twitched.

Torak was instantly alert.

Through the trees, he glimpsed the reindeer, nibbling beard-moss. He heard the crunch of its hooves, saw its misting breath. Good, they were still downwind. He forgot the feather, and thought of juicy meat and rich marrowfat.

Behind him, the faint creak of Renn's bow. He fitted an arrow to his own, then realized he was blocking her view, and dropped to one knee, since she was the better shot.

The reindeer moved behind a beech tree. They'd have to wait.

As Torak waited, he noticed a spruce, five paces below him. The way it spread its snowladen arms . . . warning him back.

Gripping his bow, he fixed his gaze on the prey.

A gust of wind stirred the beeches around him, and last summer's leaves rustled like dry, dead hands.

He swallowed. It felt as if the Forest were trying to tell him something.

Overhead, a branch shifted, and a flurry of snow hissed down. He glanced up. His heart jerked. An eagle owl. Tufted ears as sharp as spearpoints. Huge orange eyes like twin suns.

With a cry he leapt to his feet.

The reindeer fled.

Wolf raced off in pursuit.

Renn's arrow sped past Torak's hood.

The eagle owl spread its enormous wings and silently flew away.

'What were you *doing?*' shouted Renn furiously. 'Standing up like that? I might have killed you!'

3

Torak didn't reply. He was watching the eagle owl soar into the fierce blue of the noonday sky. But eagle owls, he thought, hunt by night.

Wolf came bounding through the trees and skittered to a halt beside him, shaking off snow and lashing his tail. He hadn't expected to catch the reindeer, but he'd enjoyed the chase.

Sensing Torak's unease, he rubbed against him. Torak knelt, burying his face in the deep, coarse scruff, breathing in Wolf's familiar, sweet-grass scent.

'What's wrong?' said Renn.

Torak raised his head. 'That owl, of course.'

'What owl?"

He blinked. 'But you must have seen it. The eagle owl, it was so close I could have touched it!'

When she still looked blank, he ran back up the hill, and found the feather. 'Here,' he panted, holding it out.

Wolf flattened his ears and growled.

Renn put her hand to her clan-creature feathers.

'What does it mean?' said Torak.

'I don't know, but it's bad. We should get back. Fin-Kedinn will know what to do. And Torak – ' She eyed the feather, 'leave it here.'

As he threw it in the snow, he wished he hadn't picked it up with his bare hand. A fine grey powder dusted his palm. He wiped it off on his parka, but his skin carried a whiff of rottenness that reminded him of the Raven bone-grounds.

Suddenly Wolf gave a grunt, and pricked his ears.

'What's he smelt?' said Renn. She didn't speak wolf talk, but she knew Wolf.

Torak frowned. 'I don't know.' Wolf's tail was high, but he wasn't giving any of the prey signals Torak recognized.

4

Strange prey, Wolf told him, and he realized that Wolf was puzzled, too.

An overwhelming sense of danger swept over Torak. He gave an urgent warning bark. 'Uff!' *Stay away!*

But Wolf was off, racing up the valley in his tireless lope.

'No!' shouted Torak, floundering after him.

'What's the matter?' cried Renn. 'What did he say?'

'"Strange prey",' said Torak.

With growing alarm, he watched Wolf crest the ridge and glance back at them. He looked magnificent: his thick winter pelt a rich blend of grey and black and foxy red, his bushy tail taut with the thrill of the hunt. *Follow me, pack-brother! Strange prey!*

Then he was gone.

They followed as fast as they could, but they were burdened with packs and sleeping-sacks, and the snow was deep, so they had to use their wicker snowshoes, which slowed them even more. When they reached the top, Wolf was nowhere to be seen.

'He'll be waiting for us,' said Renn, trying to be reassuring. She pointed to a thicket of aspen. 'Soon as we get down into that, he'll pounce.'

That made Torak feel a little better. Only yesterday, Wolf had hidden behind a juniper bush, then leapt out and knocked him into a snowdrift, growling and play-biting till Torak was helpless with laughter.

They reached the aspens. Wolf didn't pounce.

Torak uttered two short barks. *Where are you?*

No answer.

His tracks were plain enough, though. Several clans hunted here, and all used dogs, but there was no mistaking Wolf's tracks for a dog's. A dog runs haphazardly, because he knows his master will feed him, whereas a wolf runs with

5

a purpose: he must find prey, or starve. And although Wolf had been with Torak and the Raven Clan for the past seven moons, Torak had never given him food, for fear of blunting his hunting skills.

The afternoon wore on, and still they followed his trail: a straight-line lope, in which the hindpaws trod in the prints of the forepaws. The crunch of their snowshoes and the rasp of their breath echoed through the Forest.

'We're getting quite far north,' said Renn. They were about a daywalk from the Raven camp, which lay to the south-west, by the Widewater river.

Again Torak barked. *Where are you?*

Snow drifted from a tree, pattering onto his hood. The stillness after it settled seemed deeper than before.

As he watched the gleam die on a cluster of holly berries, he sensed that the day was on the turn. Already the brightness was fading from the sky, and shadows were stealing out from under the trees. A chill crept into his heart, because he knew that the descent into darkness had begun.

The clans call this the demon time, because it's in winter, when the great bull Auroch rears high among the stars, that demons escape from the Otherworld, and flit through the Forest, to cause havoc and despair. It only takes one to taint a whole valley; and although the Mages keep watch, they can't trap them all. Demons are hard to see. You never catch more than a glimpse, and you can't be sure what they look like, because they change, the better to slip into sleeping mouths, and possess living bodies. There they crouch in the red darkness, sucking out courage and trust; leaving the seeds of malice and strife.

It was at this moment, at the demon time, that Torak knew the omens had come true. Wolf hadn't howled a reply because he could not. Because something had happened to him.

Nightmare visions flashed through Torak's mind. What if Wolf had tried to bring down an auroch or an elk on his own? He was only twenty moons old. A flying hoof can kill a foolhardy young wolf.

Maybe he'd been caught in a snare. Torak had taught him to avoid them, but what if he'd been careless? He'd be trapped. Unable to howl as the noose tightened round his neck.

The trees creaked. More snow pattered down. Torak put his hands to his lips and howled. *Where – are – you?*

No reply.

Renn gave him a worried smile; but in her dark eyes he saw his own anxiety. 'The sun's going down,' she said.

He swallowed. 'In a while the moon will be up. There'll be enough light to track.'

She gave a doubtful nod.

They'd gone another few paces when she turned aside. 'Torak! Over here!'

Whoever had caught Wolf had done it with the simplest of traps. They'd dug a pit, and hidden it with a flimsy screen of snow-covered branches.

That wouldn't have held him for long, but in the churned-up snow around the pit, Torak found shreds of braided rawhide. 'A net,' he said in disbelief. 'They had a net.'

'But – no spikes in the pit,' said Renn. 'They must have wanted him alive.'

This is a bad dream, thought Torak. I'm going to wake

up, and Wolf is going to come loping through the trees.

That was when he saw the blood. A shocking red spatter in the snow.

'Maybe he bit them,' muttered Renn. 'I hope he did, I hope he bit their hands off!'

Torak picked up a tuft of bloody fur. His fingers shook. He forced himself to read the snow.

Wolf had approached the pitfall warily, his tracks changing from a straight-line lope to a walk, in which front and hind prints showed side-by-side. But he'd approached just the same.

Oh Wolf, said Torak silently. Why weren't you more careful?

Then it struck him that maybe it was his friendship with Wolf that had made him more trusting of people. Maybe this was his fault.

He stared at the trampled trail that led north. Ice was forming in the tracks. Wolf's captors had a head start.

'How many sets of prints?' said Renn, staying well back, as Torak was by far the better tracker.

'Two. The bigger man's prints are deeper when he ran off.'

'So – he was carrying Wolf. But why take him at all? No-one would hurt Wolf. No-one would dare.' It was strict clan law that no harm should be done to any of the hunters in the Forest.

'Torak,' she called, crouching behind a clump of juniper. 'They hid over here. But I can't make out – '

'Don't move!' warned Torak.

'What?'

'There, by your boot!'

She froze. 'What – made *that*?'

He squatted to examine it.

8

His father had taught him tracking, and he thought he knew every print of every creature in the Forest; but these were the strangest he'd ever seen. Very light and small, like a bird's – but not. The hind tracks resembled tiny, crooked, five-clawed hands, but there were no front prints, only two pock-marks: as if the creature had been walking on stumps.

'"Strange prey",' murmured Torak.

Renn met his eyes. 'Bait. They used it as bait.'

He stood up. 'They went north, towards the valley of the Axehandle. Where could they go from there?'

She threw up her hands. 'Anywhere! They could've turned east for Lake Axehead, and kept going all the way to the High Mountains. Or doubled back south, for the Deep Forest. Or west, they could be halfway to the Sea by now –'

Voices, coming their way.

They ducked behind the junipers. Renn readied her bow, and Torak drew his black basalt axe from his belt.

Whoever it was, they were making no attempt at stealth. Torak saw a man and woman, followed by a large dog dragging a sled on which lolled a dead roe buck. A boy of about eight summers plunged eagerly ahead, and with him, a younger dog with a deerhide saddle-pack strapped to his belly.

The young dog caught Wolf's scent on Torak, gave a terrified yelp, and sped back to the boy, who halted. Torak saw the clan-tattoo between his eyebrows: three slender black ovals, like a permanent frown.

Renn breathed out. 'Willow Clan! Maybe they saw something!'

'No!' He pulled her back. 'We don't know if we can trust them!'

She stared at him. 'Torak, these are *Willows*! Of course we

9

can!' Before he could stop her, she was running towards them, both fists over her heart in sign of friendship.

They saw her and broke into smiles. They were returning to their clan in the west, the woman explained. Her face was scarred, like birch canker, marking her as a survivor of last summer's sickness.

'Did you meet anyone?' said Renn. 'We're looking for –'

'"We"?' queried the man.

Torak stood up. 'You've come from the north. Did you see anyone?'

The man's eyes flicked to Torak's clan-tattoos, and his eyebrows rose. 'We don't meet many Wolf Clan these days.' Then to Renn, 'You're young to be hunting so far from your camp.'

Renn bridled. 'We're both thirteen summers old. And we have the Leader's leave –'

'Did you see anyone?' broke in Torak.

'I did,' said the boy.

'Who?' cried Torak. 'Who was it?'

The boy drew back, startled by his intensity. 'I – I'd gone to find Snapper.' He pointed at his dog, who gave a faint wag of his tail. 'He likes chasing squirrels, but he gets lost. Then I saw them. They had a net, it was struggling.'

So he's still alive, thought Torak. He'd been clenching his fists so hard that his nails were digging into his palms.

'What did they look like?' said Renn.

The boy stretched his arm above his head. 'A huge man. And another, big, with bandy legs.'

'What about their clan-tattoos?' said Torak. 'Clan-creature skins? Anything!'

The boy gulped. 'Their hoods were up, I didn't see their faces.'

10

Torak turned to the Willow man. 'Can you take a message to Fin-Kedinn?'

'Whatever it is,' said the man, 'you should tell him yourself. The Leader of the Ravens is wise, he'll know what to do.'

'There's no time,' said Torak. 'Tell him that someone has taken Wolf. Tell him we're going to get him back.'

Two

Night brought a bone-cracking frost that turned the trees white, and the snow-crust brittle underfoot.

It was past middle-night, and Torak was dizzy with tiredness. He forced himself to keep going. The trail of Wolf's captors lay like a snake in the moonlight. North, always north.

With heartstopping suddenness, seven Mages loomed before him. Lean, horned shadows cut across his path. *We will rule the Forest*, they whispered in voices colder than windblown snow. *All tremble before us. We are the Soul-Eaters . . .*

A hand touched his shoulder. He cried out.

'What's wrong?' said Renn.

He blinked. Before him, seven birch trees glittered with frost. 'A dream.'

'About what?' Renn knew something of dreams, because sometimes her own came true.

'Nothing,' said Torak.

She gave a disbelieving snort.

They trudged on, their breath smoking in the freezing air.

Torak wondered if the dream meant something. Could it be – was it possible that the *Soul-Eaters* were behind Wolf's disappearance?

But what would they want with Wolf?

Besides, no trace of them had been found. Since the sickness last summer, Fin-Kedinn had spoken to every clan in the Open Forest, and had sent word to the Deep Forest and the Sea and Mountain clans. Nothing. The Soul-Eaters had gone to ground like a bear in winter.

And yet – Wolf was still gone.

Torak felt as if he were walking in a blizzard of ignorance and fear. Raising his head, he saw the great bull Auroch high in the sky. He felt the malice of its cold red eye, and fought a rising tide of panic. First he'd lost his father. Now Wolf. What if he never saw Wolf again? What if he was already dead?

The trees thinned. Before them glimmered a frozen river, criss-crossed with hare tracks. On its banks, the dead umbels of hemlock reached spiked fingers towards the stars.

A herd of forest horses took fright and clattered off across the ice, then turned to stare. Their manes stood stiff as icicles, and in their moon-bright eyes, Torak glimpsed an echo of his own fear.

In his mind he saw Wolf as he'd looked before he vanished: magnificent and proud. Torak had known him since he was a cub. Most of the time he was simply Wolf: clever, inquisitive, and fiercely loyal. Sometimes he was the guide, with a mysterious certainty in his amber eyes. Always he was a pack-brother.

'What I don't understand,' said Renn, cutting across his thoughts, 'is why take Wolf at all?'

'Maybe it's a trap. Maybe they want me, not Wolf.'

'I thought of that, too.' Her voice dropped. 'Maybe – whoever took Wolf is after you because,' she hesitated. 'Because you're a spirit walker, and they want your power.'

He flinched. He hated being a spirit walker. And he hated that she'd said it out loud. It felt like a scab being torn off.

'But if they *were* after you,' she persisted, 'why not just take you? Two big strong men, we'd have been no match for them. So why – '

'I don't *know!*' snapped Torak. 'Why do you keep on? What good does it do?'

Renn stared at him.

'I don't *know* why they took him!' he cried. 'I don't *care* if it's a trap! I just want him back!'

After that, they didn't speak at all. The forest horses had trampled the trail, and for a while it was lost, which at least gave them an excuse to split up. When Torak found it again, it had changed. For the worse.

'They've made a sled,' he said. 'No dogs to pull it, but even without, they'll be able to go much faster down-hill.'

Renn glanced at the sky. 'It's clouding over. We should build a shelter. Get some rest.'

'You can if you want, I'm going on.'

She put her hands on her hips. 'On your own?'

'If I have to.'

'Torak. He's my friend too.'

'He's not just my *friend*,' he retorted, 'he's my pack-brother!'

He could see that he'd hurt her.

'And how,' she said between her teeth, 'is blundering about missing things going to help him?'

He glared at her. 'I haven't missed anything!'

'Oh no? A few paces back, one of them turned aside to follow those otter tracks – '

'What otter tracks?'

'*That's what I mean!* You're exhausted! So am I!'

He knew she was right. But he didn't want to admit it.

In silence they found a storm-toppled spruce, and dug out the snow at its base to make a makeshift sleeping-space. They roofed it with spruce boughs, and used their snowshoes as shovels to pack on a thick layer of snow. Finally they dragged more boughs inside, and laid their reindeer-hide sleeping-sacks on top. When they'd finished, they were trembling with fatigue.

From his tinder pouch Torak took his strike-fire and some shredded birch bark, and woke up a fire. The only deadwood he'd found was spruce, so it smoked and spat. He was too exhausted to care.

Renn wrinkled her nose at the smoke, but didn't remark on it. She took a coil of elk-blood sausage from her pack and cut it in three, then put one piece on the roof of the shelter for the clan guardian, and tossed Torak another. Tucking her own share in her food pouch, she picked up her axe and waterskin. 'I'm going to the river. There's more meat in my pack, but *don't* touch the dried lingonberries.'

'Why not?'

'Because,' she said crossly, 'I'm saving them for Wolf!'

After she'd gone, Torak forced himself to eat. Then he crawled out of the shelter and made an offering.

15

Cutting a lock of his long dark hair, he tied it round a branch of the fallen spruce. Then he put his hand on his clan-creature skin: the tattered scrap of wolf fur sewn to the shoulder of his parka. 'Forest,' he said, 'hear me. I ask by each of my three souls – by my name-soul, my clan-soul, and my world-soul – I ask that you watch over Wolf, and keep him from harm.'

It was only when he'd finished that he noticed a lock of dark-red hair tied to another branch. Renn had made her own offering.

That made him feel guilty. He shouldn't have shouted at her.

Back in the shelter, he pulled off his boots, wriggled into his sleeping-sack, and lay watching the fire, smelling the mustiness of reindeer fur and the bitter tang of spruce.

Far away, an owl hooted. Not the familiar 'bvoo-bvoo' of a grey Forest owl, but the deep 'oo-hu, oo-hu, oo-hu' of an eagle owl.

Torak shivered.

He heard Renn's footsteps crunching through the snow, and called to her. 'You made an offering. So did I.'

When she didn't answer, he added, 'Sorry I snapped at you. It's just . . . Well. Sorry.'

Still no answer.

He heard her crunch towards the shelter – then circle *behind* it.

He sat up. 'Renn?'

The footsteps stopped.

His heart began to pound. It wasn't Renn.

As quietly as he could, he wriggled out of his sleeping-sack, pulled on his boots, and reached for his axe.

The footsteps came closer. Whoever it was stood only an arm's length away, separated by a flimsy wall of spruce.

For a moment there was silence. Then – very loud in the stillness – Torak heard wet, bubbling breath.

His skin prickled. He thought of the victims of last summer's sickness. The murderous light in their eyes; the slime catching in their throats . . .

He thought of Renn, alone by the river. He crawled towards the mouth of the shelter.

Clouds covered the moon, and the night was black. He caught a whiff of carrion. Heard again that bubbling breath.

'Who are you?' he called into the dark.

The breathing stopped. The stillness was absolute. The stillness of something waiting in the dark.

Torak scrambled out of the shelter and stood, clutching his axe with both hands. Smoke stung his eyes, but for a heartbeat he glimpsed a huge form melting into the shadows.

A cry rang out behind him – and he spun round to see Renn staggering through the trees. 'By the river!' she panted. 'It stank, it was horrible!'

'It was here,' he told her. 'It came close. I heard it.'

Back to back, they stared into the Forest. Whatever it was, it had gone, leaving only a whiff of carrion and a dread memory of bubbling breath.

Sleep was now impossible. They fed the fire, then sat up together, waiting for dawn.

'What do you think it was?' said Renn.

Torak shook his head. 'But I know one thing. If we'd had Wolf with us, it would never have got that close.'

They stared into the fire. With Wolf gone, they hadn't only lost a friend. They'd lost someone to keep them from harm.

THREE

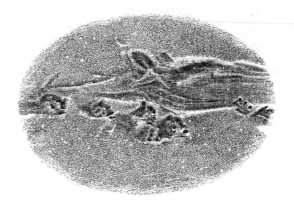

They heard nothing more that night, but in the morning they found tracks. Huge, man-like – but without any toes.

The tracks were nothing like the booted feet of the men who'd captured Wolf, but they headed the same way.

'Now there are three of them,' said Renn.

Torak didn't reply. They had no choice but to follow.

The sky was heavy with snow, and the Forest was full of shadows. With each step they dreaded seeing a figure lurching towards them. Demon? Soul-Eater? Or one of the Hidden People, whose backs are hollow as rotten trees . . .

The wind picked up. Torak watched the snow drifting across the tracks, and thought of Wolf. 'If this wind keeps up, the trail won't last much longer.'

Renn craned her neck to follow the flight of a raven. 'If only we could see what it can.'

Torak gave the bird a thoughtful stare.

They began their descent into the next valley through a silent birchwood. 'Look,' said Torak. 'Your otter's been here before us.' He pointed to a line of webbed prints and a long, smooth furrow in the snow. The otter had bounded down the slope, then slid on its belly, as otters love to do.

Renn smiled, and for a moment, they pictured a happy otter taking a snow-slide.

But the otter had never reached the frozen lake at the bottom of the hill. In the lee of a boulder twenty paces above the shore, Torak found a scattering of fish-scales and a shred of rawhide. 'They trapped it,' he said.

'*Why?*' said Renn. 'An otter's a hunter . . .'

Torak shook his head. It didn't make sense.

Suddenly, Renn tensed. '*Hide!*' she whispered, pulling him behind the boulder.

Through the trees, Torak caught movement on the lake. A creature snuffling, swaying, searching for something. It was very tall, with a shaggy pelt and a trailing, matted mane. Torak smelt carrion, and heard a wet bubbling of breath. Then it turned, and he saw a filthy one-eyed face as rough as bark. He gasped.

'It *can't* be!' whispered Renn.

They stared at one another. 'The Walker!'

The autumn before last, their paths had crossed with this terrifying, mad old man. They'd been lucky to escape with their lives.

'What's he doing so far from his valley?' breathed Torak as they shrank further behind the boulder.

'And how do we get past without being seen?' hissed Renn.

'Maybe – we don't.'

'*What?*'

'Maybe he saw who took Wolf!'

'Have you forgotten,' she said in a furious whisper, 'that he nearly killed us? That he threw my quiver in the stream, and threatened to *snap my bow*?' It was unclear which she considered worse: threatening them, or her bow.

'But he didn't, did he?' countered Torak. 'He let us go. And Renn. What if he saw something?'

'So you're just going to ask him, are you? Torak, he's *mad*! Whatever he says, we couldn't believe him!'

Torak opened his mouth to reply . . .

. . . and around them the snow exploded.

'*Give it back*!' roared the Walker, brandishing his green slate knife. 'She took his fire! She *tricked* him! The Walker wants it *back*!'

'The Walker has tricked the tricksters!' he bellowed, pinning them against the boulder. 'Now they must give it *back*!'

His mane was a tangle of beard-moss, his scrawny limbs as gnarled as roots. Loops of green slime swung like creepers from his shattered nose and his rotten, toothless mouth.

He'd left his cape on the ice to fool them, and was naked but for a hide loincloth stiff with filth, foot-bindings of mouldy wovenbark, and a rancid jerkin made from the skin of a red deer, which he'd ripped from the carcass, and then forgotten to clean. The tail, legs and hooves swung wildly as he waved his knife in their faces.

'She *took* it!' he shouted, spattering them with slime. 'She *tricked* him!'

'I – I didn't take anything,' stammered Renn, hiding her bow behind her back.

'Don't you remember us?' said Torak. 'We never stole anything!'

'Not she!' snarled the Walker. '*She!*' Quick as an eel, a grimy hand flashed out and seized Torak by the hair. His head was twisted back, his weapons tossed in the snow. 'The sideways one,' breathed the Walker, blasting him with an eye-watering stink. '*Her* fault that Narik is lost!'

'But *we* didn't do anything!' pleaded Renn. 'Let him go!'

'Axe!' spat the Walker, fixing her with his bloodshot eye. 'Knife! Arrows! Bow! In the snow, quick quick quick!'

Renn did as she was told.

The Walker pressed his knife against Torak's windpipe, cutting off his air. 'She gives him her fire,' he snarled, 'or he slits the wolf boy's throat! And he'll do it, oh yes!'

Black spots darted before Torak's eyes. 'Renn – ' he gasped, 'strike-fire – '

'Take it!' cried Renn, fumbling at her tinder pouch.

Deftly the old man caught the stone, and threw Torak to the ground. 'The Walker has *fire!*' he exulted. 'Beautiful *fire! Now* he can find Narik!'

That would have been the time to run. Torak knew it, and so did Renn. Neither of them moved.

'The sideways one,' panted Torak, rubbing his throat.

'Who is she?' said Renn.

The old man turned on her, and she dodged a flailing hoof. 'But the Walker is *mad,*' he sneered, 'so who can believe him?'

Seizing one of the deer legs, he sucked at the festering hide. 'The sideways one,' he mumbled. 'Not alone, oh no, oh no. Twisted legs and flying thoughts.' He hawked and spat, narrowly missing Torak. 'Big as as a tree, crushing the little creatures, the slitherers and scurriers too weak to fight back.' A spasm of pain twisted his ruined features. 'Worst,' he whispered, 'the Masked One. Cruellest of the cruel.'

Renn threw Torak a horrified look.

'But the Walker follows,' hissed the old man. 'Oh yes, oh yes, he listens in the cold!'

'Where are they going?' said Torak. 'Is Wolf still alive?'

'The Walker knows nothing of *wolves*! They seek the empty lands! The Far North!' He clawed the crusted tattoos on his throat. 'First you're cold, then you're not. Then you're hot, then you die.' His eye lit on Torak and he grinned. *'They are going to open the Door!'*

Torak swallowed. 'What door? Where?'

The old man cried out, and beat his forehead with his fists. *'But where is Narik?* They keep him and keep him, and Narik is *lost!'* He turned and blundered off towards the lake.

Torak and Renn exchanged glances – then snatched up their weapons, and raced after him.

Out on the ice, the Walker retrieved his shaggy cape, and resumed his snuffling search. One of his foot-bindings came loose and blew away.

Torak brought it back – and recoiled. The old man's foot was a blackened, frostbitten, toeless stump. 'What happened?'

The Walker shrugged. 'What always happens if you lose your fire. It bit his toes, so he cut them off.'

'What bit them?' said Renn.

'It! It!' He beat at the wind with his fists.

Suddenly his face changed, and for a moment Torak saw the man he'd been before the accident that had taken his eye and his wits. 'It can never rest, the wind, or it would cease to be. That's why it's angry. That's why it bit the Walker's toes.' He cackled. 'Ach, they tasted *bad*! Not even the Walker could eat them! He had to spit them out and

22

leave them for the foxes!'

Torak's gorge rose. Renn clamped both hands over her mouth.

'So now the Walker keeps falling over. But still he searches for his Narik.' He ground his knuckle into his empty eye socket.

Narik, thought Torak. The mouse who'd been the old man's beloved companion. 'Did they take Narik too?' he said, determined to keep him talking.

The Walker shook his head sadly. 'Sometimes Narik goes away. He always comes back, in new fur. But not this time.'

'New fur?' queried Renn.

'Yes, yes!' the Walker said tetchily. 'Lemming. Vole. Mouse. Doesn't matter what, still the same Narik!'

'Oh,' said Renn. 'I see. New fur.'

'Only this time,' said the Walker, his mouth ragged with grief, 'Narik never came back!' He staggered away across the ice, howling for his fosterling.

Almost with reluctance, they left him, and made their way into the woods on the other side of the lake.

'He'll be better now that he has fire,' Renn said quietly.

'No he won't,' said Torak. 'Not without Narik.'

She sighed. 'Narik's dead. An owl probably ate him for nightmeal.'

'Another Narik, then.'

'He'll find one.' She tried to smile. 'One with new fur.'

'How? How can he track a mouse, with only one eye?'

'Come on. We'd better get going.'

Torak hesitated. The sun was getting low, the trail fast disappearing beneath windblown snow. And yet – he felt for the Walker. This stinking, angry, mad old man had found one spark of warmth in his life: his Narik, his fosterling. Now that spark was lost.

Before Renn could protest, Torak dropped his gear and ran back to the lake.

The old man didn't glance up, and Torak didn't speak to him. He put down his head and began looking for signs.

It didn't take long to find a lemming burrow. He spotted weasel tracks, and followed them to a clump of willow on the shore. There he crouched, listening for the small scratchings that told him where the lemmings were burrowing.

With its many knife-prick entrance holes, their winter shelter reminded him of an extremely small badger's sett. Peering at the snow, he found one hole rimed with tiny ice-arrows of frozen breath. That meant the occupant was at home.

He marked the spot with two crossed willow twigs, and ran to fetch the old man. 'Walker,' he said gently.

The old man swung round.

'Narik. He's over there.'

The Walker squinted at him. Then he followed Torak back to the crossed sticks.

As Torak watched, he knelt and began clearing the snow with feather-light gentleness, stooping to blow away the final flakes.

There, curled in its burrow on a neat bed of dried grass, lay a lemming about the size of Torak's palm: a soft, heaving ball of black and orange fur.

'Narik,' breathed the Walker.

The lemming woke with a start, sprang to its feet, and gave a fearsome hiss to frighten off the intruder.

The Walker grinned, and extended his big, grimy hand.

The lemming fluffed up its fur and hissed again.

The Walker didn't move.

The lemming sat down and scratched its ear vigorously with its hind paw. Then it waddled meekly onto the leathery palm, curled up, and went back to sleep.

Torak left them without a word.

Back on the shore, Renn handed him his weapons and pack. 'That was a good thing you did,' she said.

Torak shrugged. Then he grinned. 'Narik's grown a bit since we saw him. Now he's a lemming.'

She laughed.

They hadn't gone far when they heard the crunch of snow, and the Walker's angry muttering.

'Oh, *no!*' said Renn.

'But I *helped* him!' said Torak.

'*Giving?*' roared the Walker. In one hand he brandished his knife; the other clutched Narik to his chest. 'Do they think they can just *give*, and wander off? Do they think the Walker has *forgotten* the old ways?'

'Walker, we're sorry,' said Torak, 'but – '

'A gift looks for a *return! That* is the way of things! Now the Walker must give *back!*'

Torak and Renn wondered what was coming next.

'Black ice,' wheezed the Walker, 'white bears, red blood! They seek the eye of the viper!'

Torak caught his breath. 'What's that?'

'Oh, he'll find out,' said the Walker, 'the foxes will tell him.'

Suddenly he bent like a wind-snapped tree, and the look he gave Torak was wise, and fraught with such pain that it pierced Torak's souls. 'To enter the eye,' he breathed, 'is to enter the dark! You may find your way out again, Wolf boy; but once you've gone in, you'll never be whole. It'll keep a part of you down there. Down in the dark.'

FOUR

The Dark crept over the Forest, but Wolf didn't even notice. He was caught in a Dark of his own: of rage and pain and fear.

The tip of his tail ached where it had been stamped on in the fight, and his forepaw hurt from the bite of the big cold claw. He couldn't move at all, because he was squashed onto a strange, sliding tree, which the taillesses were dragging over the Bright Soft Cold. He couldn't even move to lick his wounds. He was flattened beneath a tangled deerhide that was pressing down on him hard. It was unlike any hide he'd ever encountered. It had lots of holes in it, but somehow it managed to be stronger than an auroch's leg-bone.

The growls inside him were fighting to get free, but *more* hide was tangled round his muzzle, so he couldn't let them out. That was the worst of it: that he couldn't growl or snap or howl. It hurt to hear Tall Tailless howling for him, and not be able to howl back.

26

Sharp and small inside his head, Wolf saw Tall Tailless and the female, running after him. They were coming. Wolf knew that as surely as he knew his own scent. Tall Tailless was his pack-brother, and a wolf never abandons his pack-brother.

But would Tall Tailless be able to *find* him? He was clever, but he wasn't at all good at finding, because he wasn't a normal wolf. Oh, he smelt of wolf (as well as lots of other things besides), and he talked like a wolf, even if he couldn't hit the highest yips. And he had the light silver eyes, and the spirit of a wolf. But he moved slowly on his hind legs, and was very bad at catching scents.

Suddenly the sliding tree shuddered to a halt. Wolf heard the harsh bark of tailless talk; then the crunch of the Bright Soft Cold as they began to dig their Den.

Behind him on the tree, the otter woke up, and started a piteous mewing. On and on she went, until Wolf wanted to shake her in his jaws to make her stop.

He heard a tailless approaching from behind. He was too squashed to turn and see, but he caught the smell of fish. The otter stopped mewing, and started making scrunching noises. That was a relief.

A few lopes ahead, the Bright Beast-that-Bites-Hot snarled into life. Wolf watched the taillesses gather round it.

They bewildered him. Until now, he'd thought he knew their kind. At least, he knew the pack that Tall Tailless ran with, the pack that smelt of ravens. But these – these were bad.

Why had they attacked him? Taillesses are not the enemies of wolves. The enemies of wolves are bears and lynxes, who sneak into Dens to kill wolf cubs. Not taillesses.

Of course, Wolf had met some bad ones before now; and even the good ones sometimes growled and waved their forepaws when he got too close to their meat. But to attack without warning? No true wolf would do this.

Straining ears and eyes and nose, Wolf watched the bad pack crouch round the Bright Beast. He swivelled his squashed ears to listen, and sniffed, trying to sort their tangled smells.

The slender female smelt of fresh leaves, but her tongue was black and pointed as a viper's, and her sideways smile was as empty as a carcass pecked by ravens.

The other female, the big one with the twisted hind legs, was clever, but Wolf sensed that she was unsure of her place in the pack, and unsure of herself. On her overpelt lay a patch of stinking fur. It was the fur of the strange prey which had lured him into the trap.

The last in the pack was a huge male with long, pale fur on his head and muzzle, and breath that reeked of spruce-blood. He was the worst, because he liked to hurt. He'd laughed as he'd trodden on Wolf's tail, and cut his pad with the big cold claw.

It was this pale-pelt who now rose on his hind legs and came towards Wolf.

Wolf gave a muffled growl.

Pale-Pelt bared his teeth, and brought his big claw close to Wolf's muzzle.

Wolf flinched.

Pale-Pelt laughed, lapping up Wolf's fear.

But what was this? Wolf's muzzle was *free*! Pale-Pelt had cut his muzzle free!

Wolf seized his chance and lunged – but the deerhide held him back, and he couldn't get his jaws around it to bite through it.

Here came the other one, the big twisted female with the stinking fur.

Pale-Pelt jabbed at Wolf again, but Stinkfur growled at him. Pale-Pelt stared hard, to let her know who was leader, then stalked off.

Crouching beside Wolf, Stinkfur pushed a scrap of elk meat through a hole in the deerhide.

Wolf ignored it. Did these taillesses think he was stupid? Did they think he was a dog, who would take meat from anyone?

Stinkfur threw up her forepaws, and walked away.

Now the viper-tongued female left the Bright Beast, and came over to Wolf. Squatting on her haunches, she talked softly to him.

Without wanting to, he listened. Her voice reminded him a little of the female who was Tall Tailless' pack-sister, whose talk was sharp and clever, but gentle underneath. As he listened to the viper-tongued female, he smelt that she was not afraid of him; that she was *curious*.

He flinched as she reached her forepaw towards him, but she didn't touch him. Instead he felt coldness on his flank. His whiskers quivered. She was smearing his pelt with elk blood!

The smell was so muzzle-wateringly delicious that it drove all else from his head. After much struggling, he twisted round and started to lick.

He knew it was odd that the female had done this, and something in her voice made him wary, but he couldn't stop. The blood-lust had him in its grip, and already the strength of the elk was loping through his limbs. He went on licking.

Wolf was becoming *very* tired. There was black fog in his head, and he could hardly keep his eyes open. He felt as if a great stone were crushing him.

Through the fog he heard the soft, sly laugh of the viper-tongued female, and knew that she had tricked him. The elk blood she'd fed him had been bad, and now he was sinking into the Dark.

The fog grew thicker. Fear seized him in its jaws. With the last twitch of his mind, he sent a silent howl to Tall Tailless.

FIVE

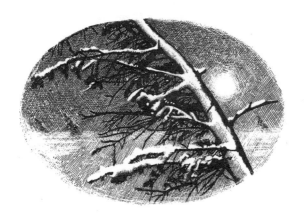

'A re you scared?' said Torak.
'Yes,' said Renn.
'Me too.'

They stood at the edge of the Forest, beneath the last –
the very last – tree. Before them stretched an empty white
land beneath an endless sky. Here and there, a stunted
spruce withstood the onslaught of the wind, but that was
the only sign of life.

They were now as far north as any of the Forest clans had
been, except for Fin-Kedinn, who as a young man had
journeyed into the frozen lands. In the two days since
meeting the Walker, they'd crossed three valleys, and
glimpsed the distant glare of the ice river at the roots of
the High Mountains – where, the winter before last, the
Ravens had camped, and Torak had gone in search of
the Mountain of the World Spirit.

They stood with the north wind in their faces, staring at

the trail of Wolf's captors: a brutal knife-slash through the snow.

'I don't think we can do this on our own,' said Renn. 'We need help. We need Fin-Kedinn.'

'We can't go back now,' said Torak. 'There isn't time.'

She was silent. Since their encounter with the Walker, she'd been unusually subdued. Torak wondered if she too had been thinking about what the old man had said. *Twisted legs and flying thoughts . . . the sideways one . . . Big as a tree . . .* It had raised echoes in his mind: echoes of Fin-Kedinn, speaking of the Soul-Eaters. But he couldn't bring himself to mention them out loud. It couldn't be them. Why would they have taken Wolf, and not him?

So in the end, all he said was, 'Wolf needs us.'

Renn didn't reply.

Suddenly, he was gripped by the fear that she would turn round and leave him to carry on alone. The fear was so intense that it left him breathless.

He watched her brush the snow off her bow, and settle it on her shoulder. He braced himself for the worst.

'You're right,' she said abruptly. 'Let's go.' Without a backwards glance, she left the shelter of the trees.

He followed her into the empty lands.

As soon as they left the Forest, the sky pressed upon them, and the north wind scoured their faces with snow.

In the Forest, Torak had always been *aware* of the wind – as a hunter he had to be – but apart from storms, it was never a threat, because the power of the Forest kept it in check. Out here, nothing could hold it back. It was stronger, colder, wilder: a malevolent, unseen spirit, come to harass these puny intruders.

The trees became smaller and sparser, until they shrank to an occasional knee-high willow or birch. Then – nothing. No green thing. No hunters. No prey. Only snow.

Torak turned, and was shocked to see that the Forest had dwindled to a charcoal line on the horizon.

'It's the edge of the world,' said Renn, raising her voice above the wind. 'How far does it go on? What if we fall off?'

'If the edge of the world is out there,' he said, 'Wolf's captors will fall off first.'

To his surprise, she gave him a sharp-toothed grin.

The day wore on. The snow was firmer than in the Forest, so they didn't need their snowshoes, but the north wind blew it into low, hard ridges, which kept tripping them up.

Then, abruptly, the wind dropped. Now it was blowing softly from the north-east.

At first, it was a relief. Then Torak realized what was happening. He couldn't see his feet. He was standing in a river of snow. Around his calves, long, ghostly streams were flowing like smoke, obliterating the trail.

'The wind's covering the tracks!' he shouted. 'It knows we need them, so it's destroying them!'

Renn ran ahead to see if the trail was any clearer. She threw up her arms. 'Nothing! Not even you could find it!' As she ran back to him, he saw her expression, and his heart sank. He knew what she was going to say, because he'd been thinking it himself. 'Torak, this is wrong! We can't survive out here. We've got to go back.'

'But people do live here, don't they?' he insisted. 'The Ice clans? The Narwals, the Ptarmigans, the White Foxes? Isn't that what Fin-Kedinn said?'

'They know how. We don't.'

33

'But – we have dried meat and firewood. And we can find our way by the North Star. We can bind our eyes with wovenbark to keep out the glare, and – and there is prey out here. Willow grouse. Hare. That's how Fin-Kedinn managed.'

'And when the wood runs out?' said Renn.

'There's that willow he talked about, the kind that only grows ankle high, but you can still – '

'Can you *see* any willow out here? It's buried under snow!'

Her face was pale, and he knew that behind what she said lay a deeper dread. The clans whispered stories about the Far North. Blizzards so powerful they carried you screaming into the sky. Great white bears that were bigger and fiercer than any in the Forest. Snowfalls that buried you alive. And Renn knew about snowfalls. When she was seven summers old, her father had ventured onto the ice river east of Lake Axehead. He'd never come back.

'We can't do this on our own,' she said.

Torak rubbed a hand over his face. 'I agree. At least, for tonight. We should make camp.'

She looked relieved. 'There's a hill over there. We can dig a snow cave.'

He nodded. 'And then I'm going to do what it takes to find the trail.'

'What do you mean?' she said uneasily.

He hesitated. 'I'm going to spirit walk.'

Her mouth fell open. 'Torak. No.'

'Listen to me. Ever since we saw that raven, I've been thinking about it. I can spirit walk in a bird, I'm sure of it. I can go high in the sky, see far into the distance. I can see the trail!'

Renn folded her arms. 'Birds can fly. You can't.'

'I wouldn't have to,' he said. 'My souls would be inside

the bird's body – say it's a raven – I'd see what the raven sees, I'd feel what it feels. But I'd still be me.'

She walked in a circle, then faced him. 'Saeunn says you're not ready. She's the Clan Mage. She knows.'

'I did it last summer – '

'By accident! And it hurt! And you couldn't control it! Torak, your souls could get stuck inside, you might never get out! Then what happens to your body? The one that's lying on the snow, with only its world-soul keeping it alive?' Her voice was shrill, and there were two spots of colour on her cheeks. 'You'd die, that's what! I'd have to sit in the snow and watch you die!'

He couldn't argue with her, because everything she said was true. So he said, 'I need you to help me find a raven. I need you to help me loosen my souls. Are you going to help me or not?'

SIX

' First,' said Torak, 'we've got to attract a raven.'

He waited for Renn to comment, but she was hacking out the snow cave, making it plain that she wanted no part of this.

'I spotted a nest at the edge of the Forest,' he said.

Her axe struck, and chunks of snow flew.

'It's a daywalk away,' he added, 'but they may come foraging out here. And I brought bait.'

She stopped in mid-swing. 'What bait?'

From his pack he pulled a squirrel. 'I shot it yesterday. While I was filling the waterskins.'

'You planned this,' she said accusingly.

He glanced at the squirrel. 'Um. I thought I might need it.'

Renn resumed her attack on the snow, hitting harder than before.

Torak laid the squirrel twenty paces from where the

shelter would be – so that, once his name-soul and clan-soul had left his body, they wouldn't have far to go, to get into a raven. Well, that was the hope. He didn't know if it would work, because he didn't know anything about spirit walking. Nobody did.

Drawing his knife, he slit the squirrel's belly, and stood back to study the effect.

'That's not going to work,' called Renn.

'At least I'm trying,' he retorted.

She wiped her forehead on the back of her mitten. 'No, I mean, you're doing it wrong. Ravens are too clever to be fooled by that, they'll think it's a trap.'

'Oh,' said Torak. 'Yes, of course.'

'Make it like a wolf kill. That's what they look for, a kill.'

He nodded, and set to work.

Renn forgot about disapproving, and helped. They used her shoulder-bone scraper to chop up the squirrel's liver, mixed it with snow, and spattered this around to resemble blood. Then Torak cut off a hind leg and tossed it to one side, 'so that it'll look as if a wolf trotted away to eat in peace.'

Renn studied the "kill". 'Better,' she said.

The shadows were turning blue, and the wind had gone into the north, leaving a light breeze wafting snowflakes over the carcass. Torak said, 'The ravens will be flying home to roost. If they come, it won't be before first light.'

Renn shivered. 'It doesn't seem possible, but according to Fin-Kedinn, there are white foxes out here, so we'll have to stay awake to keep them off the carcass.'

'And we can't have a fire, or the ravens will smell it.'

Renn bit her lip. 'You do know that you can't have anything to eat? To go into a trance, you need to fast.'

Torak had forgotten that. 'What about you?'

37

'I'll eat when you're not looking. Then I'll make the paste for loosening your souls.'

'Do you have what you need?'

She patted her medicine pouch. 'I gathered a few things in the Forest.'

His lip curled. 'You planned this.'

She didn't smile back. 'I had a feeling I might need to.'

The sky was darkening, and a few stars were glinting. 'First light,' murmured Torak.

It was going to be a long night.

Torak huddled in his sleeping-sack, and tried to stop shivering. He'd been shivering all night, and he was sick of it. Peering throught the slit in the snow cave, he saw the half-eaten moon shining bright. Dawn wasn't far off. The sky was clear – and ravenless.

In one mitten, he clutched a scrap of birch bark containing Renn's soul-loosening paste: a mixture of deer fat and herbs which he was to smear on his face and hands when she gave the word. In the other, he held a small rawhide pouch fastened with sinew. What Renn called a "smoke-potion" smouldered inside. He'd asked what was in it, but she'd said it was better not to know, and he hadn't insisted. Renn had a talent for Magecraft, which for reasons she never went into, she tried to ignore. Practising it put her in a bad mood.

His belly rumbled, and she nudged him with her elbow. He refrained from nudging back. He was so hungry that if a raven didn't come soon, he'd eat the squirrel.

A thin scarlet line had just appeared in the east, when a black shape slid across the stars.

Again, Renn nudged him.

'I see it,' he whispered.

A smaller shape glided after the first: the raven's mate. Wingtip to wingtip, they wheeled over the kill – then flew away.

Some time later, they came back for another pass, flying a little lower. At the fifth pass, they flew so low that Torak heard their wingbeats: a strong, rhythmic 'wsh wsh wsh'.

He watched their heads turn from side to side, scanning the land below. He was glad he'd buried the gear beside the snow cave, which Renn had made into a featureless mound, with only a slit for air and observation. Ravens are the cleverest of birds, with senses sharp as grass.

Yellow fire spilled over the edge of the world, but still the ravens circled, spying out the "kill".

Suddenly, one folded its wings and dropped out of the sky.

Torak slipped off both mittens, to be ready.

Silently, the raven lit down on the snow. Its breath smoked as it stared at the shelter. Its wingspan was wider than Torak's outstretched arms, and it was utterly black. Eyes, feathers, legs, claws; like the First Raven herself, who woke the sun from its winter sleep, and was burnt black for her pains.

This raven, however, was more interested in the squirrel, which it approached at a cautious, stiff-legged walk.

'Now?' mouthed Torak.

Renn shook her head.

The raven gave the carcass a tentative peck. Then it hopped high in the air, landed – and flew off. It was checking that the squirrel was really dead.

When the carcass didn't move, both ravens flew down. Warily they walked towards it.

'*Now!*' mouthed Renn.

Torak smeared on the paste. It had a sour green smell that stung his eyes and made his skin prickle. Then he unfastened the pouch and sucked in the smoke-potion.

'Swallow it all,' Renn whispered in his ear, 'and *don't* cough!'

The smoke was bitter, the urge to cough almost overwhelming. He felt Renn's breath on his cheek. 'May the guardian fly with you!'

Feeling sick, he watched the big raven tug at the frozen innards. A sharp pain tugged at his own insides – and for a moment he felt a surge of panic. *No, no I don't want to . . .*

. . . and suddenly he was tugging at the squirrel's guts with his powerful beak, slicing off delicious tatters of frozen meat.

Swiftly he filled his throat-pouch, then pecked out an eye. Enjoying its slippery smoothness on his tongue, he hitched his wings and hopped onto the wind, and it bore him up, up into the light.

The wind was freezing and unimaginably strong, and his heart swelled with joy as it carried him higher. He loved the coldness rippling under his feathers, and the smell of ice in his nostrils, and the wind's wild laughter screaming through him. He loved the ease with which he rode upwards, twisting and turning with the merest tilt of his wings – he loved the power of his beautiful black wings!

A slippery 'wsh' – and his mate was at his side. As she folded her wings and rolled off the wind, she gave a graceful twitch of her tail, asking him to sky-dance. He slid after her and locked his icy talons in hers, and together they drew in their wings and dived.

Through the streaming cold they sped, through a blur of black feathers and splintered sun, exulting in their speed as the great white world rushed up to meet them.

Of one accord they unlocked their talons, and he snapped open his wings and struck the wind, and now he was soaring again, soaring towards the sun.

With his raven eyes he could see for ever. Far to the east, the tiny speck of a white fox trotted through the snow. To the south lay the dark rim of the Forest. To the west he saw the wrinkled ice of the frozen Sea. To the north: two figures in the snow.

With a cry he sped off in pursuit.

'Cark?' called his startled mate.

He left her, and the white land flowed beneath him.

As he drew nearer, he swooped, and in an instant that burned into his mind for ever, he took in every detail.

He saw two figures straining to haul a sled. He saw Wolf strapped to the sled, unable to move. As he strained to catch the least twitch of a paw, the smallest flicker which would tell him that Wolf was still alive, he saw the bigger man pause, pull his parka over his head, and loosen the neck of his jerkin to let out the heat. He saw the blue-black tattoo on the man's breastbone: the three-pronged fork for snaring souls. The mark of the Soul-Eater.

From his raven beak came a horrified croak. *The Soul-Eaters. The Soul-Eaters have taken Wolf.*

He flew higher, and the sun blinded him. The wind gave a furious twist, and threw him off.

His courage cracked like thin ice.

The wind screamed in triumph.

A sharp pain pierced his insides – and he was Torak again, and he was falling out of the sky.

41

SEVEN

Torak woke in the blue gloom of the snow cave with the wind's angry laughter ringing in his ears.

Renn was kneeling over him, looking scared. 'Oh, thank the Spirit! I've been trying to wake you all morning!'

'All – morning?' he mumbled. He felt like a piece of rawhide that had been pummelled and scraped.

'It's midday,' said Renn. 'What *happened*? You were breathing in snow, and your eyes had turned up inside your head. It was horrible!'

'Fell,' he said. With each breath, pain stabbed his ribs, and every joint screamed. But his limbs still obeyed him; so no broken bones. 'Do I – bruises?'

She shook her head. 'But souls get bruises too.'

He lay still, staring at a droplet about to fall from the roof. *The Soul-Eaters had taken Wolf.*

'Did you see the trail?' said Renn.

He swallowed. 'North. They headed north.'

She sensed that he was keeping something back. 'As soon as you went into a trance,' she said, 'the wind blew up. It sounded angry.'

'I was flying. I wasn't supposed to.'

The drop landed on Renn's parka and lost itself in the fur: like a soul falling to earth.

'You shouldn't have done it,' she said.

Raising himself painfully on one elbow, Torak peered through the slit. The wind was blowing softly, but the ghostly snow-fingers were back.

'I don't think it's finished with us,' said Renn.

Torak lay down again, and drew his sleeping-sack under his chin. *The Soul-Eaters had taken Wolf.*

He couldn't bring himself to tell her – at least, not yet. If she knew, she might insist that they went back to the Forest for help. She might leave.

He shut his eyes.

'But who *are* the Soul-Eaters?' he'd once asked Fin-Kedinn. 'I don't even know their names.'

'Few do,' Fin-Kedinn had replied, 'and they don't speak of them.'

'Do *you* know?' Torak had demanded. 'Why won't you tell me? It's my destiny to fight them!'

'In time,' was all the Raven Leader would say.

Torak couldn't make him out. Fin-Kedinn had taken him in when his father was killed; and long ago, Fa and he had been good friends. But he rarely spoke of the past, and only ever revealed what he thought Torak needed to know.

So now all Torak knew was that the Soul-Eaters had plotted to rule the Forest. Then their power had been shattered in a great fire, and they'd gone into hiding. Two of the seven had since met their deaths – and thus, under clan law, couldn't be mentioned by name for the next five winters. One of them had been Torak's father.

Deep in his chest, Torak felt the familiar ache. Fa had joined them to do *good*; that was what Fin-Kedinn had told him. That was what Torak clung to. When they'd become evil, Fa had tried to leave, and they'd turned on him. For thirteen winters he'd been a hunted man, raising his son apart from the clans, never mentioning his past. Then, the autumn before last, the Soul-Eaters had sent the demon bear that killed him.

Now they'd taken Wolf.

But why Wolf, and not Torak? Why, why, why?

He fell asleep to the moaning of the wind.

Someone was shaking him, calling his name.

'Wha?' he mumbled into a mouthful of reindeer fur.

'Torak, wake *up*!' cried Renn. 'We can't get out!'

Awkwardly he sat up as far as the low roof would allow. Beside him, Renn was struggling not to panic.

The slit in the shelter was gone. In its place was a wall of hard-packed snow.

'I've been digging,' she said, 'but I can't break through. We're snowed in. It must have drifted in the night.'

Torak noticed that she said "it drifted", rather than "the wind did this, burying us while we slept".

'Where's my axe?' he said.

Her face worked. 'Outside. They're both outside, where we left them. With the rest of our gear.'

He took that in silence.

'I should have brought them inside,' said Renn.

'There wasn't room.'

'I should've made room. I should've thought.'

'You were looking after me, it's not your fault. We've got knives. We'll dig ourselves out.'

He drew his knife. Fin-Kedinn had made it for him last summer: a slender blade of reindeer shinbone, slotted with leaf-thin flakes of flint. It wasn't meant for digging in wind-hardened snow. Fa's blue slate knife would have been better; but Fin-Kedinn had warned Torak to keep it hidden in his pack. He regretted that now.

'Let's get started,' he said, trying to sound calm.

It was frightening, digging a tunnel with no idea how far they had to go. There was nowhere to put the hacked-out snow except behind them, so no matter how hard they worked, they remained trapped in the same cramped hole. The dripping walls pressed in, and their breath sounded panicky and loud.

After they'd moved about an arm's length, Torak put down his knife. 'This isn't working.'

Renn met his eyes. Her own were huge. 'You're right. A drift like this, it could go on for . . . We might never break out.'

He saw the effort she was making to stay calm, and guessed that she was thinking of her father. He said, 'We'll dig upwards instead.'

She nodded.

It was much harder, digging up. Chunks of snow fell in their eyes and down their necks, and their arms ached savagely. They worked back-to-back, trampling the snow beneath their boots. Torak clenched his jaw so hard that it hurt.

Gradually, the snow above him began to turn a warmer blue. 'Renn! Look!'

She'd seen it.

Feverishly they hammered with their knife-hilts. Suddenly it cracked like an eggshell – and they were through.

45

The glare was blinding, the cold burned their lungs. They stood with upturned faces, gaping like baby birds; then scrambled out and collapsed on the snow. A faint breeze chilled their sweat-soaked hair. The wind was gone.

Torak gave a shaky laugh.

Renn lay on her back, staring into nothingness.

Sitting up, Torak saw that their shelter had been buried beneath a long, sloping hill that hadn't existed the night before. 'Our gear,' he said. 'Where's our gear?'

Renn scrambled to her feet.

Apart from their knives and sleeping-sacks, everything they needed: bows, arrows, axes, food, firewood, waterskins, cooking-skins – *everything* – lay buried somewhere under the snow.

With exaggerated calm, Torak brushed off his leggings. 'We know where the shelter is. We'll dig a trench around it. Sooner or later, we'll find it.' But he knew as well as Renn that if they didn't find their gear before dark, they might not survive another night. This one mistake could be the death of them.

After so much effort digging *up*, it was a bitter blow to have to dig *down*; and as soon as they started, the wind returned, gusting snow about them in blinding, choking clouds.

Torak was beginning to lose hope when Renn gave a shout. 'My *bow*! I've found my bow!'

It was late afternoon by the time they found everything, and by then they were exhausted, drenched in sweat, and ragingly thirsty.

'We should dig in,' panted Renn, 'wait till dawn.'

'We can't,' said Torak. The need to go after Wolf was overwhelming.

'I know,' said Renn. 'I know.'

After eating a little dried meat and draining their waterskins, they tied strips of wovenbark over their eyes to keep out the glare – uncomfortably aware that they should have done this earlier – and set off, heading north by the sun, which was getting low.

Torak's head was throbbing, and he was stumbling with fatigue. He had an uneasy sense that they shouldn't be doing this – that they weren't thinking straight – but he was too tired to sort it out.

The wide plains gave way to steep hills and dizzying blue ridges of windblown snow. In places, these formed precarious overhangs that reared above them like monstrous, frozen waves. And always the north wind blew. Angry. Vengeful. Unappeased.

In the shifting snow, it became hard to judge distances. It didn't feel as if they'd walked far, but when Torak crested a hill and glanced back, he saw that the Forest was gone.

A savage gust punched him in the back and he fell, rolling all the way to the bottom.

Renn floundered after him. 'Should've used your axe to break your fall,' she mumbled as she helped him up. His axe had been stuck in his belt; there'd been no time to pull it out.

From then on, they walked with axes in hand.

They'd been tired when they set off, but now every step was an effort. Thirst returned, but they'd run out of wood for melting snow. They knew they shouldn't try eating it, but they did anyway. It blistered their mouths and gave them cramps. And still the wind blew: pelting their faces with tiny darts of ice until their cheeks cracked and their lips bled.

We don't belong here, Torak thought hazily. Everything's wrong. Nothing's as it should be.

Once, they heard the gobbling of willow grouse, startlingly close, but when they searched, the birds had vanished.

Another time, Renn saw a man in the distance; but when they reached him, he turned out to be a pile of rocks, with fluttering strands of hair and hide tied to his arms. Who had made him, and why?

Their sweat-soaked jerkins chilled them to the bone, and snow froze to their outer clothes, making them heavy and stiff. Their faces burned, then turned numb. Something the Walker had said surfaced in Torak's memory. *First you're cold, then you're not . . .* What came after that?

Renn was tugging his sleeve, pointing at the sky.

He swayed.

Purple-grey clouds were boiling up from the north.

'Storm!' she shouted. 'Keep together!' Already she was dragging a coil of rawhide rope from her pack. They'd been in a snowstorm before, and knew how easy it is to get separated.

'We've got to dig in!' she yelled as she struggled to tie one end of the frozen rope about her waist.

'Where?' he shouted, tying his end clumsily about him. The land had turned flat again.

'Down!' she shouted. 'Dig down! A snow hole!' She stamped up and down, feeling for firmer snow – and suddenly it broke beneath her, and she was gone.

'*Renn!*' shouted Torak.

The rope at his waist snapped taut, yanking him forwards. He threw himself back, dug in his heels. He couldn't see anything – just churning white chaos – but he could feel her weight on the rope, dragging him down.

Struggling, slipping, he slid inexorably forwards – and toppled . . . a few paces onto a pile of broken snow.

The snow heaved. It was Renn.

They sat up, badly shaken, but unhurt.

Craning his neck, Torak saw that they'd gone through an overhang. Without knowing it, they'd been walking on a fragile crust over thin air.

For Renn, this was the last arrow that brings down the auroch. 'I can't go on!' she cried, striking the snow with her fists.

'We have to dig in!' yelled Torak. But he knew it was hopeless. He barely had the strength to lift his axe.

With one final, wild burst of pride, he staggered to his feet and shouted at the wind. 'All right, you've won! I'm *sorry*! I'll never dare fly again! I'm *sorry*!'

The wind screamed. Terrible shapes flew at him through the snow. A twisting column whirled towards him, then blew apart . . .

Suddenly the snow seemed *not* to blow apart, but to draw *together*: thousands of tiny flakes meeting, coalescing, to form a creature unlike any he'd ever seen.

It had the staring eyes of an owl, and it flew towards him through the whiteness. Before it surged a silent pack of dogs.

Torak was too exhausted to be frightened. It's over, he thought numbly. I'm sorry, Wolf. Sorry I couldn't save you.

He sank to his knees as the owl-eyed creature bore down upon him.

EIGHT

The owl-eyed creature bellowed a command, and the dogs slewed to a halt. Whipping out a long curved knife, it started hacking a snow hole with astonishing speed. In moments, Torak and Renn were seized and thrown in, and a wall of snow was yanked down on top.

After the fury of the wind, the rasp of breath was loud in the gloom. Torak heard the creak of frozen hide; caught a rancid smell that was oddly familiar. He couldn't see Renn – the creature had leapt in between them – but he was too wretched to care.

To his surprise he found that he wasn't cold any more, he was hot. First you're cold, he thought, then you're not; then you're hot, and then you die.

He found that he liked death. It was beautifully warm and soft, like the pelt of a great white reindeer. He wanted to draw it over his head and snuggle down deep . . .

Someone was shaking him. He moaned. Owl eyes stared

into his, jolting him back from his lovely warm death.

He made out a ruff of snow-caked fur framing a round face purpled by frost. Ice crusted the brows and the short black beard. The flat nose had a dark band tattooed across it, which Torak didn't recognise. He just wanted to go back to death.

The creature snarled. Then it plucked out its eyes.

Torak saw that the owl eyes were thin bone discs on a strap. The man's real eyes were permanently slitted against the glare. Swiftly he yanked back the sleeve of his parka, took out a flint knife, and cut a vein in his stocky brown forearm. 'Drink!' he barked, pressing the wound to Torak's lips.

Salty-sweet heat filled Torak's mouth. He coughed, and swallowed blood. Strength and warmth coursed through him: real warmth, not the false heat of frostbite. With it came pain. His face was on fire. Burning needles pierced his joints.

In the gloom, he heard Renn. 'Leave me 'lone! Want to sleep!'

Now the man was chewing something. He spat a grey lump into his hand, and pushed it between Torak's teeth. 'Eat!'

It was rancid and oily, and he recognized the taste. Seal blubber. It was wonderful.

The man smeared more chewed blubber over Torak's face. At first it hurt – the man's palm was rough as granite – but amazingly soon, the pain faded to a bearable throb.

'Who are you?' mumbled Torak.

'Later,' grunted the man, 'when the wind's anger is spent.'

'How long will that be?' said Renn.

'One sleep, many, who knows? Now no more talk!'

Torak is twelve summers old, and Fa has been dead for nearly half a moon.

Torak has just killed his first roe buck, and to keep Wolf quiet while he's skinning it, he's given him the hooves; but the cub has tired of playing with them, and trots over to poke his muzzle into what Torak is doing.

Torak is washing deer gut in the stream. Wolf grabs the other end in his jaws and tugs. Torak tugs back. Wolf goes down on his forepaws and lashes his tail. A game!

Torak bites back a smile. 'No, it isn't a game.' Wolf persists. Torak tells him firmly in wolf talk to *let go* – and the cub obeys so promptly that Torak topples backwards into the water. Wolf pounces, and now they're splashing about, and Torak is laughing. His father is still dead; but he's no longer alone. He's found a pack-brother.

When he gets to his feet, the stream is frozen. Winter has the Forest in its grip. Wolf is full-grown, and trotting off through the glittering trees – trotting off with Fa.

'Come back!' shouts Torak, but the north wind carries his voice away. The wind is so strong that he can hardly stand, but it has no power to touch Wolf or Fa. Not a breath stirs Fa's long black hair; not a whisper ruffles Wolf's silver fur.

'*Come back!*' he cries. They can't hear him. Helplessly he watches them walk away through the trees.

He woke with a start. His chest ached with loss. His cheeks were stiff with frozen tears.

He was huddled in his sleeping-sack. His clothes were damp inside, and he was so cold that he was beyond shivering. Sitting up, he saw that he was no longer in the snowhole, but in a domed shelter made of blocks of snow.

On a flat stone lamp, a sludge of pounded blubber burned with a low orange flame. Above it hung a seal's bladder of melting ice. From the stillness outside, the storm had blown over. The strange man had gone.

'I had a *terrible* dream,' muttered Renn beside him. Her face was scabbed and blistered; there were dark smudges under her eyes.

'Me too,' he said. His face felt sore, and it hurt to talk. 'I dreamt that Wolf – '

The strange man crawled into the shelter. He was short and stocky, and his seal-hide parka made him look even stockier. Throwing back his hood, he revealed a flat face framed by short dark hair, with a fringe across his brow. His eyes were black slits of distrust. 'You're from the Far South,' he said accusingly.

'Who are you?' countered Torak.

'Inuktiluk. White Fox Clan. I was sent to find you.'

'Why?' said Renn.

The White Fox man tossed his head. 'Look at you! Your clothes are sopping wet! Don't you know it's not snow that kills, but wet? Here. Get out of them and into these.' He tossed them two hide bundles.

They were so cold that they didn't argue. Their limbs were as useless as sticks, and it took forever to get undressed. The bundles turned out to be sleeping-sacks of silvery seal fur, lined with an inner sack of soft birdskin, with the feathers on the inside. These were so warm that they felt better almost at once; but Torak realized with alarm that the White Fox man had disappeared, taking their clothes with him. Now they were completely in his power.

'He left us some food,' said Renn. She sniffed a strip of frozen seal meat.

Still in his sleeping-sack, Torak shuffled to the wall, and peered through a crack.

What he'd taken for the roof of the snow hole in which they'd sheltered overnight was in fact a large sled, which now stood upright. Its runners were the jawbones of a whale, its cross-bars the antlers of reindeer. A tangled harness disappeared into a smooth white hillock, and into five other hillocks a little further off. From the middle of each came a thin whisp of steam.

Inuktiluk whistled, and the hillocks erupted into six large dogs. They yawned and wagged their tails as they shook off the snow, and Inuktiluk batted away their noses as he untangled their harnesses and checked their paws for ice cuts.

With her thumbnail, Renn prised a shred of meat from between her teeth. 'The Walker said "the foxes" would tell us how to find the Eye of the Viper. Maybe he meant the White Foxes.'

Torak had thought of that too. 'But can we risk it?' he said. He wanted to trust Inuktiluk, but he'd learned the hard way that a man can do kind things, and still hide a rotten heart.

'You're right,' said Renn. 'We won't tell him anything. Not till we know we can trust him.'

Inuktiluk was turning their clothes inside out, and laying them on the sled. They froze in moments, and he beat the ice from them with the flat of his snow-knife. Then he fetched meat and tossed it to the dogs.

Five were full-grown, but the sixth was a puppy of about five moons. Its pads hadn't yet toughened, and it wore rawhide paw-boots; it squealed with pleasure as Inuktiluk flipped it onto its back, to check that they were securely fastened.

Torak thought of Wolf, and the dream returned to darken his spirit. He told Renn about it. Then he said, 'Wolf was with Fa, and Fa is dead. So was it Fa's spirit who sent the dream? Was he telling me that Wolf is dead too?'

'Or maybe,' said Renn, 'it wasn't your father's spirit that dreamed to you, but Wolf's. Maybe he's asking you for help.'

'But he must know that we're coming for him.'

She looked unhappy.

He was wondering if now was the time to tell her about the Soul-Eaters, when Inuktiluk returned.

'Get dressed,' he said sternly.

Their clothes were drier, but uncomfortably cold. It didn't help that Inuktiluk watched them with evident disapproval. 'You're much too thin. To survive on the ice, you need to be fat! Don't you even know that? Everything in the north is fat! Seals, bears, people!' Then he asked them what names they carried.

They exchanged glances. Renn told him their names and clans.

Inuktiluk seemed startled to learn that Torak was Wolf Clan. 'That makes it worse,' he murmured.

'What do you mean?' said Torak.

Inuktiluk frowned. 'We won't talk of it here.'

'I think we must,' said Torak. 'You saved our lives, and we're grateful. But please. Tell us why you were looking for us.'

The White Fox man hesitated. 'I'll tell you this. Three sleeps ago, one of our elders went into a trance to watch the night fires in the sky, and the spirits of the Dead sent her a vision. A girl with red willow hair, like the World Spirit in winter; and a boy with wolf eyes.' He paused. 'The boy was about to do a great evil. That's why I had to find you. To stop you bringing evil to the people of the ice.'

'I haven't done anything wrong,' Torak said hotly.

Inuktiluk ignored that. 'Who *are* you? What are you doing here, where you don't belong?'

When they didn't answer, he rolled up the sleeping-sacks and headed out. 'Rub more blubber on your faces, and bring the lamp. We're leaving.'

'Where?' said Torak and Renn together.

'Our camp.'

'Why?' said Renn. 'What are you going to do to us?'

Inuktiluk looked offended. 'We're not going to harm you, that's not our way! We'll just give you better gear, and send you home.'

'You can't make us go back,' said Torak.

To his surprise, Inuktiluk burst out laughing. 'Of course I can! I've got all your gear strapped to my sled!'

After that, they had no choice but to follow him outside.

He'd already put on his owl-eyed visor, and now he tossed them both a pair. Then he snatched up a supple hide whip fully twenty paces long, and at once the dogs began howling and lashing their tails, eager to be off.

'Why is the sled pointing west?' said Renn uneasily.

'That's where our camp is,' said Inuktiluk. 'On the sea ice, where the seals are.'

'West?' cried Torak. 'But we've got to go *north*!'

Inuktiluk turned on him. 'North? Two children who know nothing of the ways of the ice? You'd be dead before the next sleep! Now get on the sled!'

NINE

The north wind howled over the white hills, and blasted the hunched spruce trees on the plains. It whistled through the northern reaches of the Forest, and whipped up the snow on the banks of the Axehandle, where the Raven Clan had pitched camp. It would have woken Fin-Kedinn — except that he was already awake. Since the Willows had given him Torak's message, he'd barely slept.

Someone has taken Wolf. We're going to get him back.

'But to rush off without thinking,' said the Raven Leader. With a stick he stabbed the fire that glowed at the entrance to his shelter. 'Why didn't he come back and seek help?'

'Why didn't the girl?' said Saeunn in her raven's croak. Without blinking, she met his look of pure blue anger. She was the only member of the clan who dared brave his displeasure.

They sat in silence, while above them the wind did its best to waken the Forest. The Raven Mage tented her robe over her bony knees, and stretched her shrunken claws to the fire.

Fin-Kedinn gave it another stab – and a dog, who'd been thinking about trying to slip inside, put back his ears and slunk off to find another shelter.

'I didn't think he'd be so reckless,' said Fin-Kedinn. 'To head for the Far North . . . '

'How do you know he has?' said Saeunn.

He hesitated. 'A Ptarmigan hunting party saw them in the distance. They told me this morning.'

Thoughtfully, Saeunn stroked her spiral amulet with a fingernail as ridged and yellow as horn. 'You want to go in search of them. You want to find your brother's child and bring her back.'

The Raven Leader rubbed a hand over his dark-red beard. 'I can't risk the safety of the clan by leading them into the Far North.'

Saeunn studied him with the icy dispassion of one who has never felt affection for any living creature. 'And yet you want to.'

'I've just said that I can't,' he replied. He threw away the stick, suppressing a wince. The wind had woken the old wound in his thigh.

'Then have done with it,' said Saeunn, shrugging her shoulders like a raven hitching its wings. 'The girl has shown herself to be wilful and stubborn, I can do no more with her. As for the boy, he has allowed his – *feelings*' – her lipless mouth puckered – 'to get in the way.'

'He's thirteen summers old,' said Fin-Kedinn.

'He has a destiny,' the Mage said coldly. 'His life is not his own, he may not risk it for a *friend*! He doesn't understand that, but he will. When he fails to find the wolf, he'll return, and you can punish them both.'

Fin-Kedinn stared into the embers. 'I was going to foster him,' he said. 'I should have told him. Maybe it would have made a difference. Maybe – he would have asked me for help.'

Saeunn spat into the fire. 'Why trouble yourself? Let him go! Let him go and seek his wolf!'

TEN

Wolf is in the other Now that he goes to in his sleeps. He can lope faster than the fastest deer, and bring down an auroch on his own; and *yet*, when he wakes up, he's just as hungry as if he hadn't killed at all.

This time, he is a cub again. He's cold and wet, and his mother and father and pack-brothers are lying still and Not-Breath in the mud. The Fast Wet did this. It came roaring through while Wolf was exploring on the rise.

He puts up his muzzle and howls.

On the other side of the Fast Wet, a wolf is coming, coming to rescue him!

Wolf bursts into a frenzied welcome. Then his welcome turns to puzzlement. This is such a strange wolf. Its scent is that of a half-grown male, but it smells of other creatures too, it walks on its hind legs, *and it has no tail!*

And yet – it has the light, bright eyes of a wolf; and something in its spirit calls to his. He has found a new pack-brother. A pack-brother who will never abandon him . . .

Wolf woke with a snap.

He was back on the sliding tree, squashed beneath the hated deerhide, jolting over the Bright Soft Cold. He longed for that other Now, in which he was a cub again, being rescued by Tall Tailless.

His head ached, and he'd been sick in his sleep, but he couldn't move to lick himself clean. His wounded pad hurt. His trodden-on tail hurt more.

Stinkfur came and pushed in another piece of meat – which Wolf ignored. On and on they dragged him, while the Light sank, and the Bright Soft Cold came drifting down from the Up.

After a while, Wolf smelt that they'd entered the range of a pack of stranger wolves. That meant danger.

The big pale-pelted male went off on his own, and hope leapt in Wolf's heart. Maybe Pale-Pelt would be foolish enough to attack the stranger wolves, and they would defend themselves, and he would be killed!

Much later, Pale-Pelt returned – unharmed. He was smiling his terrible smile, and carrying a small deerhide Den which wriggled and snarled. Wolf smelt the rank fury of a wolverine. A wolverine? What did this mean?

But he couldn't hold onto that for long, because he was getting tired again, sliding down into sleep.

A great owl hooted – and he woke. Without knowing why, his fur prickled with dread.

The owl fell silent. That was worse.

Wolf was now fully awake. While he'd slept, the Dark had come, and the sliding tree had stopped. The bad taillesses were some paces away, crouching round the Bright Beast-that-Bites-Hot. Wolf sensed that they were waiting for something. Something bad.

Around him the strange white land lay windless and still. He smelt a hare nibbling willow buds many lopes away. He heard the tiny scratchings of lemmings in their Dens, and the hiss of the Bright Soft Cold falling, falling.

Then through the Dark he heard a tailless approaching. His claws twitched with eagerness. Could it be Tall Tailless, come to rescue him?

His hope was swiftly torn to pieces. It wasn't his pack-brother. It was a female whom Wolf hadn't smelt before. He knew that she was part of the bad pack, for he saw the others rise on their hind legs to wait for her. He felt their dread as she came gliding through the hissing whiteness.

She was tall and very thin, and the pale fur of her head hung about her like worms. Her voice was as the rattle of dry bones, and her smell was of Not-Breath.

The others greeted her quietly in tailless talk; but although they hid it, Wolf smelt their fear. Even Pale-Pelt was afraid. So was Wolf.

Now she turned, and came towards him.

He cowered. His very spirit shrank from hers.

She came closer. He wanted to look away, but he couldn't. There was something terribly wrong with her face. It was blank as stone, and it didn't move at all, not even a twitch of her muzzle when she spoke. And her eyes were not eyes, but holes.

Wolf growled and tried to pull away, but the deerhide held him fast.

Now she was leaning over him, and her Not-Breath smell was dragging him down into a black fog of loneliness and loss.

Slowly she brought one forepaw close to his muzzle. She was holding something – he couldn't see what – but he caught the scent of that which has lain long in the deep of the earth. Through her pale flesh he glimpsed a grey light, and he knew, with the strange certainty that came to him sometimes, that what she held bit as fiercely as the Bright Beast-that-Bites-Hot. Except that it bit *cold*.

His growl became a terrified whimper. He shut his eyes and tried to think of Tall Tailless coming for him through the Bright Soft Cold: coming to rescue him, just as he'd done when Wolf was a cub.

ELEVEN

Inuktiluk's sled hurtled west, carrying Torak and Renn the wrong way. The only sounds were the panting of dogs and the scrape of runners on crusted snow; and an occasional gasp from Renn as they banked on a slope, and leaned in hard to avoid toppling over.

'You can't watch us all the time,' Torak told Inuktiluk when they'd stopped to rest by a wide, frozen lake. 'Sooner or later, we'll get away.'

'Where would you go?' retorted Inuktiluk. 'You'd never make it north, you'd never get round the ice river.'

They stared at him. 'What ice river?'

'It's about a sleep from here. No-one in the Ice clans has crossed it and lived.'

Torak set his teeth. 'We've crossed an ice river before.'

Inuktiluk snorted. 'Not one like this.'

'Then we'll go around it,' said Renn.

Inuktiluk threw up his hands. Whistling to his lead dog,

he started across the lake. 'We cross on foot,' he told them. 'Walk behind me, and do exactly as I say!'

Burning with frustration, they followed – and were soon absorbed in the difficult task of simply staying upright.

'Keep to the white ice,' called Inuktiluk.

'What's wrong with the grey ice?' said Renn, eyeing a patch to her right.

'That's new ice. Very dangerous! If you ever have to cross it, stay apart – and *keep moving*.'

Torak and Renn glanced at each other, and widened the gap between them.

Even the white ice was wind-polished to a treacherous slipperiness, and they slowed to an anxious shuffle. Inuktiluk's boots seemed to grip the ice, allowing him to stride ahead, and the dogs' sharp claws proved best of all; but the puppy slithered about in his seal-hide boots, reminding Torak painfully of Wolf. As a cub, he'd been forever tripping over his paws.

'How deep is the lake?' asked Renn.

Inuktiluk laughed. 'It doesn't matter! The cold will kill you before you can shout for help!'

It was a relief to reach the shore and climb onto solid snow. While Inuktiluk checked the dogs' paws, Torak drew Renn aside. 'There's more cover up ahead,' he whispered, 'we might be able to get away!'

'And go where?' she replied. 'How do we get round the ice river? How do we find the Eye of the Viper? Face it, Torak, we need him!'

The land became harder to cross, with jagged ridges and swooping declines. To help the dogs, they jumped off and ran up the slopes, leaping back on the sled as it sped downhill, while Inuktiluk slowed it by digging in the tines of a reindeer-antler brake.

The cold sapped their strength, but the White Fox man was tireless. Clearly he loved his strange, icy land, and he seemed troubled that they knew so little about it. He insisted that they drink often, even when they weren't thirsty, and he made them carry their waterskins *inside* their parkas, to stop them freezing. He also made them ration the amount of blubber they ate or smeared on their faces. 'You'll need it for melting ice,' he said. 'Remember, you only have as much water as you have blubber for melting ice!'

Seeing their puzzled expressions, he sighed. 'If you're to survive, you need to do as we do. Follow the ways of the creatures of the ice. The willow grouse burrows a shelter in the snow. We do too. The eider duck lines her nest with her feathers. We do the same with our sleeping-sacks. We eat our meat raw, like the ice bear. We borrow the strength and endurance of reindeer and seal, by making our clothes from their hides. This is the way of the ice.' He squinted at the sky. 'Above all, we pay heed to the wind, which rules our lives.'

As if in answer, it began blowing from the north. Torak felt its icy touch on his face, and knew that it was not appeased.

Inuktiluk must have guessed his thoughts, because he pointed to the far shore of the lake, where one of the stone men stood. 'We build those to honour it. Sooner or later, you'll have to make an offering.'

Torak worried about that. At the bottom of his pack lay Fa's blue slate knife, and in his medicine pouch, his mother's medicine horn. He couldn't imagine parting with either.

Around noon, they came to an eerie land where giant slabs of ice tilted crazily. From deep within came hollow groans and echoing cracks. The dogs flattened their ears, and Inuktiluk gripped an eagle-claw amulet sewn to his parka.

'This is the shore ice,' he said in a low voice, 'where land ice and sea ice fight for mastery. We must get through quickly.'

Renn craned her neck at a jagged spike looming overhead. 'It feels as if there are demons here.'

The White Fox looked at her sharply. 'This is one of the places where Sea demons get close to the skin of our world. They're restless. Trying to get out.'

'Can they?' said Torak.

'Sometimes one slips through a crack.'

'It's the same in the Forest,' said Renn. 'The Mages keep watch, but a few demons always escape.'

Inuktiluk nodded. 'This winter it's been worse than most. In the Dark Time, when the sun was dead, a demon sent a great island of ice surging inland. It crushed a Walrus Clan shelter, killing everyone inside. A little later, another demon sent a sickness that took the child of a woman of my clan. Then her older boy went onto the ice. We searched, but we never found him.' He paused. 'This is why we must send you south. You bring great evil.'

'We didn't bring it,' said Torak.

'We followed it,' said Renn.

'Tell me what you mean,' urged the White Fox.

They stayed silent. Torak felt bad, as he was growing to like Inuktiluk.

They pressed on through the broken mountains of ice. At last the shore ice gave way to flatter, crinkled ice. To Torak's surprise, Inuktiluk squared his shoulders and breathed deeply. 'Ah! Sea ice! *Much* better!'

Torak didn't share his ease. The ice before him seemed to be *bending*. Bewildered, he watched it gently rising and falling, like the hide of some enormous creature.

'Yes,' said Inuktiluk, 'it bends with the breath of the Sea Mother. Soon, in the Moon of Roaring Rivers, the thaw will begin, and this place will become deadly. Great cracks – tide cracks, we call them – appear beneath your feet, and swallow you up. But for now, it's a good place to hunt.'

'To hunt what?' said Torak. 'Back at the lake I saw hare tracks, but there's nothing here.'

For the first time, Inuktiluk looked at him with approval. 'So you noticed those? I hadn't thought a Forest boy would.' He pointed straight down. 'This prey is *under* the ice. We do as the ice bear. We hunt seal.'

Renn shivered. 'Do ice bears eat people?'

'The Great Wanderer eats anything,' said Inuktiluk, sticking the antler in the ice to tether the dogs. 'But he prefers seal. He's the best hunter there is. He can smell a seal through an arm's length of ice.'

'Why have you stopped?' said Torak.

'I'm going hunting,' said the White Fox.

'But – you can't! We can't stop to hunt!'

'Well what are you going to eat?' replied Inuktiluk. 'We need more blubber, and meat for the dogs!'

That shamed Torak into silence; but inside, he burned with impatience. It was six days since Wolf had been taken.

Inuktiluk unhitched his lead dog, and slowly paced the ice. Soon the dog found what it sought. 'A seal's breathing-hole,' Inuktiluk said quietly. It was tiny: a low molehill with a hole in the top about half a thumb wide, its edges grooved, where the seal had gnawed to keep it open.

From the sled, Inuktiluk took a piece of reindeer hide and laid it with the furry side on the ice, downwind of the hole. 'To muffle the sound of my boots, like the ice bear's furry pads.' He laid a swan's feather across the hole. 'Just before the seal surfaces, it breathes out – and the feather moves. That's when I've got to act fast. The seal only takes a few gulps of air before it's gone again.'

He motioned them back to the shelter of the sled. 'I must stand and wait, like the ice bear, but in those clothes you'd freeze. Stay out of the wind, and *stay still!* The slightest tremor will warn the seals.' He took up position, standing motionless, with his harpoon raised.

As Torak crouched behind the sled, he began to unpick the knots that fastened his pack to the runners.

'What are you doing?' whispered Renn.

'Getting out of here,' he said. 'Are you coming?'

She started untying her pack.

They were behind Inuktiluk, so they were able to shoulder their packs and sleeping-sacks without being seen; but as they rose, he turned his head. He didn't move or speak. He just looked.

Defiantly, Torak stared back. But he didn't stir. This man had opened a vein to save them. He was a hunter, like them. And they were about to spoil his hunt.

'We can't do this,' breathed Renn.

'I know,' replied Torak.

Slowly, they unhitched their packs.

Inuktiluk turned back to the breathing-hole.

Suddenly the feather twitched.

With the speed of a striking heron, Inuktiluk thrust in the harpoon. The harpoon head came off the shaft, and stuck like a toggle under the seal's hide. With one hand Inuktiluk hauled on the rope tied to the head, and with the other he used the shaft of the disarmed harpoon to enlarge the breathing-hole.

Dropping their packs, Torak and Renn ran to help. One tremendous pull – and the seal was out, and dead of a blow to the head before it hit the ice.

'Thanks!' panted Inuktiluk.

They helped him haul the streaming silver carcass away from the hole.

The dogs were in a frenzy to get at it, but Inuktiluk silenced them with a word. Easing the harpoon head from the wound, he stitched it shut with a slender bone that he called a "wound plug", so as not to waste blood. Then he rolled the seal onto its back, and tilted its snout into the hole. 'To send its souls down to the Sea Mother, to be born again.' Taking off his mitten, he stroked the pale, spotted belly. 'Thank you, my friend. May the Sea Mother give you a fine new body!'

'We do the same thing in the Forest,' said Renn.

Inuktiluk smiled. Slitting the seal at just the right place, he slipped in his hand and brought out the steaming, dark-red liver.

Behind them a bark rang out, and they saw a small white fox sitting on the ice. It was shorter and fatter than the red Forest foxes, and it was watching Inuktiluk with inquisitive golden-brown eyes.

He grinned. 'The guardian wants his share!' He threw it a piece, and the fox caught it neatly, and downed it in a gulp. Inuktiluk handed chunks of liver to Torak and Renn. It was firm and sweet, and slid down easily. The White Fox man tossed the lungs to the dogs, but Torak noticed that they only sniffed them, and seemed too restless to eat.

'We were lucky,' said Inuktiluk through a mouthful of liver. 'Sometimes I wait a whole day for a seal to come.' He raised an eyebrow. 'I wonder if you'd have the patience to wait that long.'

Torak thought for a moment. 'I want to tell you something.' He paused. Renn nodded. 'We came north to find our friend,' he went on. 'Please. You have to let us go.'

Inuktiluk sighed. 'I know now that you mean well. But you must understand, I can't do this.'

'Why not?' said Renn.

70

On the other side of the sled, the dogs were whining and tugging at their tethers.

Torak went to see what was troubling them.

'What is it?' said Renn.

He didn't reply. He was trying to make out the dogs' talk. Compared to wolf talk, it was much simpler, like the speech of puppies. 'They can smell something,' he said, 'but the wind's gusting, so they're not sure where it is.'

'What is it they smell?' said Renn, reaching for her bow.

Inuktiluk's jaw dropped. 'Do you – does he *understand* them?'

Torak never got the chance to reply. A ridge of ice to his left suddenly rose – and became a great white bear.

TWELVE

The ice bear raised its head on its long neck, and tasted Torak's scent.

With an effortless surge, it reared on its hind legs. It was taller than a tall man standing on the shoulders of another, and each paw was twice the size of Torak's head. One swat would snap his spine like a willow twig.

Swinging its head from side to side, it slitted its hard black eyes, and snuffed the air. It saw Torak standing alone on the ice; Renn and Inuktiluk moving to take cover behind the sled. It smelt the bloody snow beyond them, and the half-butchered carcass of the seal. It heard the dogs howling and straining at their tether in their foolish lust to attack. It took in everything with the unhurried ease of a creature who has never known fear. The power of winter was in its limbs, the savagery of the wind in its claws. It was invincible.

The blood roared in Torak's ears. The sled was ten paces

in front of him. It could have been a hundred.

In silence the ice bear dropped to all fours, and a ripple ran through its heavy, yellow-white pelt.

'Don't run,' Inuktiluk told Torak quietly. 'Walk. Towards us. Sideways. Don't show it your back.'

Out of the corner of his eye, Torak saw Renn nocking an arrow to her bow; Inuktiluk gripping a harpoon in either hand.

Don't run.

But his legs ached to run. He was back in the Forest, running from the wreck of the shelter where his father lay dying, running from the demon bear. *'Torak!'* shouted Fa with his final breath. *'Run!'*

Summoning every shred of will, Torak took a shaky step towards the sled.

The ice bear lowered its head and fixed its gaze upon him. Then – at a lazy, inturned walk – it ambled between him and the sled.

He swayed.

The ice bear made no sound as it set down each foot. Not a click of claws on ice. Not a whisper of breath.

Hardly knowing what he did, Torak slid his hand out of his mitten and felt for his knife. It wouldn't come free of its sheath. He pulled harder. No good. He should have heeded Inuktiluk's advice, and kept it inside his parka. The leather sheath had frozen solid.

'Torak!' called Inuktiluk softly. 'Catch!'

A harpoon flew through the air, and Torak caught it in one hand. The slender bone point looked feeble beyond measure. 'Will it be any use?' he said.

'Not much. But at least you'll die like a man.'

The ice bear breathed out with a rasping 'hssh' – and Torak caught a flash of yellow fangs, and knew with a cold

73

clutch of terror that the harpoon had been a mistake. This bear would not be intimidated; but it could be goaded to attack.

He caught a flicker of movement. Renn pushing up her visor to take aim. 'Don't,' he warned. 'You'll only make it worse.'

She saw that he was right, and lowered her bow. But she kept the arrow nocked in readiness.

The dogs were barking and snapping at their traces. The bear twisted its head on its long neck, and snarled: a deep, reverberating thunder that shook the ice.

It locked eyes with Torak – and the world fell away. He couldn't hear the dogs, couldn't see Renn or Inuktiluk, couldn't even blink. Nothing existed but those eyes: blacker than basalt, stronger than hate. As he gazed into them he knew – he *knew* – that to the ice bear, all other creatures were prey.

His hand on the harpoon shaft was slippery with sweat. His legs wouldn't move.

The bear champed its great jaws, and slammed the ice with its paw. The force of the blow shuddered through Torak. Somehow he stood his ground.

A Forest bear snarls if it means only to threaten; but if it's hunting in earnest, it comes on in lethal silence. Did the same hold true on the ice?

No.

The ice bear leapt for him.

He saw the scarred black hide of its muzzle, the long, purple-grey tongue. He felt hot breath burning his cheek . . .

With fearsome agility the bear swerved – reared – and pounded the ice with both forepaws.

Torak's knees buckled and he nearly went down.

Now the ice bear was turning from him, rounding on the sled, clouting it out of the way as easily as if it were birch bark. Inuktiluk dived to one side, Renn to the other – but as the sled crashed down, it caught her on the shoulder and she fell with a cry, one arm trapped beneath a runner, directly in the path of the bear.

Torak launched himself forwards, waving his harpoon and yelling, 'Here I am! Not her, me! Me!'

Inuktiluk, too, was shouting and making stabbing feints with his harpoon – and in the instant the bear turned towards him, Torak wrenched the sled off Renn and grabbed her arm, half-dragging her out of its path. At that moment, one of the dogs snapped its trace and flew at the bear. A great paw batted it away, sending it flying through the air, to land with a sickening crack on the ice. As Torak and Renn threw themselves down, the bear leaped clean over them, bounded to the seal's carcass – and snatched its head in its jaws. Then it raced off across the ice, carrying the seal as easily as if it were a trout.

'The dogs!' shouted Renn. 'Hold them!'

The puppy was cowering under the sled, but the others were reckless in their blood-lust and hampered only by their traces – and now, as they strained together, they snapped them and hurtled off in pursuit, ignoring Inuktiluk's shouted commands. The trailing traces snagged his boot, and Torak and Renn watched in horror as he was dragged across the ice.

The dogs were strong and fast, too fast to catch. Torak put his hands to his lips and *barked*: the loud, sharp command that in wolf talk means: *STOP!*

His voice cut like a whiplash, and the dogs obeyed at once, cowering with their tails clamped between their legs.

Far away, the ice bear vanished among the blue hills.

Torak and Renn ran to where Inuktiluk was already sitting up, rubbing his forehead.

He recovered fast. Grabbing the traces in his fist, he drew his knife and with its hilt, dealt the dogs punishing blows that made them squeal. Then, breathing hard, he nodded his thanks to Torak.

'We should thank *you*,' Renn said shakily. 'If you hadn't distracted it . . .'

The White Fox shook his head. 'We only lived because it let us live.' He turned to Torak. The distrust was back in his face. 'My dogs. You *can* speak to them. Who are you? *What* are you?'

Torak wiped the sweat off his upper lip. 'We need to get going. That bear could be anywhere.'

Inuktiluk studied him for a moment. Then he gathered his remaining dogs, shouldered the body of the dead one, and limped back to the sled.

Torak dropped his harpoon with a clatter, and bent double with his hands on his knees.

Renn rubbed her shoulder.

He asked if she was all right.

'Hurts a bit,' she said. 'But at least it's not my draw arm. What about you?'

'Fine. I'm fine.' Then he sank to his knees and started to retch.

The sinking sun burned golden on the dark-blue ice as the dogs flew towards the White Fox camp.

Night fell. The slender moon rose. Torak kept glancing at the sky, but not once did he catch sight of the First Tree:

the vast, silent green fires that show themselves in winter. He longed for it as never before; he needed some link with the Forest. But it didn't come.

They passed dark, fanged ice hills, and heard distant cracks and groans. They thought of demons hammering to break free. At last, Torak spotted a speck of orange light. The weary dogs scented home, and picked up speed.

As they neared the White Fox camp, Torak saw a large, humped snow shelter with three smaller ones linked to it by short tunnels. All were honeycombed with light shining through the blocks. Around them, many little humps sprang to life, scattering snow and barking a noisy welcome.

Torak stepped stiffly from the sled. Renn winced and rubbed her shoulder. They were too numb with exhaustion to feel apprehensive of what lay ahead.

Inuktiluk insisted that they beat every flake of snow from their clothes and even pick the ice from their eyebrows, before crawling into the low entrance tunnel that was built like a dog-leg to keep out the wind. On hands and knees, Torak smelt the bitter stink of burning seal oil, and heard a murmur of voices, abruptly cut short.

In the smoky lamplight, he saw whalebone racks around the walls with many boots and mittens hung up to dry; a glittering haze of frozen breath; and a circle of round faces glistening with blubber.

Swiftly, Inuktiluk told his clan how he'd found the interlopers in the storm, and everything that had happened since. He was fair – he mentioned that Torak had saved him from being dragged across the ice – but his voice shook when he told how the "wolf boy" had spoken the tongue of dogs.

The White Foxes listened patiently, asking no questions, and studying Torak and Renn with inquisitive brown eyes not unlike those of their clan-creature. They didn't seem to have a leader, but four elders huddled close to the lamp, on a low sleeping-platform piled with reindeer hides.

'It's them,' shrilled one, a tiny woman, her face dark as a rosehip shrivelled by frost. 'These are the ones I saw in my vision.'

Torak heard Renn's sharp intake of breath. Placing both fists on his heart in sign of friendship, he bowed to the old woman. 'Inuktiluk said that in your vision, you saw me about to do evil. But I haven't. And I won't.'

To his surprise, laughter ran through the shelter, and all four elders gave toothless grins.

'Who among us,' said the old woman, 'knows what evil we will or won't do?' Her smile faded, and her brow furrowed with sadness. 'I saw you. You were about to break clan law.'

'He wouldn't do that,' said Renn.

The elder didn't seem annoyed at this interruption; she merely waited to see if Renn had finished, then turned back to Torak. 'The fires in the sky,' she said calmly, 'never lie.'

Torak was bewildered. 'I don't understand! What was I going to do?'

Pain tightened the ancient face. 'You were about to take an axe to a wolf.'

THIRTEEN

'*Attack Wolf?*' cried Torak. 'I'd never do that!'

'I saw it too,' Renn blurted out. 'In my dream, I saw it!' She couldn't help herself. But as soon as she'd said it, she wished she hadn't.

Torak was staring at her as if he'd never seen her before. 'I could never hurt Wolf,' he said. 'It isn't possible.'

The White Fox elder spread her hands. 'The Dead don't lie.'

He opened his mouth to protest, but the old woman spoke first. 'Rest now, and eat. Tomorrow we send you south, and this evil will pass.'

Renn thought he'd fight back, but instead he went quiet, with that stubborn look which always meant trouble.

The White Foxes bustled about, taking food from niches cut in the walls. Now that their elders had spoken, they seemed happy to prepare a feast, as if Torak and Renn had simply happened by for a night of storytelling. Renn saw

Inuktiluk regaling the others with the tale of how the ice bear had stolen his seal, which made everyone roar with laughter. 'Don't worry, little brother,' someone cried, 'I managed to hang onto mine, so we still get to eat!'

'Why didn't you *tell* me?' said Torak. His face was taut, but she could see that beneath his anger he was badly shaken.

'I was going to,' she said, 'but then you told me about *your* dream, and –'

'Do you really believe I could hurt Wolf?'

'Of course not! But I did see it. You had an axe. You were standing over him, you were going to strike.' All day she'd carried the dream inside her. And it wasn't the everyday kind which didn't always mean what it appeared to; it was the kind with the glaring colours, which she had maybe once every thirteen moons. The kind which came true.

Someone passed her a chunk of frozen seal meat, and she discovered that she was ravenous. As well as the seal, there was delicate whale skin with a chewy lining of blubber; sour pellets of ground-up willow buds from the gizzards of ptarmigans; and a delicious sweet mash of seal fat and cloudberries, her favourites. The shelter rang with talk and laughter. The White Foxes seemed extremely good at forgetting their worries and enjoying themselves. But it was disconcerting to have Torak sit beside her in glowering silence.

'Arguing won't help us find Wolf,' she said. 'I think we need to tell them about the Eye of the Viper –'

'Well I don't.'

'But if they knew, they might help.'

'They don't want to help. They want to get rid of us.'

'Torak, these are good people.'

He turned on her. 'Good people can smile, and be rotten inside! I know, I've seen it!'

She stared at him.

'I can't lose him again,' he said. 'It's different for you. You've got Fin-Kedinn and the rest of your clan. I've only got Wolf.'

Renn blinked. 'You've got me too.'

'That's not the same.'

She felt the heat rising to her ears. 'Sometimes,' she said, 'I wonder why I even like you!'

At that moment, a stout woman called her to come and try on her new clothes – and she left without a backwards glance.

His words were ringing in her ears as she crawled through a tunnel into a smaller shelter where four women sat sewing. *It's different for you.* No it isn't! she wanted to shout. Don't you know that you and Wolf are the first friends I've ever had?

'Sit by me,' said the woman, whose name was Tanugeak, 'and calm down.'

Renn threw herself onto a reindeer skin and started plucking out hairs.

'Anger,' Tanugeak said mildly, 'is a form of madness. And a waste of strength.'

'But sometimes you need it,' muttered Renn.

Tanugeak chuckled. 'You're just like your uncle! He was angry too, when he was young.'

Renn sat up. 'You know Fin-Kedinn?'

'He came here many summers ago.'

'Why? How did you meet him?'

Tanugeak patted her hand. 'You'll have to ask him.'

Renn sighed. She missed her uncle terribly. He would know what to do.

'These visions of yours,' said Tanugeak, examining Renn's wrist. 'They can be dangerous, you should have lightning marks for protection. I'm surprised your Mage hasn't seen to that.'

'She wanted to,' said Renn, 'but I never let her.'

'Let me. I'm a Mage too. And you'll need them, I think. You carry a lot of secrets.' Turning to a woman who sat apart from the others, she asked for her tattooing things. Then, without giving Renn time to protest, she laid her forearm on her ample lap, stretched the skin taut, and began swiftly pricking it with a bone needle, pausing to dip a scrap of gull hide in a cup of black dye, and rub it into the punctures.

It hurt at first, but Tanugeak kept up a stream of stories to keep Renn's mind off it. Soon her anger slipped away, leaving only the worry that Torak might do something stupid, like trying to escape without her.

She felt safe in here. On the sleeping-platform, three children slept in a heap, like puppies. Over the blubber lamp, a baby dangled in a seal's bladder snugly stuffed with moss. The women chatted and laughed, spangling the air with specks of frozen breath; only the one who sat apart, Akoomik, kept silent.

As the drowsy peace stole over her, Renn felt cared for in a way she'd never experienced before: as if the prickly shell she'd grown to protect herself were being gently peeled away.

Tanugeak started on the other wrist, and the women laid out Renn's new clothes, stroking them with weathered brown hands.

There were outer leggings and a parka of shimmering silver sealskin, to which someone had sewn her clan-creature feathers. There was a warm jerkin and inner leggings of eider duck hide, with the soft feathers worn against the skin. There were under-mittens of hare fur, and sturdy outer mittens; ptarmigan-down slippers, to be worn over fluffy stockings made from the pelts of young seals. And to keep out the wet, there were magnificent boots of dehaired seal-hide, with criss-cross bindings of braided sinew, and finely pleated soles.

'Beautiful,' murmured Renn. 'But I've nothing to give you in return.'

The women looked astonished, then laughed. 'We don't want anything in return!' said one.

'Come back in the Dark Time,' said another, 'and we'll make you a set of winter clothes. These are just for spring!'

Akoomik didn't join in the laughter as she packed her needles in a little bone case. Renn noticed tiny toothmarks on it, and asked who'd made them.

'My baby,' replied Akoomik. 'When he was teething.'

Renn smiled. 'Is he over the worst?'

'Oh, yes,' said Akoomik in a voice that made Renn shiver. 'That's him over there.' She pointed to a ledge cut in the wall, on which lay a small, stiff bundle wrapped in hide.

'I'm sorry,' said Renn. She was scared, too. In the Forest, the clans carried their Dead far from their shelters, so that their souls couldn't trouble the living.

'We keep our Dead with us till spring,' said Akoomik, 'to save them from the foxes.'

'And to stop them feeling left out,' Tanugeak added comfortably. 'They like chatting just as much as we do. When you see a star travelling very fast, that's one of them setting off to visit their friends.'

Renn found that a comforting thought; but Akoomik pinched the bridge of her nose to hold back her grief. 'The demons took his breath a moon ago. Now they've taken my elder son, too.'

Renn remembered what Inuktiluk had said about the boy lost on the ice.

'My mate died of fever in the Moon of Long Dark,' Akoomik went on. 'Then my mother felt death coming, and went out to meet it, so that she wouldn't take food from the young ones. If my son doesn't return, I'll have no-one.' Her eyes were dull: as if a light had gone out. Renn had seen that before, in people whose souls were sick.

If I lose Wolf, I'll have no-one.

At last she understood what Torak had meant. His mother had died when he was born. He'd lost his father to the bear. He'd never even met the rest of his clan. He was more alone than anyone she knew. And although she too had lost people, she realized that with Torak, as with Akoomik, the grief was still raw. If he lost Wolf . . .

Once again, she wondered how she could bring herself to tell him what she suspected.

'Finished,' said Tanugeak, making her jump.

Renn studied the neat black zigzags on the inside of her wrists. They made her feel stronger, better protected. 'Thank you,' she said. 'Now I need to find my friend.'

'First, take this.' Tanugeak gave her a small pouch made from the scaly skin of swans' feet, with the claws left on.

'What's in it?' asked Renn.

'Things you might need.' She leaned closer. 'Listen well,' she said under her breath. 'The elders saw something else in the sky that night. We're not sure what it means, but I have a feeling you might know.' She paused. 'It was a three-pronged fork, of the kind a healer might use for catching the souls of the sick. But this one felt bad.'

Renn's fingers tightened on the pouch.

'Ah,' said Tanugeak, 'I see that you've been dreading this.' She touched Renn's hand. 'Go. Find your friend. When the time is right, tell him the secrets you carry.'

When Renn got back to the main shelter, the White

Foxes had settled down for the night. Most slept huddled together, while a few sat softening sinew between their teeth, or flexing stiff boots to make them wearable for the morning. Torak was fast asleep at one end of the sleeping-platform.

Renn got into her sleeping-sack, wondering what to do. The White Fox vision had confirmed the fear she'd been harbouring for days. The Soul-Eaters had taken Wolf.

She dreaded telling Torak. How much more could he bear?

She was woken by Inuktiluk shaking her shoulder.

Everyone else was asleep, but through a chink in the shelter she saw that the moon was low: it would be dawn soon. Torak was gone.

She shot upright.

'He's waiting outside,' mouthed Inuktiluk. 'Follow me!'

Quietly they made their way into the smaller shelter, where Renn exchanged her old clothes for the unfamiliar new ones.

The night air cut like a knife, but there was no wind. The snow glinted in the faint glow of the dying moon. The crust had frozen, so they had to tread carefully. A few dogs stirred, caught their scent, then slumped down again.

Torak was waiting. Like Renn, he had new clothes: she hardly recognized him in his silvery parka. 'They're helping us get away!' he whispered, his eyes glinting with excitement.

'Who's they?' hissed Renn. 'And *why?*'

Inuktiluk had vanished into the dark, and it was Torak who answered. 'I told him everything. You were right, they

do know about the Eye of the Viper! And there's a woman –
Akoomik? She's going to tell us where it is!'

Renn was astonished. 'But – I thought you didn't trust
them. What changed your mind?'

'You did.' He gave her one of his rare, wolfish grins. 'I do
listen to you sometimes.'

Inuktiluk was beckoning, so they followed him west till
they came to a rent in the ice. Renn saw the dark gleam of
water, and caught the tang of the Sea.

They tracked the channel as it steadily broadened, then
Torak touched her arm. 'Look.'

She gasped. 'A *skinboat*!'

It was ten paces long, sturdily built of dehaired seal-hide
stretched over a whalebone frame. Their packs were neatly
stowed at either end, and two double-bladed paddles lay
on top.

'This channel leads to the open Sea,' said Inuktiluk.
'Once you reach it, keep the land in sight, but stay clear of
the mouth of the ice river.'

'You told us that no-one had ever crossed it,' said Torak.

The round face split in a grin. 'But plenty have paddled
around it!' Then his grin faded. 'Watch out for black ice. It's
denser than white, and it'll sink you in moments. If you see
a piece in the water, you've already passed several that you
missed.'

Renn wondered how they were going to spot black ice in
a black Sea.

Torak was hefting his paddle, keen to make a start. 'How
do we find the Eye of the Viper?'

Akoomik emerged from the shadows, and with her knife
began carving marks in the snow. 'Follow the North Star
past the ice river,' she said, 'about a day's paddling from
here. When you see a mountain shaped like three ravens

perched on an ice floe, put in at the frozen bay below it, and head up the ridge that curls round its north-west flank.'

'But what *is* it?' said Renn. 'How will we know we've found it?'

Both White Foxes shivered, and made the sign of the hand. 'You'll know,' said Akoomik.

'And may the guardian save you,' said Inuktiluk, 'if you venture inside.' He helped them into the skinboat.

Torak handled his paddle confidently, but Renn was uneasy. She hadn't had as much practice in boats. 'Why are you helping us?' she asked the White Foxes.

'The elders don't know you as I do,' said Inuktiluk. 'When I explain, they won't be angry. Besides,' he added, 'if I don't help you, you'll go anyway!'

Akoomik peered into Torak's face. 'You've lost someone. So have I. If you find what you seek, maybe I will too.'

Torak thought for a moment, then rummaged in his pack, and pressed something into her mittens. 'Take these.'

She frowned. 'What are they?'

'Boar tusks. I'd forgotten I had them; but they're special. They belonged to a friend of mine. Offer them to the wind. For both of us.'

Inuktiluk grunted in approval, and Akoomik's white teeth showed in the first smile Renn had seen her give. '*Thank you!* May the guardian run with you!'

'And also with you!' whispered Renn.

Then they were off, slicing through the black water and heading for the open Sea, to find Wolf.

FOURTEEN

The stranger wolves were howling many lopes away, and as Wolf listened, he felt the bite of loneliness.

He heard that it was a big pack, and that each wolf was cleverly varying its howls to make it sound as if there were even more of them. Wolf knew that trick; he'd learned it when he'd run with the pack on the Mountain.

In his head he saw the wolves lifting their muzzles joyfully to the Bright White Eye. He longed to howl back. But he was squashed beneath the hated deerhide. Howling was only a memory.

The sliding tree lurched as the taillesses crested a ridge. Wolf forced himself to stay alert, to be ready for when his pack-brother came. But it was getting harder. Thirst scratched his throat. Pain gnawed his tail. When they'd been on the Great Wet in the terrible floating hides, he'd been sick. His belly still hurt.

The other creatures were feeling no better. The otter

had fallen into despairing silence, although Wolf smelt that she wasn't yet Not-Breath. The lynx and fox – whom Pale-Pelt had caught and crammed onto another sliding tree – hadn't yowled since the Light. Only the wolverine gave the occasional furious snarl.

The stranger pack ended its howl, and the white hills sang with silence. Wolf knew that now the wolves would be licking and snuffling each other in readiness for the hunt. Before he and Tall Tailless went hunting, they always snuffle-licked and touched noses, although of course only Wolf wagged his tail.

The sliding tree turned into the wind, and he smelt mountains drawing near. He sensed a shiver of excitement run through the taillesses, and guessed they were reaching the end of their long lope.

Stinkfur came to trot beside him, and thrust a chunk of the Bright Soft Cold through the deerhide. Awkwardly, Wolf took it in his cramped jaws, and crunched it up. He no longer had the will to refuse what he was given.

Up ahead, Pale-Pelt spoke to Viper-Tongue, and they glanced at him and broke into the yip-and-yowl of tailless laughter. Rage bit his belly. In his head he burst free of the deerhide and leapt at Pale-Pelt, tearing out his throat so that the hot blood gushed . . .

But only in his head. He was getting weaker. Even if he could break free, he wouldn't have the strength to bring down Pale-Pelt. He worried that when Tall Tailless and his pack-sister finally came, he would be too weak to fight alongside them.

As the Light fled, a mountain loomed. The wind dropped. Wolf smelt that there was little prey here, and no wolves. His pelt crawled with dread.

The sliding tree juddered to a halt.

There, against the flank of the mountain: a Bright Beast-that-Bites-Hot was snarling, and beside it – silent, unmoving – waited the Stone-Faced One.

She stood with her forepaws clenched at her sides, and Wolf sensed that in one she held the grey, glowing thing that bit cold. She was very still, and yet her shadow on the mountainflank leapt like tattered wings.

Wolf hadn't seen or smelt her since the time when she'd come through the hissing whiteness. Now, one glimpse of her terrible face made him a whimpering cub again.

In silence the other taillesses left the sliding trees, and went to join her. They were fearful, but as before, they hid their fear from each other.

The Stone-Faced One spoke in her rattling voice, and the whole pack crouched around the Bright Beast-that-Bites-Hot, and began to rock back and forth. Back and forth, back and forth. Watching them made Wolf dizzy, but he couldn't look away. Then they started a low, steady growling that thudded through Wolf like the hooves of reindeer galloping over hard ground. On and on it went, faster, louder, till his heart beat painfully in his chest.

And now from the mountain came a smell of Dark and demons, flowing over him like an unseen Fast Wet.

Suddenly Stone-Face raised her forepaw – the paw in which she held the grey thing that bit cold. Then – as Wolf watched in amazement – *she thrust her paw right into the jaws of the Bright Beast!*

Frozen with horror, he watched Stinkfur thrust in her forepaw, then Pale-Pelt, then Viper-Tongue. He watched them rocking back and forth, still growling that fast, stony growl, with their paws sunk deep in the crackling jaws of the Bright Beast.

All at once they gave a triumphant howl – and wrenched their paws out again.

Wolf could not believe what he was smelling! Their forepaws didn't stink of meat that has been bitten by the Bright Beast! They smelt cool and fresh! *What were these taillesses, whom even the Bright Beast feared to bite?*

Terror crushed Wolf: terror not only for himself but for his pack-brother.

Tall Tailless and the female were clever and brave, and they had Long Claws-that-Fly-Far. But if they attacked these strange, bad taillesses, they would be torn to pieces.

FIFTEEN

'What's that in the water?' hissed Renn.

'A seal,' said Torak over his shoulder.

'Are you sure?'

' – No.'

'It looked like an ice bear.'

'If it was an ice bear, we'd know it by now.'

But she had seen it. A great pale shape sliding through the dark water under the skinboat.

'Inuktiluk told me there are white whales,' said Torak. 'Maybe that's what you saw.'

To Renn's annoyance, he didn't seem frightened. But he was a better skinboater, and too intent on finding Wolf to be scared.

The swell lifted the boat and she dug in her paddle, trying not to think what lay beneath. The Sea Mother could drown them with one flick of her fin. Down they would sink into the bottomless black, their mouths open in a scream that had no end; and when the fishes had nibbled their bones bare, the Hidden People would roll them forever in their long green hair . . .

'Watch out,' said Torak, 'you're splashing me.'

'Sorry.'

Her arms ached, and despite her owl-eyed visor, her head was pounding from the glare. They'd reached the open Sea shortly after dawn, and were now in an eerie world of dark-green water and drifting blue ice mountains. To the east stretched the white expanse of the shore; to the north, the vast, shattered chaos of the ice river.

'Too slow,' muttered Torak. Picking up speed, he steered them behind a floating mountain.

'I don't think we should get so close,' said Renn.

'Why not? It keeps us out of the wind.'

She applied herself to her paddle. On the pale-green foot of the ice mountain, three seals lay basking. She fixed her eyes on them, and told herself not to worry.

It was no good. She *was* worried. Torak's need to find Wolf was all-consuming; she'd begun to wonder where it would lead. And she hadn't yet told him about the Soul-Eaters.

A smaller ice mountain slid past them on its mysterious journey. She felt its freezing breath, heard the slap and suck of the Sea carving a cavern in its flank. The cavern was a searing blue oval. Like an eye, she thought.

'The Eye of the Viper,' she said suddenly.

'I've been thinking about it too,' said Torak. 'It can't be anything to do with a real viper, there aren't any this far north –'

' – and Inuktiluk said, "if you venture *inside*".'

He turned to her, his owl eyes making him startlingly unfamiliar. 'I think I can guess what he meant.'

93

'Me too,' said Renn.

He shivered. 'I hope we're wrong. I *hate* caves.'

They paddled on in silence.

To keep up her spirits, Renn rummaged in her pack for food. The White Foxes had provisioned them well. Along with half a skin of blubber, she found frozen seal ribs and blood sausages. She cut two slices, and handed one to Torak. It tasted gritty, and she missed the tang of juniper berries. She missed the White Foxes more. 'I feel bad about them,' she said.

'Why?' said Torak, with his mouth full.

'They gave us so much, and we repaid them by running away.'

'They were going to send us south!'

'But all this gear. Snow-knives. Lamps. Better waterskins. A new strike-fire for me, and a beautiful case for my bow. There's even a repair kit for the boat.' She held up a pouch made from a seal's flipper.

Torak wasn't listening. He'd lowered his paddle, and was staring ahead.

'What is it?' said Renn.

Ahead of them on the ice mountain, the seals had woken up.

Renn was puzzled. 'But we've got enough food,' she whispered, 'we can't stop to hunt now!'

He ignored her.

Suddenly the seals slithered off the ice and into the water. At the same moment Torak plunged in his paddle and yelled, 'Turn! Turn!', swinging the skinboat hard to the left. A bewildered Renn did the same, and they shot sideways – out from the wake of the ice mountain – as a rending roar split the sky, and the mountain tilted and crashed into the Sea, sending a wall of water thundering over where they'd been a heartbeat before.

Panting, they bobbed up and down. In place of the ice mountain there was now a heaving white slush.

'How did you know that would happen?' said Renn.

'I didn't,' said Torak. 'The seals did.'

'How did you know they knew?'

'He hesitated. 'They feel it in their whiskers. Last summer I spirit walked in a seal. Remember?'

Uneasily, Renn licked the salt from her lips. She'd forgotten; or she hadn't wanted to remember. She hated being reminded of how different he was.

He saw it in her face. 'Come on,' he said. 'Long way to go.'

They moved off, steering clear of ice mountains. Renn felt the distance between them of things unsaid. She'd have to tell him soon.

The wind picked up, blowing cold in their faces. But in her White Fox clothes, she hardly felt it. The seal hide cut out the wind, but was lighter than reindeer hide, while the eider-feather underclothes kept her snug, but let out the sweat, so that she didn't get chilled. The dog-fur ruff around the hood kept her face warm, but never became clogged with frozen breath; and her inner mittens had slits in the palms, so she could slide her fingers out for fiddly work like opening pouches. The clothes were beautiful, too, the silver fur shimmering in the sun. But they made her feel like someone else.

The zigzag tattoos on her wrists also made her feel different, and she wondered just why Tanugeak had given them to her. The White Fox Mage had seemed to know things about her that she thought only Saeunn and Fin-Kedinn knew; things that Renn kept hidden in a deep corner of her mind.

But it was Tanugeak's final gift which puzzled her most. The swansfoot pouch contained a dark powder that smelt of soot and seaweed. What was she supposed to do with that?

'Look,' said Torak, cutting across her thoughts.

He'd been steering them further out to Sea, and now she saw why.

To the east lay the glaring white of the ice river. Jagged peaks towered over dizzying cliffs riven with deep blue cracks. Renn heard a distant booming – and saw a great spur break away and crash into the Sea. Clouds of powdered ice shot into the sky. A green wave rolled towards them, rocking the skinboat.

If we'd been closer, she thought, we'd have been crushed. Like my father.

'Try not to think about it,' Torak said quietly.

She picked up her paddle and stabbed at the water.

The sun was low and the ice river far behind them when they finally glimpsed the mountain. From the dead white land it rose: three stark peaks piercing the sky, like ravens perching on ice.

Renn had never seen anything so lonely. Two winters ago, her clan had journeyed to the northern-most end of the High Mountains, and she'd felt as if she'd reached the edge of the world. Now she felt as if she'd fallen over it.

Torak sensed it too, and slipped one hand out of his mitten to touch his clan-creature skin.

South of the mountain's western flank, they found the iced-in bay which Akoomik had drawn in the snow. It was a relief to get out of the skinboat, although their legs were stiff. Once again, they were grateful to the White Foxes. The boat was easy to carry, and their boots' rough soles stopped them slipping on the ice.

Hiding the boat in the lee of a snow hill, they over-turned it and propped it up on four forked driftwood sticks. 'Inuktiluk called them shoresticks,' Torak told Renn. 'We can use them to make the boat into a shelter, too.'

Renn knew better than to suggest that they should do exactly that, right now, since it was mid-afternoon, and the shadows were turning purple. Already, Torak was scanning for tracks.

He soon found them: a broad swathe of churned-up snow. '*Two* sleds,' he said with a frown. 'Heavily laden, and heading for the mountain. Quite fresh.' He straightened up. 'Let's go.'

Renn shivered. All at once, the Soul-Eaters felt very close. 'Wait,' she said. 'We need to think about this.'

'Why?' he said impatiently.

She hesitated. 'One of the White Fox women told me something. I've been wanting to tell you all day.'

'Yes?'

She lowered her voice to a whisper. 'Torak. It's the Soul-Eaters. They're the ones who took Wolf.'

'I – know,' he said.

'*What?*'

He told her what he'd seen when he'd spirit walked in the raven.

'But – why didn't you *tell* me?' she cried. 'You've known for *days!*'

He scowled, and hacked at the snow with his heel. 'I know I should have, but I couldn't risk it. I thought you might go back to the Forest.' His scowl deepened. 'If you'd left . . .'

Suddenly she felt sorry for him. 'I've suspected for days, but I didn't leave. And I won't now.'

He met her eyes. 'So – we go on.'

She swallowed. 'Yes. We go on.'

They looked at the trail of the Soul-Eaters, winding up the mountain.

Renn said, 'What if this *is* some kind of trap?'

'I don't care,' he muttered.

'What if they've heard rumours of the Wolf Clan boy who's a spirit walker? If they catch you, if they take your power, it could endanger the whole Forest.'

'I don't *care*,' he repeated. 'I've got to find Wolf!'

She had an idea. 'What about a disguise?'

'What?'

'That'd throw them off the scent. And maybe Tanugeak had that in mind, too. At least, she gave me what we need.'

Torak took a few paces, then turned back to her. 'What do we do?'

It didn't take long to change their appearance. Their clan-tattoos weren't a problem, as their cheeks were still so blistered from the snowstorm that the fine marks hardly showed. Renn made a black stain by mixing Tanugeak's powder with water, then finger-painted a White Fox band across Torak's nose. She also cut his hair to shoulder length, with a fringe across the brow. He was too thin to make a truly convincing White Fox, but with luck, his clothes would conceal that.

She dyed her own hair black by combing in more of the stain, which she also used to darken her face. Then she got Torak to turn her into a Mountain Hare by painting her forehead with a zigzag band tinged with earthblood from his medicine horn.

He seemed disconcerted. 'You don't look like Renn any more.'

'Good,' she said. 'And you don't look like Torak.'

They stared at one another, both more unsettled than

they cared to admit. Then they set off on the trail of the Soul-Eaters.

The sleds had been dragged up a ridge that snaked round the western flank of the mountain, just as Akoomik had said. As they climbed higher, the shadows deepened from purple to charcoal. Often they paused to listen, but no living thing stirred. No eagles wheeled, no ravens cawed.

The air grew colder. The wind dropped. Their boots creaked in the stillness.

Then – with appalling suddenness – they came upon the sleds, casually piled at the side of the trail.

After so many days of following the faintest of clues, it was a shock to find solid structures of wood and hide. It made the Soul-Eaters solid, too.

Sensing they were nearing the end, they hid their packs and sleeping-sacks in the snow a few paces from the sleds. Renn saw what a wrench it was for Torak to leave behind his father's blue slate knife. 'But it's too dangerous,' she told him. 'They knew him, they might recognize it.'

They decided to take the waterskins the White Foxes had packed for them, a little food, and knives. Renn would also take her bow, and she wanted to take the axes as well, but Torak feared the White Fox vision too much to risk it.

Twenty paces beyond the sleds, the trail rounded a spur – and they halted.

Above them reared the gaunt mountain, lit crimson by the last rays of the sun. In its flank, a black hole gaped. Before it, like a warning, stood a tall grey pillar of stone.

White mist seeped from the darkness of the cave. Clammy tendrils reached for them, stinking of dread and demons. Hope fled. If the Soul-Eaters had taken Wolf in there . . .

Glancing over her shoulder, Renn saw the shape of the

whole mountain for the first time. She saw how it rose out of the snow like the head of some giant creature. She saw how the ice river uncoiled its sinuous bulk east, before twisting round to lose itself in the Sea.

Torak had seen it too. 'We've found the Viper,' he whispered.

'We're standing on it,' breathed Renn.

They turned back to the mountain: to the glaring black hole split by the standing stone.

'And there's the Eye,' she said.

Torak took off his owl visor and stowed it in his medicine pouch. 'They're in there,' he said, 'I can feel it. So is Wolf.'

Renn chewed her lower lip. 'We need to think about this.'

'I've done enough thinking,' he snapped.

Taking his arm, she drew him behind a rock, out of sight of the Eye. 'There's no sense going in,' she said, 'unless we know for sure that – that Wolf is still alive.'

He didn't reply. Then – to her horror – he put his hands to his mouth to howl.

She grabbed his wrist. '*Are you mad?* They'll hear you!'

'What if they do? They'll think I'm a wolf!'

'You don't know that! Torak, these are *Soul-Eaters*!'

'Then what?'

'There is another way.' Slipping her hand out of her mitten, she fumbled at the neck of her parka, and brought out the little grouse-bone whistle he'd given her once. She blew on it – and no sound came, as they had known it wouldn't; but if Wolf was alive, he would hear it.

Nothing. Not a breath of wind stirred the dead air.

'Try again,' said Torak.

She tried. And again. And again.

Still nothing. She couldn't meet his eyes.

Then – from deep inside the mountain – the faintest of howls.

Torak's face lit up. 'I told you! I *told* you!'

The howl was long and wavering, and even Renn could hear its misery and pain. It rose to a peak . . .

And cut off.

SIXTEEN

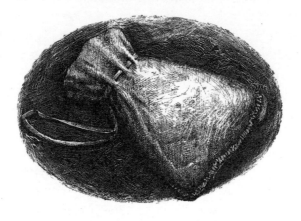

'*Wolf!*' cried Torak, throwing himself forwards.

Renn yanked him back. 'Torak, no! They'll hear you!'

'I don't care, let me go!' He pushed her away with such force that she went flying.

She landed on her back, and they stared at one another, both shocked by his violence.

He offered her his hand, but she got to her feet unaided. 'Don't you understand,' she hissed in a furious whisper, 'if you go into that cave, you might be walking right into their hands!'

'But he needs me!'

'And how does it help if you get yourself killed?' She dragged him down the trail, out of sight of the Eye. 'We have to *think!* He's down there. We know that. But if we blunder in, who knows what might happen?'

'You heard that howl,' he said through his teeth. 'If we don't go in now, he may die!'

Renn opened her mouth to protest – then froze.

Torak had heard it too. The crunch of footsteps coming up the slope.

Of one accord, they ducked behind the sleds.

Crunch, crunch, crunch. Unhurried. Coming closer.

Quietly, Torak drew his knife. Beside him, Renn slipped her hands out of her mittens and nocked an arrow to her bow.

A thickset man came into view. He was clad in mottled sealskin, and carried a grey hide pouch over one shoulder. His head was bowed. His hood concealed his face. He bore no weapons that they could see.

As Torak watched, rage choked him. His eyes misted red. This was one of them. This man had taken Wolf.

In his mind he saw Wolf standing proudly on the ridge above the Forest, his fur limned golden by the sun. He heard again that agonized howl. *Pack-brother! Help me!*

Crunch, crunch, crunch. The man was almost level with them. He stopped. Looked over his shoulder, as if reluctant to go on.

It was too much for Torak. Scarcely knowing what he did, he leapt forwards, head-butting the man in the belly, sending him crashing into the snow.

He lay winded, but then – with astonishing speed – rolled sideways, kicked Torak's knife from his hand, and grabbed his hood, twisting it backwards in a vicious choke-hold. Torak felt strong legs pinioning his arms, squeezing the breath from his chest; flint digging painfully into his throat.

'I wouldn't,' Renn said coldly. She took a step closer, her arrow aimed at the attacker's heart.

Torak felt the grip on his ribs loosen. His hood was released, the knife withdrawn.

'Please,' whined his attacker, 'don't hurt me!'

With her arrow still poised to shoot, Renn nudged Torak's knife towards him with her boot, then told her captive to get up.

'No, no!' whined the captive, cowering at her feet, 'I may not look upon the face of power!'

Torak and Renn exchanged startled glances.

The captive grovelled, scrabbling for the pouch he'd dropped in the attack. Torak was surprised to see that he wasn't a man, but a boy about his own age, although twice as heavy. He bore the black nose tattoo of the White Foxes, and his round face glistened with blubber and terror sweat.

'Where is he?' said Torak. 'What have you done with him?'

'Who?' bleated the boy. He saw Torak's tattoo, and his mouth fell open. 'You're not one of us. Who *are* you?'

'What are you doing here?' snapped Renn. 'You're no Soul-Eater!'

'But I will be!' retorted the boy with unexpected ferocity. 'They promised!'

'For the last time,' said Torak, advancing with his knife, 'what have you done with Wolf?'

'Get away from me!' squealed the boy, scrambling backwards like a crab. 'If – if I scream, they'll hear. They'll come to my rescue, all four of them! Is that what you want?'

Torak stared at Renn. *Four?*

'Get away from me!' The boy edged up the slope. 'I *chose* to do this! No-one can stop me!'

He sounded as if he were trying to convince himself. It gave Torak an idea. 'What have you got in that pouch?' he said, to keep the boy talking.

'A – an owl,' stammered the boy. 'They want it for sacrifice.'

'But an owl is a hunter,' said Renn accusingly.

'So is a wolf,' said Torak. 'And an otter. What are your masters doing in there? Tell us or we'll – '

'I don't *know!*' cried the boy, moving further up the slope.

As they followed him, the Eye came into view.

'Your masters,' Renn said quietly, 'do they talk of the one who is a spirit walker? Tell the truth! I'll know if you lie!'

'A *spirit walker?*' The boy's eyes widened. 'Where?'

'Do they ever speak of this?' demanded Torak.

'No, no, I swear it!' He was sweating freely now, stinking of blubber. 'They came to make a sacrifice! That's all I know, I swear on my three souls!'

'And for this you'd break clan law by catching hunters for sacrifice?' said Renn. 'For an empty promise of a power that will never be yours?'

Sheathing his knife, Torak took a step towards the boy. 'Your mother wants you back,' he said.

He'd guessed right. The boy's body sagged.

Renn was puzzled, but Torak ignored her. If she got an inkling of what he meant to do, she'd try to stop him. 'Get out of here,' he told the boy. 'Go back to Akoomik while you still can.'

Terror and ambition fought in the blubbery face. 'I can't,' he whispered.

'If you don't go now,' said Torak, 'it'll be too late. Your clan will make you outcast. You'll never see them again.'

'I *can't*,' sobbed the boy.

From deep within the Eye, a voice boomed. 'Boy! It is time!'

'I'll make it easy for you,' snarled Torak. Wrenching the pouch from the boy's grip, he pushed him down the trail. 'Go on, go!' He hoisted the pouch over his shoulder. 'Renn, I'm sorry, but I've got to do this.'

Realization dawned in her face. 'Torak – no – it'll never work, they'll kill you!'

Turning his head, he shouted an answer to the Soul-Eaters. 'I'm coming!'

Then he raced up the trail and into the Eye of the Viper.

SEVENTEEN

After the twilit mountainside, the darkness hit Torak like a wall.

'Shut your eyes,' said a voice in front of him. 'Let the dark be your guide.'

Torak just had time to draw down his hood before a figure lurched towards him bearing a sputtering pine-pitch torch.

From the voice he expected a man, but when he stole a glimpse from under his hood, he was startled to see a woman.

She was heavy and squat, with legs so badly bowed that she rocked as she walked. Her features were at odds with the rest of her: small, darting eyes in a sharp-snouted face. Pointed ears that reminded Torak of a bat. He didn't recognize her clan; the spiky tattoo on her chin was unknown to him. What drew his gaze was the bone amulet on her breast: the three-pronged fork for snaring souls.

'You were a long time,' said the Soul-Eater. 'Did you get it?'

Hiding his face, Torak held up the pouch. Inside, the owl wriggled feebly.

The Soul-Eater grunted, then turned and hobbled further into the cave.

Glancing back, Torak saw that the last glimmer of daylight was far behind. He slung the pouch over his shoulder, and started after her.

The Soul-Eater moved fast, despite her bow legs, and in the swinging torchlight he caught only flashes as they went deeper. Ridged red walls like a gaping maw. A tunnel as pale and twisted as guts. Yellow hand-prints that flared, then faded in the gloom. And always the echoing drip, drip of water.

As he stumbled on, the folly of what he'd done sank in. When the Soul-Eaters saw his face, they would know he wasn't the White Fox boy. Maybe, too, they would detect some trace of his father in his features. Or maybe they already knew who he was, and this was all a trap.

Down, down they went. An unclean warmth seeped from the rocks and clung to his face like cobwebs. An acrid stink stole into his throat.

'Breathe through your mouth,' muttered the Soul-Eater.

Fa used to give him the same advice. It was terrible to hear it repeated by the enemy.

Above him, Torak saw thin sheets of reddish stone hanging down like flaps of bloody hide. In their folds, unseen creatures shrank from the light.

His head struck a rock and he fell, crying out in disgust as his fingers plunged into soft blackness seething with thin grey worms.

A strong hand grabbed his arm and hauled him to his

feet. 'Quiet!' said the Soul-Eater, 'you'll startle them!' Then to the darkness, 'There, there, my little ones.' As if in answer came the squeak and rustle of thousands of bats.

'The warmth makes them wakeful,' murmured the Soul-Eater. Laying her palm on the tunnel wall, she made Torak do the same.

He recoiled. The rock had the lingering warmth of a fresh carcass. He knew only one reason for that. The Otherworld.

'Yes, the Otherworld,' said the Soul-Eater, as if she'd heard his thoughts. 'Why do you think we came all this way?'

He didn't dare reply, which seemed to irritate her. 'Don't let the bats see your eyes,' she snarled. 'They go for the glitter.'

Abruptly, the tunnel widened into a long, low cavern the colour of dried blood. It had the eye-watering stink of a midden in high summer, and Torak's gorge rose.

Then he forgot about the smell. The walls were pitted with smaller hollows, some blocked with slabs of stone. From inside one he caught the hiss of a wolverine.

His heart quickened. Where there was a wolverine, maybe there was also a wolf.

He gave a low grunt-whine that Wolf would be sure to recognize. *It's me!*

No answer. Disappointment crashed over him like a wave. If Wolf was still alive, he wasn't here.

'Stop whining,' growled the Soul-Eater, 'and keep up! If you get lost down here, we'll never find you again.'

More tunnels, until Torak's head whirled. He wondered if the Soul-Eater had chosen a winding route on purpose, to make him lose his bearings. Behind that sharp face, he sensed a quick mind. *Twisted legs, flying thoughts.* That was what the Walker had said.

They emerged into a vast cavern – and Torak faltered. Before him loomed a forest. A forest of stone.

Shadowy thickets reached upwards, seeking sunlight they would never find. Stone waterfalls froze in an endless winter. As Torak followed the lurching torchlight, a sickly warmth made the sweat start out on his brow. He heard a furtive trickling; glimpsed still pools and twisted roots. He caught nightmare flashes of figures draped in stone: some crouching above him, some half-hidden in water. When he looked again, they were gone, but he felt their presence: the Hidden People of the Rocks.

The Soul-Eater led him to a massive trunk of greenish stone that looked as if it had been hacked to a stump by some act of unimaginable violence. He heard movement, and knew he was being watched.

His foot caught on a root, and he tripped and fell. Laughter rang through the cavern.

'What's this, Nef?' said a woman's mocking voice. 'Have you brought us your fosterling at last?'

Torak's heart began to pound. He'd managed to deceive one Soul-Eater. He'd need all his wits to deceive the others.

Grovelling where he lay, he began to whine. 'No, no, don't make me look upon the face of power!'

'Not that again!' grunted Nef. 'He won't even dare look at me!'

Torak felt a flicker of hope. If they hadn't seen the White Fox boy's face . . .

A cold finger slid down his cheek, making him flinch. 'If he daren't look at Nef the Bat Mage,' a woman whispered in his ear, 'dare he look upon Seshru, the Viper Mage?'

She drew back his hood, and he found himself staring into the most perfect face he'd ever seen. Slanting lynx eyes of fathomless blue; a mouth of daunting beauty. Dark hair, drawn back from a high white brow, revealed a stark black line of tattooed arrowheads, like the markings on a snake.

Fascinated yet repelled, he met the peerless gaze, while the Viper Mage studied him as a hunter regards its kill.

Her lovely features tightened with contempt – but nothing more. She didn't know who he was. 'He's thin for a White Fox,' she said. 'Nef, you disappoint me. You've found us a runt.' Her chill fingers slid inside the neck of his parka, and she smiled. 'What's this? He has a knife!'

'A knife?' said the Bat Mage.

The knife which Fin-Kedinn had made for him hung in its sheath from a thong about his neck. Now it was gone: lifted over his head and tossed to Nef.

'He has a *knife!*' jeered a man's voice as rich and deep as an oak wood. An enormous figure loomed from the darkness, and before Torak could resist, he was seized, and his arms twisted so viciously that he screamed.

More laughter, blasting him with the eye-stinging tang of spruce-blood. 'Should I be frightened, Seshru?' mocked the man. In his bulky reindeer-hide clothes, he seemed to fill the cavern. 'Does he mean to threaten the Oak Mage?'

Torak stared into a face as hard as sun-cracked earth. The beard was a twiggy thicket, the mane a russet tangle. The eyes that bore into his were a fierce leaf-green. 'Does he mean to threaten?' repeated the Oak Mage in a tone of menacing softness.

Torak felt as helpless as a lemming trapped by a lynx.

'Thiazzi, leave him!' snapped the Bat Mage. 'We need him alive, not dead of fright!'

The Viper Mage arched her white throat and laughed. 'Poor Nef! Always so eager to play the mother!'

111

'What would you know about mothering?' Nef threw back at her.

Seshru's beautiful lips thinned.

'Let's see what it's brought us, shall we?' said Thiazzi, grabbing the pouch from Torak's hand. He pulled out a small, half-grown white owl, and shook it until its eyes darkened with shock. From that moment, Torak hated Thiazzi the Oak Mage, who delighted in tormenting creatures weaker than himself.

The Bat Mage didn't seem to like it either. Shambling forwards, she snatched the owl from the Oak Mage and stuffed it back in the pouch. 'We need this one alive, too,' she muttered. Then she turned to Torak, indicated a birchbark bowl on the floor, and told him to eat.

To his surprise, he saw that the bowl contained a strip of dried horse meat and some hazelnuts.

'Go on,' urged Seshru with a curious sideways smile. 'Eat. You have to keep up your strength.' Her glance slid to Thiazzi, and Torak caught a flicker of amusement between them.

He pretended to eat, but his throat had closed. It seemed as if only a moment ago, he'd been out in the snow with Renn. Now he was in the bowels of the earth with the Soul-Eaters.

The Soul-Eaters. They had haunted his dreams. They had killed his father. Now, at last, here they were: mysterious, unknowable – and yet more *real* than he could ever have imagined.

Thiazzi the Oak Mage sprawled on the rocks, chewing spruce-blood, flecking his beard with golden crumbs. He could have been any hunter in the Forest; except that he tortured for pleasure.

Seshru the Viper Mage moved to lean against him:

slender, graceful, her supple seal-hide tunic shimmering like moonlight on a lake. The emptiness of her smile made Torak shudder. When she licked her lips, he glimpsed a little, pointed black tongue.

Nef the Bat Mage puzzled him most of all. Her small eyes darted suspiciously from Thiazzi to Seshru, and she seemed at odds with them both – and with herself.

Far away, an owl hooted.

Seshru's smile faltered.

Thiazzi went still.

Nef murmured under her breath, and put her hand to the dusky clan-creature fur on her shoulder.

The torchlight dipped.

With a start of terror, Torak saw that a *fourth* Soul-Eater sat in the deep of the cave – where before there had been only shadow.

'Behold,' whispered Seshru, 'the Masked One is come.'

'Eostra,' said Thiazzi hoarsely, 'the Eagle Owl Mage.'

Nef grasped a stone sapling and rose to her feet, hauling Torak with her.

The Masked One, thought Torak. He remembered the pain in the Walker's face. *Cruellest of the cruel.*

Through the gloom he made out a tall grey mask. From it glared the unblinking eyes of the greatest of owls. Owl feathers covered the head, from which rose two sharp owl ears. Long coils of ashen hair hung about a feathered robe. Only the hands could be seen. The nails were hooked, and tinged with blue, like those of a corpse. The flesh had the pale-green sheen of rotting meat.

'Bring it close,' said a voice as harsh as a death-rattle.

Torak was pushed nearer, and thrown to his knees. He caught a whiff of decay, like the smell of the Raven bone-grounds. Dread froze his heart.

With appalling slowness, the owl mask bent over him, and he felt a fierce and evil will beating at his mind.

Just when he could bear it no longer, the mask withdrew. 'It is well,' it said. 'Take it away.'

Torak breathed out shakily, and crawled back towards the light. The torches flared. When he dared look again, Eostra the Eagle Owl Mage was gone.

But the change in the cave was palpable. The Oak Mage and the Viper Mage moved with sharpened purpose among the stone trees, fetching baskets and pouches whose contents Torak couldn't see.

'Come, boy,' said Nef. 'Help me feed and water the offerings. Then you and I will make the first sacrifice.'

EIGHTEEN

The dread of Eostra's presence clung to Torak as he followed the Bat Mage through the forest of stone.

Nef handed him the pouch that held the owl. 'Put it there,' she said, indicating a ledge near the altar, 'and follow me.'

As he set down the pouch, Torak loosened the neck a little, to give the owl some air. Nef barked mirthlessly. 'It makes you uneasy to harm a hunter. You'll have to do worse if you want to be a Soul-Eater.' Snatching a torch, she set off through the twisting tunnels. 'You'll have to take on the burden of sin for the good of the many. Could you do that, boy?'

'– Yes,' Torak said doubtfully.

'We'll find out,' said Nef. 'Tell me. How old are you?'

He blinked. 'Thirteen summers.'

'Thirteen.' Her brow furrowed. 'My son would have been fifteen, if he'd lived.'

For a moment, Torak almost felt sorry for her.

'Thirteen summers,' repeated the Bat Mage. With a faraway look, she reached into a pouch at her belt and brought out a handful of dead flies. On her shoulder the clan-creature fur stirred – stretched its neck – and snapped them up. 'There, my beauty,' she murmured. She caught Torak staring. 'Well go on,' she said, 'let her sniff you!'

He offered it his finger. The bat's crumpled ears quivered, delicate as new leaves, and he felt the brief warmth of a tiny tongue tasting his skin. *Strange prey*, he thought. He pictured how the bat would move over snow: its claws digging in, its elbows making tiny stump-like tracks. With a pang he thought how the ever-curious Wolf would have raced to investigate.

'She likes you,' growled Nef. 'Odd.' Abruptly she headed off again, and Torak had to run to keep up.

'How did your son die?' he asked.

'He starved,' said Nef. 'The prey fled our part of the Forest. We must have done something to displease the World Spirit.' Her scowl deepened. 'I wanted to die too. I tried to, but the Wolf Mage saved me.'

At the mention of his father, Torak nearly fell over.

'He saved my life,' Nef said bitterly. 'Now he's dead, and I can never repay him. Gratitude is a terrible thing.'

Suddenly she seized Torak's hands and pressed them to the wall of the tunnel, crushing them under her own. 'That's why we're here, boy, to make things right with the World Spirit! Quick! Tell me what you feel!'

He struggled, but her hands imprisoned his. Beneath his palms the rock was clammy and warm. Deep within, he felt something squirm. 'It lives!' he whispered.

'What you feel,' said Nef, 'is the skin that separates our world from the Other. There are places under the earth where that skin has worn thin.'

Torak thought of a cave he'd once ventured into. He asked if there were such places in the Forest.

'There's one,' said Nef. 'We tried it, but the way was shut.'

'Why do you need it?' he said. 'Why are you here?'

The small eyes glinted. 'You know why.'

He licked his lips. 'But – I need to learn more if I'm to be a Soul-Eater.'

Nef leaned closer, engulfing him in the acrid smell of bat. 'First we must find the Door,' she said. 'The place where the skin is thinnest. Then we must make the charm to protect us from what will come forth. Last,' her voice sank to a whisper, 'in the dark of the moon – we must open the Door.'

Torak swallowed. Once again he heard the voice of the Walker. *'They are going to open the Door!'*

'But – why?' he breathed. 'Why do you – '

'No more questions!' snarled Nef. 'We've got work to do!'

They hurried on, emerging after a time into the stinking cavern where Torak had heard the wolverine. He saw a stream that he'd missed before, pooling in a hollow before vanishing down a crevice. Beside it stood a birchbark pail and a wovenbark sack of dried cod.

Nef told him to take them both and follow her. Shambling to the first of the hollows, she shifted the slab that blocked it by a hand's width. She tossed in a scrap of cod, drew out a small birchwood bowl, filled it, and pushed it in again.

Torak caught a gleam of eyes. An otter: the one whose joyful snow-slide he'd tracked in the Forest. Her sleek coat was matted, and she shrank from them. His pity for Nef drained away. If she could do this . . .

The Bat Mage pushed back the slab, leaving a narrow

gap for air, and limped to the next hollow. Slowly they made their way through the cavern. Torak glimpsed a white fox curled in exhausted slumber. An eagle: all ruffled feathers and glaring yellow rage. A lynx so cramped that it couldn't turn round. The spitting fury of a wolverine.

Finally, in a deep pit almost completely sealed by an enormous slab of stone, he glimpsed the awesome, unmistakeable bulk of an ice bear.

'That one gets only water,' said Nef, taking the pail and splashing some into the hole. 'We need to keep it starved, or it'll be too strong.'

The bear gave a thunderous growl, and hurled itself against the slab. The slab held firm. Not even the power of an ice bear could move it.

'How did you catch it?' said Torak.

Nef snorted. 'Seshru has some skill with sleeping-potions. Thiazzi's strength has its uses.'

Torak turned, and took in the length of the cavern. He'd begun to realize that what the Soul-Eaters were doing went far beyond threatening Wolf. 'Hunters,' he said. 'They're all hunters.'

'Yes,' said the Bat Mage.

'Where's the wolf?'

Nef went still. 'How do you know there is one?'

He thought quickly. 'I heard it. A howl.'

The Bat Mage lurched back the way they'd come. 'The wolf will be brought in tomorrow, in the dark of the moon. When it's time.'

Covertly, Torak glanced about him to see if some hollow remained unexplored.

Again Nef seemed to read his mind. 'He isn't here. We're keeping him apart from the others.'

'Why?'

That earned him a sharp glance. 'You ask a lot of questions.'

'I want to learn.'

The bat on Nef's shoulder squirmed, and she watched it lift off and flit away into the darkness. 'Because of Seshru,' she said. 'Last summer she received a strange message from our brother across the Sea. *The Wolf lives.*' We don't know what it means. But that's why we keep the wolf separate.'

Torak's thoughts whirled. Did they know something? Maybe not enough to tip them off that he was a spirit walker, but something . . .

He realized that Nef was watching him keenly, so he asked the question to which he thought he already knew the answer. 'All these creatures. What are you going to do to them?'

'What do you think we're going to do?'

'Kill them,' he said.

The Bat Mage nodded. 'The blood of the nine hunters is the most dreadful – the most potent of sacrifices.'

His temples pounded. The cave walls pressed in on him.

'You say you want to be one of us,' said Nef. 'Well, that begins now.' She raised her torch, and Torak saw that she'd brought him full circle, back to the forest of stone. It was deserted. The other Soul-Eaters had gone. On the ledge at his shoulder, the owl in the pouch lay still. Awaiting sacrifice.

The breath caught in his throat. 'But – you said tomorrow. In the dark of the moon.'

'For the full charm, yes. But first we have the *finding* of the Door – and for that, too, we must protect ourselves. The blood of the owl will do that. And it will help us hear what lies within.'

Wedging the torch in a crevice, she reached for the pouch, and drew out the bird. With one hand she held it down. With the other she extended her knife-hilt to Torak. 'Take it,' she ordered. 'Cut off its head.'

Torak stared at the owl, and the owl stared back at him: bedraggled, limp with fright.

Nef jabbed the knife-hilt in his chest. 'Are you so weak that you fail at the first test?'

A test . . .

He saw now that everything the Bat Mage had done had been leading up to this. She meant to find out if he was who he pretended to be: a White Fox boy determined to step over into the murky world of the Soul-Eaters.

'But it isn't prey,' he said. 'We're not going to eat it. And we're not hunting. It hasn't had a chance to get away.'

The eyes of the Bat Mage were bright with a terrible certainty. 'Sometimes,' she said, 'the innocent must suffer for the good of the many.'

Good? thought Torak. What's this got to do with good?

'Take the knife,' commanded Nef.

He couldn't breathe. The air in his lungs was hot and heavy with sin.

'Come!' said Nef. 'We are the Soul-Eaters, we speak for the World Spirit! Are you with us or against us? There is no middle path!'

Torak took the knife. He knelt, and placed his free hand on the owl. He'd never felt anything so soft as those feathers, so delicate as the fragile bones that sheltered the small, racing heart.

If he refused to do this, Nef would kill him. And the Soul-Eaters would open the Door, and unleash who knew what horrors upon the world.

And Wolf would die.

He took a deep breath – silently begged the World Spirit for forgiveness – and brought down the knife.

NINETEEN

'It's done,' said the Bat Mage.

'Is that the blood?' said the Oak Mage.

'Of course.'

Hardly daring to breathe, Renn shrank deeper into her hiding-place: a dank fissure behind a thicket of stone saplings. Where was Torak? What had they done to him?

She watched the Soul-Eater bearing a sputtering torch in one hand and a horn cup in the other. In the flickering light, the bow-legged shadow was vast. Overhead, thousands of bats stirred.

'Where's the boy?' said the Oak Mage, taking his place before the altar.

'With the offerings,' said the Bat Mage. 'He seemed shaken. Seshru is watching him.'

Renn's skin crawled.

'So he's shaken, is he?' sneered the Oak Mage. 'Nef, he's a coward! I hope that won't affect the charm.'

'Why should it, Thiazzi?' retorted the Bat Mage. 'He came to *us*, he offered himself. He'll serve the purpose well enough.'

What purpose? thought Renn. From what she'd heard, Torak's disguise had succeeded; they didn't know who he was, or that he was a spirit walker. But why did they need him?

She wondered, too, how many Soul-Eaters there were in these caves. There had been seven when they'd banded together, and two were now dead, which left five; but the White Fox boy had mentioned only four. Where was the fifth?

Then she forgot about that. The Bat Mage set the torch in a cleft, dipped her forefinger in the cup, and daubed a streak of darkness on her brow. She did the same for the Oak Mage.

'The blood of the owl,' she chanted, *'for keenest hearing.'*

'And to protect us from those who rage within,' intoned the Oak Mage.

Renn stifled a gasp. *The blood of the owl* . . . So they'd killed it, just as the White Fox boy had said. But why? To kill a hunter angers the World Spirit, and brings bad luck on oneself and one's clan.

Resting her hand on a sapling, she was startled to feel a sickly warmth. She knew instantly what it was. The heat of the Otherworld.

To protect us from those who rage within . . . Did they mean demons? Demons from the Otherworld?

If only she'd followed Torak at once! But instead she'd paced the snow: furious with him, arguing with herself. By the time she'd made up her mind – had hidden her bow and found her courage – the cave had swallowed him.

That was when she'd heard the echoing tread of a man. She'd barely had time to slip inside before he'd loomed from the darkness: big as an auroch, his face hidden in a tangle of hair and beard. The Oak Clan tattoo had been plain on the back of his hand. The smell of spruce-blood had hung about him like mist in the Forest.

In awe she'd watched him put his shoulder to a slab of rock five times her size, and slide it across the cave mouth as if it had been a wicker screen. They were shut in. She'd had no choice but to follow him into the twisting tunnels: fearing to get too close, or worse – to be left behind in the dark.

At last they'd emerged into this forest of stone. Around her she felt the presence of shadowy figures watching, waiting. Even the drip, drip of water sounded stealthy. Worst of all was the flutter and squeak of thousands of bats. Did they know she was here? Would they tell the Soul-Eaters?

Peering between two stone saplings, she watched the Bat Mage take up her torch and touch it to others wedged around the altar. Firelight flared – then suddenly dipped, as if in homage. The bats fell silent. The air grew heavy with evil.

Renn jammed her knuckles in her mouth.

A *third* Soul-Eater sat at the head of the altar. In the gloom, Renn made out feathered robes that seemed to grow from the stone itself; the fearsome orange glare of an eagle owl.

Behind the mask, a chill voice spoke. 'The souls. Give me the souls.'

The Bat Mage placed something small on the altar – and the shadowy robes moved to cover it. Renn guessed that the Bat Mage had worked some kind of binding charm, and trapped the owl's souls in its feathers.

'It is well,' said the voice behind the mask.

Renn thought of the owl's souls, caught – perhaps for

ever – in the grip of the Eagle Owl Mage. She wondered if they would ever escape, to flutter into the sky, seeking the shelter of the First Tree . . .

Dread dragged at her heart as she watched the Mage place something dark and curved on the altar. It was the Walker's strike-fire: the stone claw that he'd taken from a cave in the Forest long ago.

Next, the Oak Mage reached into a pouch, and held up a small black pebble with the sheen and smoothness of an eye. *'This is the owl,'* he chanted as he laid it beside the strike-fire. *'The first of the nine hunters.'*

The nine hunters?

Renn's fingers closed about a slender twig of stone. Feeling sick, she watched the Oak Mage upend the pouch. More pebbles rattled onto the altar.

The Bat Mage chose one and laid it beside that which betokened the owl. *'This,* she chanted, *'is the eagle. For keenest sight.'*

'And to protect us from those who rage within,' chanted the others.

Another pebble was set beside the second. And another. And another. As Renn listened, the hideous extent of the impending sacrifice revealed itself.

'This is the fox. For cunning . . .
This is the otter. For water-skill . . .
This is the wolverine. For rage . . .
This is the bear. For strength. .
This is the lynx. For leaping . . .
This is the wolf . . . '

Renn shut her eyes.

' . . . For wisdom . . . '

A hush fell. The ninth pebble lay waiting to be set in its place: to close the ring of eyes encircling the strike-fire.

The Eagle Owl Mage extended a talon to grasp it. *'This,'* she chanted, *'is the man. For cruelty.'*

Man.

Renn's grip tightened on the stone. At last she knew why the Soul-Eaters had let the White Fox boy join them. And now Torak had taken his place . . .

The stone snapped. The bats exploded in a fluttering, squeaking cloud.

'Someone's there!' cried Nef, leaping to her feet.

'It's the boy!' boomed Thiazzi. 'He's been listening!'

Torchlight slid between the stone trees as the Soul-Eaters began to search the cave.

Wildly Renn cast about for an escape; but in choosing her hiding-place, she'd crept too far from the tunnel. She couldn't get back without being seen.

Nearer and nearer came the light, reaching for her. Nearer came the heavy tread of the Oak Mage.

She did the only thing she could. She climbed up.

The fissure was jagged as an axe-cut, and she skinned her palms as she groped for handholds. She raised her head – couldn't see anything – scrambled higher into the dark.

The footsteps were almost upon her.

Her fingers found a ledge. No time to think. She heaved herself onto it, praying that the rustling of the bats would mask the frantic scrabbling of her boots.

It wasn't a ledge, it was a tunnel, she'd found a tunnel! Too low to stand up – she bumped her head – dropped to all fours, and crawled in.

The tunnel bent to the right, good, if she could get inside, the light wouldn't find her. But it was so narrow that she could barely squeeze in, and the roof was getting lower – she had to crawl on her belly, and push herself ahead on her elbows.

Squirming like a lizard, she wriggled deeper. As she

twisted her head to look back, she saw the yellow light flickering closer, nearly touching her boots. She wasn't far enough in, it was going to find her . . .

With a tremendous heave she pulled herself round the bend – just as the light snapped at her heels.

Below her, a man's harsh breathing. The sharp tang of spruce-blood.

She bit down hard on her lower lip.

Then – from the other side of the cave – the thud of running feet.

'It wasn't the boy!' panted the Bat Mage. 'He's been with Seshru all the time!'

'Are you sure?' said the Oak Mage, his voice shockingly close.

'It must have been the bats,' said Nef.

'Well from now on,' growled Thiazzi, 'we'd better keep watch.'

His voice receded, taking the light with it. Darkness flooded back.

Weak with relief, Renn slumped on her belly. For a long time she lay in the blackness, listening to the Soul-Eaters moving about, talking in low voices.

At last, their voices faded. They had left the forest of stone. The bats fluttered, then sank into silence. Still Renn waited, fearing a trap.

When she was as certain as she could be that she was alone, she started to wriggle backwards out of the tunnel.

The hood of her parka snagged on the roof, and she kicked forwards to unhook it – but the tunnel was too low, she couldn't move far enough to free herself.

Irritated, she tried again. And again. She tried wriggling from side to side. The tunnel was too narrow, it didn't do any good.

She lay on her belly, struggling to take in what had happened. Her arms were folded awkwardly beneath her chest. Against her fists she felt the thunder of her heart.

The truth crashed upon her.

She was stuck.

TWENTY

She thought about screaming for help; but that would bring the Soul-Eaters. She thought about lying in this stinking weasel hole, dying of thirst. A quick death or a slow one. That was the choice.

She was soaked in sweat, and the tunnel walls blew back the smell of her fear. She could no longer hear the drip of water; only her ragged breath, and a strange, uneven 'drum-drum-drum' that was keeping pace with the thunder of her heart.

It *was* her heart, she realized: her heart echoing through the rock as it thumped against her ribs.

Suddenly she was horribly aware of the vast weight of stone that pressed upon her, of the utter impossibility of movement. The earth had swallowed her. It had only to give the slightest twitch to crush her like a louse.

No-one would ever know. No-one would find her bones and lay them to rest in the Raven bone-ground. No-one would put the Death Marks on her, to keep her souls together.

Darkness lay on her face like a second skin. She shut her eyes. Opened them. No difference. She dragged her hand from under her, held it before her nose. Couldn't see her fingers. They didn't exist. *She* didn't exist.

She couldn't get enough air. She took a great, shuddering breath – and the rock shrank tight around her.

She panicked. Clawing, kicking, moaning, drowning in a black sea of terror. She collapsed, exhausted, grinding her mouth into the unyielding stone to keep back the whimpers.

Deep in the earth, there is no time. No winter. No summer. No moon. No sun. There is only the dark. Renn lay for so long that she wasn't Renn anymore. Whole winters drifted over her. She became part of the rock.

She heard demons cackling on the other side. Lights flashed. Red eyes glared at her, coming nearer. She was dying. Soon her souls would be scattered, and she'd become a demon: squeaking and gibbering in the endless heat of the Otherworld, hating and desiring all living things.

But now more lights were coming: tiny, brilliant green needle-pricks that shimmered and danced, chasing the red eyes away. There was a humming in her ears, a humming of . . .

Bees?

She jerked awake. Bees? In winter, in a cave in the Far North?

The humming was nearer, and it was definitely bees. Although she couldn't see them, she could feel them, brushing against her cheeks. What were they? A message from her clan-guardian? The spirits of her ancestors? Or a trick of the demons, waiting behind the rock?

But they didn't feel evil. Shutting her eyes, she lay and listened to the humming of the bees . . .

It's the Moon of the Salmon Run, and the blackthorn trees are in bloom, and the bees are humming. Renn is eight summers old: hunting with Fin-Kedinn, eager to try out the beautiful new bow he has made for her. She pauses on the riverbank to admire its gleaming golden curve, and the blackthorn blossom drifts down like summer snow, and catches on the manes of the forest horses who stand in the shallows.

When she drags her eyes away from her bow, she's startled to see that Fin-Kedinn has crossed the river and gone on ahead. Hurriedly she tumbles down the bank and splashes after him.

The mares don't like her coming so close to their foals. They show the whites of their eyes, ready to kick.

Renn isn't frightened, but to avoid them she flounders deeper, and the mud sucks at her boots. She's stuck.

She panics. Since her father died, she's had nightmares about being trapped. What if the horses trample her? What if the Hidden People of the river pull her under?

Suddenly the sunlight is blotted out, and Fin-Kedinn is standing over her. His face is as impenetrable as ever, but in his blue eyes there's a glint of laughter.

'Renn,' he says calmly, 'there's an answer to this. But you won't find it if you don't use your head.'

She blinks. Glances down. Then – wobbling – she steps out of her boots.

Laughing, her uncle swings her high in his arms. And now she's laughing too, and squealing as he swings her down in a dizzying swoop to pluck her boots from the mud. Still laughing, he sets her on his shoulders, and wades to the bank, and around them the blossom is drifting, and the bees are humming . . .

The bees were still humming, but she couldn't see them any more because she was back in the weasel hole. The thought of Fin-Kedinn was like a beam of light in the dark. Her fingers touched the polished slate wrist-guard on her forearm. He'd made it for her when he'd taught her to shoot.

'There is an answer,' she whispered. 'Use your head . . .'

Her breathing slowed. Her chest was no longer heaving. The walls didn't seem to grip quite as tightly as before.

Of course! she thought. Don't breathe so deeply, and you won't take up so much space!

Keeping her breathing shallow was a small victory, and it cheered her greatly. She wasn't dead yet. If only there was some way of making herself narrower still.

Maybe it *was* possible. Yes! Why hadn't she thought of it before?

Slowly – painfully – she uncurled her right arm and stretched it forwards as far as she could. Then she tilted her left shoulder back. Now she really *was* narrower, because she wasn't blocking the tunnel face on, but tilting sideways.

The next bit would be harder. Bending her right arm back over her head, she clutched at her parka. Missed. Tried again, and grabbed the hood. Tugged. It was mercifully loose: Tanugeak had told her that the White Foxes made them like that because loose clothes are warmer. Like a snake sloughing off its skin, Renn wriggled and pulled, wriggled and pulled – and at last the parka slid over her head.

She lay panting, and the bees hummed giddily.

Now for the birdskin jerkin. This was harder – no hood to grab hold of – but without the parka she could move much more easily.

131

The relief when the jerkin came off was overwhelming. For a while she lay gasping, feeling the sweat chilling her skin, touching the clothes bunched up in front of her. But now she was resting with a purpose. In only her leggings, she was half the size she had been, and could slip through the tunnel like an eel. She could get back to the forest of stone, and find Torak and Wolf.

She started wriggling backwards, but her leggings snagged on a spur. It didn't stop her for long, but to her surprise, the buzzing of the bees turned as fierce as hornets. What did that mean? Didn't they want her to go back?

Stretching her hand into the darkness before her, she felt cool air stinging her raw fingers. It wasn't merely the chill of drying sweat, it was a current of cold air. And if it was cold, it must be coming from outside.

Pushing with her toes, she edged forwards through the tunnel. It sloped steeply up, but now that she had more room to squirm, it was easier, and she could grasp projections jutting from the rocks, and pull herself along.

Still she hesitated. If she went forwards – wherever that led – it would mean leaving Torak behind. She couldn't do that. She had to warn him that he was the ninth hunter in the sacrifice.

And yet – if she went back, she would find herself once again in the cavern of the Soul-Eaters; and even if she could evade them, and somehow find Torak – even if they could rescue Wolf, and make their way through the tunnels to the mouth of the cave – how would they get out, when it was blocked by that great slab which only Thiazzi could move?

She chewed her lip, wondering what to do.

Fin-Kedinn often said that when things went wrong, the worst you could do was nothing. 'Sometimes, Renn, you have to make a choice. Maybe it's a good one, maybe not.

132

But it's better than doing nothing.'

Renn thought for a moment. Then she started wriggling forwards.

TWENTY-ONE

In the forest of stone, the Soul-Eaters were making ready for the finding of the Door.

Nef hobbled about dipping torches in pitch and setting them in place, while her bat flitted overhead. The veins in Thiazzi's temples bulged as he hauled rocks into a circle about the altar. Seshru fitted three masks with gutskin eyes for seeing into the Otherworld. Of Eostra there was no sign.

Torak dreaded the return of the Eagle Owl Mage – and yet he needed it, too. He had to be certain that all four Soul-Eaters were here in this cave, before he could slip away and find Wolf. Until then, he had to be the apprentice Soul-Eater: grinding earthblood on a slab, while the blood of the owl stiffened on his forehead.

After he'd killed it, Nef had put her heavy hand on his shoulder. 'Well done. You've just taken the first step to becoming one of us.'

No I haven't, Torak had told her in his head.

But he knew what Renn would have said. 'Where will it end, Torak? How far will you go?'

He remembered an argument he'd had with Fin-Kedinn, when he'd begged the Raven Leader to let him go in search of the Soul-Eaters. In vain.

'Your father tried to fight them,' Fin-Kedinn had said, 'and they killed him! What makes you think you'd be any stronger?'

At the time, Torak had raged against the Raven Leader's refusal, but now he understood what lay behind it. It wasn't only the evil of the Soul-Eaters which Fin-Kedinn feared. It was that within Torak himself.

Once, the Raven Leader had told him the story of the first winter that ever was. 'The World Spirit fought a terrible battle with the Great Auroch, the most powerful of demons. At last the World Spirit flung the demon burning from the sky; but as it fell, the wind scattered its ashes, and a tiny speck settled in the marrow of every creature on earth. Evil exists in us all, Torak. Some fight it. Some feed it. That's how it's always been.'

Torak thought of that now: a tiny black seed in his marrow, waiting to burst into life.

'Bring me the earthblood,' said Seshru, startling him. 'Quickly. It's almost time.'

He lifted the heavy slab and carried it to the altar.

How long before he could escape and find Wolf?

The plan he'd come up with was dangerous – it might even kill him – but it was the only one he could think of. First he had to return to the stinking tunnel where the "offerings" were held; then he had to get as close to the ice bear as he dared, and then –

'Put it there,' ordered Seshru.

He did as he was told, and made to withdraw – but her cold hand clasped his wrist.

'Stay. Watch. Learn.'

He had no choice but to kneel beside her.

She'd painted the mask with lime, turning it glaring white. Now she dipped her forefinger in a paste of alder juice and earthblood, and reddened the mouth. Her finger worked in slow circles that made Torak dizzy. As he watched, the face began to live. The scarlet lips glistened with spittle. The mane of dead grass rustled and grew.

'Don't touch,' whispered the Viper Mage.

He jerked back with a cry.

Laughter rippled through the Soul-Eaters. They were playing with him, making him feel one of them for some purpose of their own.

'You want to know why we're doing this,' said Nef, guessing the question in his mind.

'Why are we going to open the Door?' murmured Seshru. 'Why are we going to let out the demons?'

'To rule,' said Thiazzi, coming to stand beside her. 'To unite the clans and rule.'

Torak licked his lips. 'But – the clans rule themselves.'

'Much good it does them,' growled Nef. 'Have you never asked yourself why the World Spirit is so fickle, so unpredictable? Why does it send the prey at some times, but not others? Why does it kill one child with sickness, but spare another? Because the clans don't live as they should!'

'They have different ways of sacrificing,' said Thiazzi, 'of sending their Dead on the Journey. This displeases the World Spirit.'

'There's no *order* to it,' said Nef.

Thiazzi drew himself up to his full height. '*We* know the

true way. We will show them.'

'But to do that,' said Seshru, fixing Torak with her unfathomable gaze, 'we must have power. The demons will give it to us.'

He tried to look away, but her eyes held his. 'No-one can control demons,' he said.

Thiazzi's laugh echoed through the cave. 'You're wrong. If only you knew how wrong!'

'The mistake others made in the past,' said Seshru, 'was to overreach themselves. Our brother who is lost summoned an elemental and trapped it in a great bear. Of course he couldn't control it. It was a magnificent madness.'

Magnificent? thought Torak. That madness had cost his father his life.

Nef hobbled towards him. 'The demons *we* summon,' she declared, 'will be as many as the bats that darken the moon –'

' – as many as the leaves in the Forest,' boomed the Oak Mage. 'We will flood the land with terror!'

'And after that . . . ' the Viper Mage stretched out her hands, then drew them towards her, as if grasping an invisible bounty, 'we will call them back, and the demons will do *our* bidding, because we – and only we – possess that which forces them to our will.'

Torak stared at her. 'What do you mean?'

The beautiful mouth curved. 'Ah. You'll see.'

Torak looked from Nef to Seshru to Thiazzi. Their faces were alight with fervour. While he had been plotting to rescue Wolf, they had been hatching a plan to gain dominion over the Forest.

'Soul-Eaters, they call us,' said Thiazzi. He spat out a crumb of spruce-blood.

'A foolish name,' said Nef.

'But useful,' murmured Seshru with her sideways smile, 'if it keeps them in fear.'

Torak rose uncertainly to his feet. 'I – should go,' he said. 'I should guard the offerings.'

'From what?' said Thiazzi, blocking his path. 'The Eye is shut. Nothing can get in.'

'Or out,' said Seshru.

Torak swallowed. 'One of them might escape.'

The Viper Mage slid him a mocking glance. 'He wants to get away from us.'

'I told you he was a coward,' sneered Thiazzi.

'Here.' Nef held out a length of shrivelled black root. 'Take it. Eat.'

'What is it?' said Torak.

Seshru licked her lips, showing her little pointed tongue. 'It'll send you into a trance.'

'This is part of being a Soul-Eater,' said Thiazzi. 'That is what you want. Isn't it?'

All three were watching him.

He took the root and put it in his mouth. It tasted sweet, but with an undertow of rottenness that made him gag.

They had trapped him. First the owl. Now this. Where would it end? How was he ever going to find Wolf?

TWENTY-TWO

There was black fog in Wolf's head, and it told him that Tall Tailless wasn't coming to rescue him, not ever ever ever.

Something had happened. He'd fallen prey to a Fast Wet, or been attacked by the bad taillesses. Otherwise he would have come by now.

As Wolf paced the tiny stinking Den, he shook his head to get rid of the fog, but only succeeded in bumping his nose on a rock. The Den was far away from all the other creatures, and so small that he could only take a single pace before he had to turn round and go back again. Pace, turn. Pace, turn.

He *ached* to run. In his sleeps, he loped up hills and down into valleys; he rolled about in ferns, waggling his paws and growling with delight. Sometimes he leapt so high that he soared into the Up, and snapped at the Bright White Eye. But always when he woke, he was back in the stinking Den.

He could have howled – if he'd had the spirit to howl. But what was the use? Nobody would hear him except the bad taillesses and the demons.

Pace, turn. Pace, turn.

Hunger gnawed at his belly. In the Forest, when he hadn't made a kill for a long time, hunger sharpened his nose and ears, and put a spring in his lope that sent him flying between the trees. But this hunger was so bad that it didn't even hurt.

All the pacing was making him giddy, but he couldn't stop, even though it got harder with every step. His tail was much, much worse. He'd tried licking it better, but it didn't taste like himself any more, and it didn't carry his scent. It smelt like Not-Breath prey that's lain in the Forest for many Lights and Darks. It tasted bad. The badness was making him sick. He could feel it seeping through him, eating up his strength.

Pace, turn. Pace, turn.

He was deep in the guts of the earth, and far from all other creatures. He missed the whimpering of the otter, and the fury of the wolverine; he even missed the stupid snarling of that stupid bear. And yet – he wasn't alone. His ears rang with the squeaking of bats and the gibber of demons. He could smell them behind the rocks, hear the scrabbling of their claws. There were so many. It was a torment not to be able to attack: to bite and snap and tear, as he was meant to do. Hunting demons was what he was *for*.

Pace, turn. Pace, turn.

It was demons that had put the badness in his tail; it was demons that were blowing black fog through his head. Because of them, he'd begun to see and hear things that weren't there. Sometimes he saw Tall Tailless crouching beside him. Once he'd heard the high, thin yowl that the female made when she put the grouse bone to her muzzle.

Now, beneath the bat-squeaks and the scratching of demons, he caught a new sound, a real one. Two taillesses coming closer: one small, one heavier.

For a moment, hope leapt. *Could it be Tall Tailless and the female?*

No. This wasn't his pack-brother coming to rescue him. It was the bad taillesses: Viper-Tongue and Pale-Pelt.

Knowing he was too weak to fight, Wolf cowered in the Den. He heard the covering being scraped back, and saw a lump of bark lowered onto the floor. He snapped up the wet. There was just enough to waken thirst, but not enough to send it back to sleep.

And yet – what was this? Another scent clung to Viper-Tongue's overpelt. A clean, well-loved scent: *the scent of Tall Tailless!*

Wolf's joy swiftly turned to horror as he realized that this could only mean one thing. The bad taillesses had caught his pack-brother!

He went wild. Yowling, hurling himself against the Den. He put up his muzzle to howl, but strong paws grabbed his head. He twisted – tried to bite – but he was too weak and they were too strong. Once again the hated tree bark was wound about his muzzle.

Once again he was unable to howl.

TWENTY-THREE

The forest of stone was growing before Torak's eyes.
Rocky trunks thrust upwards with splintering cracks.
Brittle branches spread with the jerky shudder of broken
fingers.

He shut his eyes, but still he saw it. He wondered if this
was the "inner eye" which Renn had told him about: the
one you used for Magecraft. He wished savagely that she
was with him now.

The black root was sweet and rotten in his mouth. He
could feel it tugging at his souls, although he'd only
chewed it for a moment, then hidden it under his tongue.
He felt dizzy and sick, but more alert than ever before in
his life.

He watched the Soul-Eaters circling the altar. Like the
forest of stone, they had changed beyond recognition. The
Bat Mage snarled through a wrinkled muzzle as she spread
her leathery wings to shadow the cave. The Oak Mage

towered over the stone trees, his gnarled bark crackling as he brandished twin rattles made of teeth and skulls. The Viper Mage glared with dead gutskin eyes through a hissing mane of serpents.

Only the Eagle Owl Mage remained unchanged, as if rooted in stone.

Forgotten in the shadows, Torak hung back. Now was the time to slip away: to go in search of Wolf. But the black root held him fast in an invisible web. He couldn't move.

Sounds came to him more keenly than ever before. He heard every drip from the stone trees; every bat-squeak, every flicker of wet snake tongues. He knew why, and the knowledge sickened him. The blood of the owl had sharpened his hearing.

Hating himself for doing nothing, he watched the Viper Mage whirl round and round, thrashing her snake head in dizzying circles. A serpent slithered past his face. He caught its split yellow stare, the black lightning of its tongue.

Suddenly the Viper Mage moved to the altar, and plunged both hands in a hollowed stone – then drew them out, spattering red. Thrashing, swaying, she glided to the back of the cavern, and planted her palms on the rock.

The Oak Mage and the Bat Mage bayed in ecstasy.

Torak gasped.

As the Viper Mage sprang away, her handprints smoked. The red stain was eating through the skin between this world and the Other.

At last he understood the meaning of the yellow handprints he'd glimpsed on his way into the caves. They'd been made by someone trying to find the Door.

And now, behind the serpent hiss and the rattle of tooth on bone – behind the groans of the earth itself – Torak heard a sound that made his knees give, and the back of his neck crawl as if a spider were scuttling across it. A sound to suck the hope from the marrow, and stop the heart with dread: harsh, malevolent, rasping *breath*.

Demons. Demons on the other side of the rock, lusting to be let loose.

In helpless horror he stared at the whirling, chanting Soul-Eaters. What should he do? He had to find Wolf. He had to stop them engulfing the world in terror.

The Viper Mage was clutching the Walker's strike-fire and tapping it over the rock, pausing now and then to listen. Faster went the rattles. Faster went the 'tap-tap-tap' of the black stone claw.

Torak's head swam. He tried to move, but the invisible web had him in its grip.

'Tap-tap-tap.'

Between the outstretched arms of the Viper Mage, *the rock began to move*.

Torak blinked. It had to be just a flicker of torchlight . . .

No. There it was again: like a hand pushing up beneath taut-stretched hide. Pushing up *beneath* the rock.

This time there was no mistaking it. Behind the rock – in the burning chaos of the Otherworld – the demons were straining to break through. Smooth, blind heads tented and stretched the stone. Cruel mouths gaped and sucked. Savage claws scrabbled. The wall of the cavern was buckling, fragile as a day-old leaf. Not for long could it withstand such terrible, insatiable hunger.

The Eagle Owl Mage rose and raised one arm, and Torak saw that she held a black oak mace surmounted by a fiery stone.

The Soul-Eaters paused in their dance. *'The fire-opal,'* they breathed.

Bewildered and fascinated, Torak sank to his knees – and the fire-opal filled the cavern with crimson light. It was the blistering heat at the heart of the fiercest ember. It was the clamorous scarlet of fresh blood on snow. It was the blaze of the angriest sunset, and the glare of the Great Auroch in the deep of winter. It was beauty and terror, ecstasy and pain – and the demons wanted it. Their howls shook the cavern as they hurled themselves at the rock, redoubling their onslaught in their frenzy.

Torak swayed. *This* was the secret power of the Soul-Eaters. With this they would bend the demons to their will.

'The fire-opal,' they whispered, as the Eagle Owl Mage held the mace on high, and around her the stone trees thrashed in a soundless wind.

As Torak watched, the Oak Mage and the Bat Mage gnashed their teeth until black spittle flew, and the Viper Mage planted her smoking palms against the rock – and threw up her head and cried, 'The Door – is – found!'

She staggered back, and Torak saw that on the rock she'd completed a great ring of handprints – and inside the ring, the demons were on the point of bursting through.

At that moment, the Eagle Owl Mage lowered the fire-opal, shrouding it in her robes – and its scarlet light was quenched. The taut-stretched rock sprang back. The howls of the demons sank to a furious panting.

'The Door is found,' hissed the Viper Mage, and slumped to the ground in a faint.

The invisible web holding Torak snapped.

He leapt to his feet and ran.

TWENTY-FOUR

Torak raced through the tunnels, skinning his knuckles and barking his shins. He stumbled, and the torch he'd snatched from the forest of stone lurched wildly. As he righted himself, a leathery wing fluttered past his face. He bit back a cry and staggered on.

Twice he thought he heard footsteps, but when he paused, he caught only his own echo. He doubted that the Soul-Eaters would follow him. They didn't need to. Where would he go? The Eye of the Viper was shut.

He closed his mind to that and ran on.

Fragments of what he'd witnessed flashed before his eyes. The thrusting snouts of the demons, fighting to break open the Door. The awful beauty of the fire-opal.

He couldn't believe that it had held him for so long. What spell had it cast, that had made him forget Wolf? Was this how it had been for his father? Drawn in by his curiosity, by his fatal need to know – until it was too late.

Too late. Terror seized him. Maybe it was already too late for Wolf.

As he ran, he spat out the black root, then bit it in two; crammed half in his medicine pouch, and chewed the other. The rotten undertaste made him gag, but he forced himself to swallow. No time for hesitation. He'd seen what the root had done to the Soul-Eaters. Now it had to work for him.

With alarming suddenness the first cramps gripped. Clutching his belly, he staggered into the tunnel of the offerings, jammed the torch in a crack, and fell on all fours.

He retched, spewing up a gobbet of black bile. His eyes were streaming, the tunnel was spinning. His souls were beginning to tug loose.

Still retching, he crawled to the pit that held the ice bear. He caught the sound of furred pads on stone.

Memory reached from the dark and pulled him down. A blue autumn dusk in the Forest. His father laughing at the joke he'd just made. Then, out of the shadows, the bear –

No! he told himself. Don't think about Fa, think about Wolf! *Find* Wolf.

Shivering, he crawled closer, and rested his burning forehead against the rock, peering through the chink between the floor and the slab that covered the pit.

Flinty eyes glared back at him. A growl shuddered through the rock. His spirit quailed. Even starved and weakened, the ice bear was all-powerful. Its souls would be too strong.

More cramps convulsed him. He retched . . .

. . . and suddenly he was trapped in the pit, slitting his eyes against the painful blur of light. He was so hot, so terribly hot. Above him the frail body of a boy taunted him with the maddening scent of fresh meat. The blood-smell was so strong that his claws ached as he paced and turned, and paced again.

He caught the distant murmur of man-voices, and for a moment his mind turned from the blood-smell, and he bared his teeth. He knew those voices. It was the evil ones who had taken him from the ice.

As he remembered his lost home, dull pain coursed through him. They had robbed him of his beautiful cold Sea, where the white whales sleep and the succulent seals swim; of the faithful wind which never failed to waft the blood-smell to his nose. They had stolen his ice, his never-ending ice, which hid him when he hunted, and carried him wherever he wished to go, which was all he'd ever known. They had brought him to this terrible, burning place where there was no ice; where the blood-smell was everywhere, but never within reach.

He growled as he thought how he would seize the heads of the evil ones and crush them in his jaws! He would slash their bellies and feast on their smoking guts and their sweet, slippery fat! Like the pounding of the Sea, the blood-urge thundered through him, and he roared till the rocks shook. He was the ice bear, he feared *nothing*! All, *all* was prey!

Deep inside the marrow of the ice bear, Torak's souls struggled to gain mastery. The bear's spirit was the strongest he'd ever encountered. Never had he been so engulfed by the feelings of another creature.

With a tremendous effort of will, he overcame – and the ice bear ceased to rage at the evil ones, and turned to the blood-smells: the tantalizing web of scent trails which led out into the dark, like the drag-marks after he'd hauled a walrus over the ice.

Close – maddeningly close – he smelt the blood of lynx

and otter, bat and boy; of wolverine and eagle. Further off, he smelt wolf.

Its scent was fainter than the others, and tainted with a badness he didn't understand – but for a bear who could scent a seal through the thickest ice, it was easy to trace.

The trail led down through the dark, and round to the side of his striking-paw – then up again, to where the air smelt cooler. They thought they were cunning to hide the wolf, but he would find it. And when he'd broken free and killed all the others, he would kill the wolf, too. He would catch it in his jaws and shake it till its spine cracked . . .

No! shouted Torak silently.

For a moment the great bear faltered, and in the pulsing marrow of its bones, Torak's souls struggled to escape. He'd smelt enough. His plan had worked. He knew where the Soul-Eaters had hidden Wolf.

The bear's souls were too strong.

He couldn't get out.

TWENTY-FIVE

Renn burst from the weasel hole and toppled headfirst into the snow.

After the heat of the caves, the cold was a knife in her lungs. She didn't care. She rolled onto her naked back and stared up into a blizzard of stars.

From high overhead came the caw of a raven. She gasped a fervent thanks – and her clan-guardian cawed back, warning her that it wasn't over yet.

Her teeth were chattering. She was losing heat fast. Getting to her feet, she discovered that she couldn't find her parka, jerkin or mittens, which she'd pushed before her out of the hole.

After an increasingly desperate search, she fell over them. She bundled them on, and they warmed her in moments. She blessed the skill of the White Fox women.

Above her the stars glimmered as clouds sped across the sky. No sign of the First Tree. And no moon, either.

No moon? But surely it couldn't be the dark of the moon already?

Yes it could. With a shiver she realized that she had no idea how long she'd been underground. She stared at the shadowy bulk of the mountain. Torak and Wolf were somewhere inside, bound for sacrifice in the dark of the moon. Which was now.

She had to find them. She had to go back inside.

As her eyes accustomed to the starlight, she realized that she didn't recognize her surroundings. Before her the weasel hole was a circle of blackness, but she couldn't see the standing stone, or the Eye of the Viper; only humped snow and charcoal rockfaces. For all she knew, she could be on the other side of the mountain.

Frantic, she felt her way forwards – tripped – and pitched into a snowdrift.

A very hard snowdrift, with something solid underneath.

She got to her knees and started to dig.

A skinboat. No. *Two* skinboats: both bigger than the one the White Foxes had given them, and stowed with paddles, harpoons, and rope. The Soul-Eaters had thought of everything. Drawing her knife, she slit the belly of each boat. There. See how far they got now!

From deep within the mountain came a roar.

She ran to the weasel hole. There it was again: the unmistakeable roar of an ice bear. She remembered the murderous chant of the Soul-Eaters. *A bear for strength.*

The roars fell silent. She strained to listen, but from the dark came only a warm uprush of bat-stink. She pictured Torak, alone against the might of the Soul-Eaters. She had to find him.

She thought fast. On her way through the weasel hole, she'd climbed steadily upwards. That must mean that she was now higher up the mountain than when she'd started.

'So head *down!*' she cried.

She ran, plunging into snowdrifts, pulling herself out, but heading down, always down.

With breathtaking suddenness she rounded a spur – and there was the standing stone and the Eye of the Viper. She never thought she'd be so glad to see them.

The Eye was shut, blocked by the slab which the Oak Mage had pushed across it. But maybe she could move it just enough to crawl in.

She put her shoulder against it and heaved. She might as well have tried to shift the mountain itself.

Steam misted from the bottom corner of the slab, where it didn't quite fit across the cave mouth. She tried to squeeze through the gap. It would be big enough for Wolf, but was just a few fingers too narrow for her.

As she stood before the Eye, the truth settled upon her as stealthily as snow. There was only one way back inside. The way she had come.

'I can't,' she whispered. Her breath swirled eerily in the gloom.

She ran back up the trail, and stood panting before the weasel hole. It was tiny. A tiny, cruel mouth waiting to swallow her.

She put back her head. 'I *can't!*'

Moonlight hit her smartly in the face.

She blinked. She'd got it wrong. It wasn't the dark of the moon. Not yet. There – riding above the clouds – was the thinnest of silver slivers: the very last bite that the Sky Bear hadn't yet caught. She still had one day left. And so did Torak and Wolf.

As she gazed up at the pure, steady white light, Renn felt new courage steal into her. The moon was the eternal prey:

eternally in flight across the sky, eternally caught and eaten, but always reborn, always faithfully lighting the way for hunters and prey – even in the very deep of winter, when the sun was dead. Whatever happened, the moon always came back. And so would she.

Before she could change her mind, she raced down the trail to the Soul-Eaters' sleds, where she and Torak had hidden their gear. Luckily there hadn't been any fresh snow, so she easily found her pack.

First she gobbled down a few mouthfuls of blubber, which steadied her a little. Then she packed more blubber in her food pouch for Wolf and Torak, stuck her axe in her belt, and crammed the rest of what she thought she might need in her medicine pouch. Then she raced back to the weasel hole.

The breath sawed painfully in her chest as she yanked her parka and jerkin over her head and rolled them up as small as they would go. The sweat on her skin froze instantly, but she ignored that as she tied her mitten strings round the bundled-up clothes, then fastened the other end to her ankle, so that she'd be dragging them behind her. She allowed herself one final glance at the moon, and muttered a quick prayer of thanks.

The wind burned like ice, but the unclean warmth of the weasel hole was worse. As she crawled into the blackness, panic rose in her throat. She choked it back down.

You did it once, she told herself. You can do it again.

She put down her head and began to crawl.

⼭

She never knew how long it took her to find her way back inside. Back through the ever-shrinking weasel hole, back through that final, heart-stopping narrowness – then out into the forest of stone, where – amazingly – the Soul-Eaters were nowhere to be found: only a flicker of torchlight, and a grim circle of red handprints on the wall that turned her sick with fear.

Something – maybe her clan-guardian wheeling far overhead – guided her through the twists and turns and sudden jolting drops, until she stumbled into a foetid stench, and the uncertain light of a guttering torch.

She was in a low tunnel with blood-coloured walls and smaller caves branching off it, blocked by slabs of stone. From behind the slabs she caught the scrabbling of claws, and guessed that this was where the "offerings" were confined.

'Torak?' she whispered.

No answer; but the scrabblings stilled.

'Wolf?'

Still nothing. Groping with her hands, she made her way through the gloom.

The torch went out, plunging her into blackness – and she tripped over something lying on the floor.

She lay winded, waiting for disaster to strike. When it didn't, she slipped off her mitten to investigate. Her hand touched the softness of seal-hide. It was a body in a seal-hide parka, lying on the floor.

'Torak?' she whispered.

Silence. He was either sleeping, or . . .

Dreading what she might find, she moved closer. *If he was dead*.

Her mind reeled. His souls might be thronging the dark: angry, bewildered, unable to stay together without Death Marks. His clan-soul might have got separated, leaving behind a demon. A terrible thought, that her friend might have turned against her.

No. She wouldn't believe it. Bringing her hand closer, she held it over where she guessed the face would be – and felt a faint warmth. Breath. He was alive!

Abruptly she drew back her hand. *Maybe it wasn't Torak. Maybe it was a Soul-Eater.*

Warily, she touched the hair. Thick, short, with a fringe across the forehead. A thin face, no beard; but scabbed, which could be snow-burn. It *felt* like Torak. But if she was wrong . . .

She had an idea. If it was Torak, she'd find a scar on his left calf. Last summer he'd been gashed by a boar, and had sewn it up quite badly, then forgotten to take out the stitches. In the end she'd had to do it for him, and he'd become impatient, and they'd bumped their heads, and burst out laughing.

Sliding her hand inside the boot, she ran it over the skin. *Yes.* Beneath her fingers she found the warm, smooth ridges of scarred flesh.

Trembling with relief, she grabbed him by the shoulders. 'Torak! Wake up!'

He was heavy and unresponsive.

She hissed in his ear. 'Stop it! Wake *up!*'

What was *wrong* with him? Had they given him a sleeping-potion?

'Who's there?' a woman called gruffly.

Renn froze.

A faint glow of torchlight appeared at the end of the tunnel.

'Boy?' called the woman. 'Where are you? Answer me!'

Wildly, Renn groped in the dark for a hiding-place. Her fingers found the edge of a slab blocking one of the hollows, but it was too heavy, she couldn't move it. Find another. Fast.

The footsteps came nearer. The torchlight grew brighter.

Renn found a slab that she could just move, pushed it back – quietly, *quietly* – crawled inside, and pulled it shut.

A thin line of light showed through the slit that remained. She held her breath.

The footsteps paused. Whoever it was, they were close.

She turned her head from the torchlight, in case they felt her staring, and fixed her gaze blindly on the dark.

From the back of the hiding-place, a pair of yellow eyes glared back at her.

TWENTY-SIX

In one horrified heartbeat, Renn glimpsed a beak sharp enough to slit a whale's belly; talons that could carry a reindeer calf to a clifftop eyrie.

Drawing in her legs, she shrank against the rock. The hollow was tiny: there was barely space for them both. Her weapons were useless. She pictured lightning-fast talons shredding her face and hands; the Soul-Eaters peering in at her ruined flesh, then finishing off what the eagle had begun.

'Boy!' called the Soul-Eater on the other side of the slab.

The eagle hunched its huge wings and fixed its eyes on Renn.

She heard the scrape of a torch being stuck in a crack; the thin squeak of a bat.

'There you are!' said the Bat Mage.

Renn froze.

'Boy! Wake up!'

'So you found him,' said another woman a little further off. Her voice was low and musical, like water rippling over stones. Renn's skin prickled.

'I can't wake him up,' said the Bat Mage. To Renn's surprise, she sounded concerned.

'He took too much root,' the other said scornfully. 'Leave him. We don't need him till tomorrow.'

The eagle spread its wings as far as it could, warding Renn back. Back where? She had nowhere to go. She tried to make herself even smaller, and an eagle pellet crunched beneath her palm.

The Soul-eaters went silent. Had they heard?

'What are you doing?' said the soft-voiced Soul-Eater.

'Turning him over,' replied the Bat Mage. 'Can't let him sleep on his back. If he's sick, he'll choke.'

'Oh Nef, why bother? He isn't worth – ' she broke off.

'What is it?' said Nef.

'I feel something,' said the other. 'Souls. I feel souls, in the air around us.'

Silence. Again that high, thin squeak.

Renn blinked. The stink of birdlime was making her eyes water and her nose run. She tried not to sniff.

'Your bat feels them too,' said the soft-voiced one.

'There, my beauty,' crooned the Bat Mage. 'But whose souls? Could one of the offerings be dead?'

'I don't think so,' murmured the other. 'It's more . . . No, it doesn't feel like one of them.'

'Still, we'd better check them.'

Terror settled on Renn like a covering of ice.

'Hold my torch,' said the Bat Mage, her voice receding as she moved away.

Renn heard the scrape of stone a few paces away, then the ferocious hiss of a wolverine.

'Well *he's* not dead yet!' laughed the soft-voiced one.

The Bat Mage grunted as she pushed back the stone.

Another slab was scraped aside, nearer Renn's hiding-place. She caught the squeak of an otter.

One by one, the Soul-Eaters checked the offerings, drawing steadily closer to where she huddled. Her mind raced. There was no way out. If she bolted, they'd see her. If she stayed where she was, she'd be caught like a weasel in a trap. She had to stop them looking inside. If she didn't, she was dead.

A fox barked in the hollow next to hers. They were almost upon her. *Think.*

Only one thing to do.

Screwing her eyes shut, she crossed her arms over her face – and kicked the eagle.

It lashed out with an ear-splitting 'klek-klek-klek' – and she felt a chill on her wrists as talons sliced a hair's breadth from her skin.

On the other side of the slab, the Soul-Eaters stopped.

The eagle shook itself angrily, and began preening its ruffled feathers.

Renn cowered with her arms over her face, unable to believe that she was unhurt.

'No point checking that one,' said the Bat Mage. 'Though it sounds like she's hungry again.'

'Oh, leave her!' cried the other impatiently. 'Leave the boy, leave them all! I need rest, and so do you! Let's *go!*'

Yes, go! Renn pleaded silently.

The Bat Mage hesitated. 'You're right,' she said. 'After all, they've only got to live one more day.'

Their footsteps receded down the tunnel.

Renn sagged with relief. With her fingertips she traced the zigzag tattoos on her wrists, and saw again Tanugeak's round, shrewd face. *You'll be needing them, I think.*

It was some time later, and the eagle was becoming restive again, before Renn dared to move. As she rubbed the feeling back into her legs, she heard someone stir on the other side of the slab.

'You can come out now,' whispered Torak.

Ⴇ

He still couldn't believe it was really her.

'*Renn?*' he mumbled.

'Thank the Spirit, you're awake!' With her hair stained black, she looked eerily unfamiliar. But she was Renn all right: showing her small, sharp teeth in a wobbly smile, and giving him awkward little pats on the chest.

'Renn . . . ' he said again. The dizziness seized him, and he shut his eyes.

He wanted to tell her everything. About spirit walking in the ice bear, and getting trapped. About hearing Wolf howling – howling *inside* his head – and breaking free of the bear. Above all, he wanted to tell her how incredible, how wonderful it was that she'd made her way through the darkness, and found him.

But when he tried, the bitter bile rose in his throat, and all he managed was, 'I'm – going to be sick.'

He got on all fours and retched, and she knelt beside him, holding back his hair.

When it was over, she helped him stagger to his feet. As they moved into the torchlight, she saw his face for the first time. 'Torak, what *happened* to you? Your lips are black! There's blood on your forehead!'

He flinched from her touch. 'Don't, it's – tainted.'

'What happened?' she said again.

He couldn't bring himself to tell her. Instead he said, 'I know where they've got Wolf. Let's go.'

But as he staggered down the tunnel, she held him back. 'Wait. There's something I've got to tell you.' She paused. 'The Soul-Eaters. They're not only after Wolf. They want to sacrifice you, too!'

Then she told him a story that turned him sick all over again, about a chant she'd overheard in the forest of stone. 'It's a charm that will give them great power, and protect them from the demons.'

His knees buckled, and he leaned against the wall. 'The nine hunters. I heard them say it, but I never thought . . . ' With a scowl, he snatched up the torch. 'Come on. Not much time.'

Renn looked puzzled. 'But – isn't Wolf here, with the others?'

'No. I'll tell you as we go.'

His head was clearing fast, and as he led her through the tunnels – trying to remember the scent trails smelt by the bear, and pausing to listen for sounds of pursuit – he told her of the message from across the Sea, which had prompted the Soul-Eaters to keep Wolf separate. Then he told her what he'd witnessed in the caves. The finding of the Door. The Soul-Eaters' plan for flooding the land with terror. The fire-opal.

Once again, Renn halted. 'The *fire-opal*? They've found the fire-opal?'

He stared at her. 'You know about it?'

'Well – yes. But not much.'

'Why haven't you told me?'

'I never thought . . . ' She hesitated. 'It's something you hear about in stories, if – if you grow up in a clan.'

'Tell me now.'

She moved closer, and he felt her breath on his cheek. 'The fire-opal,' she whispered, 'is light from the eye of the Great Auroch. That's why the demons are drawn to it.'

He met her gaze, and in the fathomless black he saw two tiny, flickering torches. 'So whoever wields it,' he said, 'controls them.'

She nodded. 'As long as it touches neither earth nor stone, the demons are in thrall, and must do the bidding of the bearer.'

He remembered the crimson glow in the forest of stone. 'But it was so beautiful.'

'Evil can be beautiful,' said Renn with startling coldness. 'Didn't you know that?'

He was still trying to take it in. 'How old is it? When did it –'

'No-one knows.'

'But now it's found,' he murmured.

She licked her lips. 'Who has it?'

'Eostra, the Eagle Owl Mage. But after they found the Door, she disappeared.'

They fell silent, listening to the flutter of bats overhead, and a distant trickle of water; wondering what else thronged the dark.

It was Torak who spoke first. 'Come on. We're nearly there.'

Again, Renn was puzzled. 'How do you know where to go?'

He hesitated. 'I just do.'

They climbed higher, and eventually reached a dank little

cave where a dirty brown stream pooled before disappearing down an echoing hole. A birchbark pail stood beside it, with a wovenbark pouch containing a few scraps of mouldering cod. In a corner they found what appeared to be a pit, covered by a sturdy wattle screen weighted with rocks. Torak's heart raced. He knew – he *knew* – that Wolf was in the pit.

Handing the torch to Renn, he rolled the rocks away, and threw the screen aside.

Wolf lay in a tiny, filthy hole scarcely bigger than he was. He was painfully thin: the bones of his haunches jutted sharply. From his matted fur rose a stink of rottenness. He lay on his belly with his head on his paws, not moving at all, and for one terrible moment, Torak thought he was dead.

'*Wolf!*' he breathed.

The great silver head twitched – but the amber eyes were dull.

'His muzzle,' whispered Renn, 'look at his muzzle!'

It was bound with a length of rawhide, cruelly tight.

Rage burned in Torak's breast. 'I'll fix that,' he said between his teeth. 'Give me your knife.'

Jumping into the pit, he cut the binding. '*Pack-brother,*' he said in a shaky grunt-whine, '*it's me!*'

Wolf's tail didn't even twitch.

'Torak,' Renn said uneasily.

'*Pack-brother,*' Torak said again, more urgently.

'Torak!' cried Renn. '*Get out!*'

Wolf's lips drew back in a snarl, and he staggered to his feet. The instant before he sprang, Torak grabbed the edge of the pit and heaved himself up – while Renn seized his parka and pulled with all her might. He shot out, and they shoved the screen and the rocks back on top just as Wolf leapt, hitting it with a thud.

Renn clamped both hands over her mouth.

Torak stared at her, aghast. 'He doesn't know me,' he said.

TWENTY-SEVEN

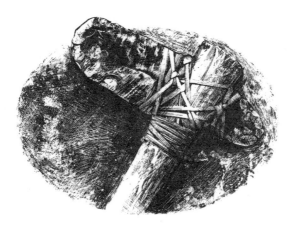

Wolf leapt at the strange, half-grown tailless – but the Den snapped shut, and he fell back onto the stone.

The badness in his tail wouldn't let him rest. He circled until his hind legs shook so much that he had to lie down. His pelt felt hot and tight, and there was a buzzing in his ears. The black fog was hurting his head.

From above him came the yip-and-yowl of the strange taillesses. He twitched his ears in bewilderment. He *knew* those voices. Or he thought he did. But although these taillesses *sounded* familiar, they smelt all wrong. The female smelt of fish-dog and eagle, and the male – who sounded so like Tall Tailless – stank of the bad ones and of the great white bear. Was it Tall Tailless, or wasn't it? Wolf didn't know. He couldn't untangle it in his head.

And yet, not long ago, he *had* caught the scent of his pack-brother, he was sure of it. He'd caught it on the overpelt of the Viper-tongued female; and even though she'd wound the hated deerhide about his muzzle, he had howled for his pack-brother, howled for him inside his head. And for a moment – the swiftest of snaps – he'd heard an answer; and the sound of his pack-brother's rough, beautiful howls had been like gentle breath whiffling through his fur.

Then the black fog had closed in again, and the beautiful howls had changed to the dull roar of a bear. *I am angry!* the bear had roared. *Angry! Angry!* Like all bears, this one was no good at talking, so it just kept saying the same thing over and over.

A scraping above him. Light stung his eyes. Then the lump of birch bark dangled before his nose, and came to rest. Listlessly, he lapped up the wet.

The strange taillesses were peering in at him. He smelt their confusion and fear. Now the half-grown male was leaning down almost within snapping range, giving soft grunt-whines. *'Pack-brother! It's me!'*

That voice . . . so familiar. So soothing to Wolf's aching head, like the feel of cool mud on sore pads.

But maybe Wolf was in the *other* Now, the one he went to in his sleeps. Maybe when he woke up, he would be alone again in this stinking Den.

Or maybe it was another trick of the bad taillesses.

Again the male was leaning in. Wolf saw the short fur on his head: much shorter than Tall Tailless. But he also saw a beloved, flat face, and bright wolf eyes.

Confused, Wolf sniffed the furless paw which reached towards him. It *smelt* a little like Tall Tailless – but was it? Should Wolf lick it? Or snap?

Wolf gave a warning growl, and Torak withdrew his hand.

'He doesn't recognize you,' said Renn.

Torak's fists clenched. 'But he will.' He stared into the tiny, squalid hole. The Soul-Eaters would pay for this. He didn't care if it took him the rest of his life, he would hunt them down and make them pay for what they'd done to Wolf.

'How much time do we have?' said Renn, wrenching him back to the present. 'Where are the Soul-Eaters?'

He shook his head. 'We're well out of earshot from the forest of stone; and from what Seshru said, they'll be resting. I don't think they'll come up here until – until tomorrow, when they open the Door. But that's just a guess.'

Renn nodded grimly. 'One thing's for sure. We won't get far with Wolf like this. He needs food and medicine. Fast.'

Opening her food pouch, she withdrew a slab of blubber, and dropped it into the pit. Wolf fell on it and gulped it down without even chewing.

'Good that you thought to bring food,' said Torak.

'I haven't finished,' muttered Renn. She pulled up the birchbark bowl on its cord, filled it with small, dark pellets from her food pouch, and lowered it into the pit. Wolf's black nose twitched. He heaved himself to his feet, and snuffled them up.

'Lingonberries,' said Renn.

For the first time in days, Torak grinned. Then his gaze returned to Wolf, and his grin faded. 'He will get better. Won't he?'

He saw her struggling to compose her face in an encouraging smile.

'But – Renn,' he faltered, 'it can't be that bad.'

Taking the sputtering torch, she held it over the pit. 'Look at his tail!'

Wolf gave a fierce growl. *Stay away!*

Torak went cold. The tip of Wolf's bushy silver tail was matted with dried blood; but it wasn't that which turned him ill with fear. It was the slimy greenish-black flesh which showed through in patches. Flesh which stank of rottenness.

'It's the blackening sickness,' said Renn. 'It's poisoning him. The worms of sickness are eating him up from inside.'

'But once we get him out into the snow, he'll be better –'

'No, Torak, no. We've got to stop this now, or it'll be too late.'

He knew what she meant, but he couldn't face it. 'There must be something you can do! After all, you know Magecraft!'

'If there was, don't you think I'd have done it? Torak, it's killing him! You know this!' She met his eyes. 'There's only one thing to do. We've got to cut it off.'

Ψ

'You know I'm right,' Renn said again, but she could see that Torak wasn't listening.

Fearfully, she glanced over her shoulder. So far, there had been no sign of the Soul-Eaters.

She turned back to him. 'Do you trust me?' she said.

'What?'

'Do you trust me?'

'Of course I do!'

'Then you must know that I'm telling the truth! Now tell him. Tell Wolf what we have to do to make him better.'

He hesitated; then, slowly, he lowered himself into the pit, talking quietly in wolf talk.

Wolf raised his head and gave a warning growl. To

Renn's horror, Torak ignored it. He crouched, keeping his eyes steady but his gaze soft.

Wolf's hackles were stiff, his ears flat back.

Suddenly he lunged, snapping the air a hand's breadth from Torak's face. The clash of the great jaws rang through the cave.

Torak put his head still closer, and snuffled at the black lips.

Wolf went on growling, staring at Torak with eyes grown dark and threatening.

Torak drew back, and rose to his feet. 'He didn't understand,' he said dully.

'Why not?'

'I – I couldn't find a way to say it; to tell him this will make him better. Because in wolf talk there is no future.'

'Oh,' said Renn.

Slowly, she drew the axe from her belt: the axe she had known – with the knowledge which came to her sometimes – that she would need. 'Take it.'

Torak didn't answer. He was staring at the axe.

'We'll only – cut off the tip,' she said. 'About the length of your thumb.' She swallowed. 'Torak. You've got to. He's your pack-brother.'

He took the axe. Weighed it in his hand.

Wolf raised his head, then slumped onto his side, his flanks heaving.

Torak braced his legs and raised the axe.

Renn felt sick. It was the vision of the White Fox elder.

Slowly, Torak lowered the axe. 'I *can't*,' he whispered. He glanced up at her, his eyes glistening. 'I can't.'

After a moment's hesitation, Renn let herself down into the pit. There was just enough room for her to stand beside him. She took the axe from his hand.

Wolf cast her a narrow glance, and drew back his lips to show his fearsome teeth.

'We should bind up his muzzle,' she breathed.

'No,' said Torak.

'He'll bite!'

'*No!*' he said fiercely. 'If I bind his muzzle now, he'll think I'm no better than the Soul-Eaters! If I don't – if I trust him not to hurt me – then maybe – *maybe* – he'll trust me to let us help him.'

For a moment they stared at one another. She saw the conviction in his face, and knew his mind was made up.

'I won't let him bite you,' he said, placing himself between her and Wolf's jaws. As he went down on his knees, Wolf raised his head and sniffed his fingers, then lay back again.

With his left hand, Torak stroked the fluffy fur behind Wolf's ears, whiffling and grunt-whining under his breath. His right hand passed gently over Wolf's flank, then over the haunch. When he reached the base of the tail, Wolf's muzzle wrinkled in a snarl.

Torak's hand continued – slowly – down the tail.

Wolf growled until his whole body shook.

Torak froze.

Then his fingers moved a little further, till they'd nearly reached the rottenness at the tip. His hand closed over the tail, holding it down.

With blinding speed, Wolf lunged – and seized Torak's other wrist in his jaws. His teeth clamped tight around the bone, denting the skin but not piercing it: poised to crush.

Renn held her breath. She'd once seen Wolf crack the thighbone of an elk. He could sever Torak's wrist as easily as snapping a twig.

Wolf's great amber eyes fixed on Torak's: waiting to see what he would do.

Torak's face glistened with sweat as he met Wolf's gaze. 'Get ready,' he told Renn.

She rearranged her icy fingers on the axe-hilt.

Torak never took his eyes from Wolf's. 'Do it,' he said.

TWENTY-EIGHT

Wolf's tail still hurt, but it was a clean hurt, and the badness was gone.

The black fog was gone too, and with it the last of his doubts. This half-grown male really was Tall Tailless.

It was the black fog which had made him glare at his pack-brother, and take his forepaw in his jaws. *If you harm me*, Wolf had told him with his eyes, *I bite*. But the gaze of Tall Tailless had been steady and true; and suddenly Wolf had remembered the time when he was a cub, and was choking on a duck bone, and Tall Tailless had grabbed his belly and squeezed. Wolf had been so outraged that he'd twisted round to bite, but Tall Tailless had kept squeezing, and the duck bone had shot out of Wolf's muzzle – and he'd understood. Tall Tailless had been *helping* him.

This was why Wolf had let the pack-sister cut his tail with the big stone claw. This was why he hadn't bitten his pack-brother's forepaw. Because they were helping him.

Now it was over, and the pack-sister was leaning against the side of the Den, panting, while Tall Tailless sat with his head in his forepaws, shaking all over.

Wolf went to sniff the bit of tail which lay upon the stone: the bit of tail which had been Wolf, but was now just a scrap of bad meat, not worth eating. Then he nose-nudged Tall Tailless under the chin to say sorry for glaring at him, and Tall Tailless made an odd gulping noise, and buried his muzzle in Wolf's scruff.

After that, things got better. The pack-sister gave Wolf more lingonberries, and delicious slithery chunks of fish-dog fat, and he felt his strength racing back. Tall Tailless sat beside him, scratching his flank, and the pack-sister dipped the bitten end of his tail in a thin mud that smelt of honey and wet ferns. Wolf let her do this, because he knew that she was making him better.

Putting his muzzle between his paws, he shut his eyes, and gave himself up to the scratching of his pack-brother, and the wonderful cool mud that was chasing away the last of the badness.

山

Wolf recovered with a speed that astonished and gratified Renn.

Already his fur seemed sleeker, and his nose had lost that dull, hot look. At the end of his tail – now a thumblength shorter than before – the wound smelt clean and fresh. To her surprise, Wolf had let her dress it with a salve of elder and meadowsweet in chewed blubber. He'd even let her bind it in wovenbark, which he'd made only a half-hearted attempt to eat.

It was Torak who couldn't watch; who seemed unable to

bear the sight of the wound, as if he felt the pain more than Wolf himself.

'He really is getting better,' said Renn, to reassure him. 'I think wolves heal faster than we do. Do you remember last autumn in the Moon of Roaring Stags, when he went after blackberries and tore his ear? Three days later, there wasn't even a scab.'

'I'd forgotten that.' He forced a smile. 'And your salve is helping, too.'

'He's getting stronger all the time,' she said, drawing her medicine pouch shut. 'I think we should –'

A bat fluttered overhead, and of one accord they paused to listen.

Nothing.

Three times during the day – this strange underground day that felt more like night – Torak had made his way back to the forest of stone, and stolen a freshly dipped torch, and checked that the Soul-Eaters were still sleeping off their trance. But they couldn't count on that for much longer.

'We should get him out of this pit,' said Renn. 'We can make a sling of our belts, and haul him out. If he'll let us.'

'He'll let us. You said Thiazzi's blocked the cave mouth?'

'Yes. We *might* be able to shift it.'

'We'll have to. It's the only way out.'

'No it isn't.' Reluctantly, she told him about the weasel hole.

Normally he would have wanted to know everything about it, including why she hadn't told him sooner; but instead he seemed distracted. She wondered if he was worrying about the same thing that had begun to trouble her.

She watched him nuzzle Wolf's scruff. Wolf flicked one

ear, and they exchanged one of those speaking glances that used to make her feel left out; but she didn't mind any more, she was just glad that Torak had his pack-brother back.

'The blood of the nine hunters,' he said suddenly. 'It's to protect them from the demons, isn't it, when they open the Door?'

She nodded. 'I've been thinking about that, too. Even for the Soul-Eaters, it's going to be incredibly hard to keep the Door open for more than a few heartbeats. But that'll be enough.'

They pictured demons spreading like a black flood over the snow. Across the ice. Towards the Forest.

'And the fire-opal,' said Torak, 'it will give them control once the demons are out.'

'Yes.'

He passed his hand over Wolf's flank, and Wolf stirred his tail in acknowlegement, taking care not to thump it.

'How can it be destroyed?' said Torak. 'Hammered? Thrown into the Sea?'

Her fingers tightened on her medicine pouch. 'Nothing so simple. You can only rob it of its power by burying it under earth or stone. And – ,' she hesitated. 'It needs a life. A life buried with it. Otherwise it won't be appeased.'

Torak rested his chin on his knees and frowned. 'When I put the Death Marks on my father,' he said, surprising her, 'I didn't do it very well. Especially not here, for the clan-soul.' He touched his breastbone. 'He had a scar, where he'd cut out the Soul-Eater tattoo.'

Renn swallowed.

'I couldn't go back and make things right for him,' he went on. 'Gather his bones, lay them to rest in the Wolf Clan bone-ground – wherever that is – because ever since then, in one way or another, I've been fighting the Soul-Eaters.' He paused. 'I left him because he told me to. Because he knew it was my destiny to fight the Soul-Eaters. I don't think I can turn my back on that destiny now.'

Renn didn't reply. This was what she'd feared.

She wished desperately that they could find their way out of these horrible caves, retrieve their skinboat, and get back to the White Foxes. Then Inuktiluk could take them on his dog sled to the Forest, and they would be with Fin-Kedinn again, and it would be over. But she knew this wasn't going to happen.

Torak raised his head, and his grey eyes were steady. 'This isn't about rescuing Wolf any more. I can't just run off and leave them to open the Door.'

'I know,' said Renn.

'Do you?' His face was open and vulnerable. 'Because I can't do this on my own. And I can't ask you to help. You've already done so much.'

That annoyed her. 'I know what we've got to do just as well as you do! We've got to make sure that Wolf is free, and then,' she caught her breath, 'then *we've* got to stop them opening the Door.'

TWENTY-NINE

After something of a struggle, they managed to haul Wolf out of the pit, and headed off. Their way led through the tunnel of the offerings, where they were relieved to find no sign of the Soul-Eaters, although they'd been there recently. The hole which had held the lynx was empty.

Torak was wondering what this meant when Wolf gave a low, urgent 'uff'!

'Hide!' he whispered – but Renn knew enough wolf talk to recognize the warning, and was already scrambling into the lynx's hollow. Torak pushed the slab across it, and an instant later, Nef's bat flitted past his face.

'Boy?' called Nef from the end of the tunnel. 'Where are you?'

Torak glanced behind him at Wolf, whose amber eyes glowed in the torchlight. If Nef saw him . . .

As the Bat Mage limped towards them, Wolf turned and

melted into the dark. Torak breathed out in relief. He shouldn't have doubted Wolf. If he didn't want to be seen, it didn't happen.

'I'm here,' he said, struggling to keep his voice steady.

'Where have you been?' snapped Nef.

Rubbing his face, he tried to look bleary. 'I was asleep. That root . . . my head hurts.'

'Of course it hurts! You've got to be strong to be a Soul-Eater!'

To Torak's alarm, she stopped right outside Renn's hiding-place, and leaned her hand on the rock.

He edged away, in the hope that she would follow.

She didn't. Propping her torch against the wall, she squatted on her haunches. 'Strong,' she repeated, as if to herself, 'you've got to be *strong*.' She opened her hands and stared at them. They were dark with blood.

'The lynx,' said Torak. 'You've killed it. The sacrifice has begun.'

As Nef held her tainted hands before her, her fists clenched. 'It has to be done! The few *must* suffer for the good of the many!'

Torak licked his lips. He had to get rid of the Bat Mage before she discovered Renn. And yet . . .

'You don't have to do this,' he said.

Nef's head jerked up.

'The sacrifice. The Door.'

'*What?*' snarled the Bat Mage.

'These are demons!'

'That's the beauty of it! Demons don't *know* right from wrong! We can bend them to our will! Don't you see? This is our chance to make things right! To enforce the way of the World Spirit!'

'By breaking clan law?'

Nef stared at him. Suddenly she lurched to her feet, snatched the torch, and brought it close to his face: so close that he heard the sputtering hiss of pine-pitch. 'You were a coward,' she said, 'grovelling, whining – but not any more. Why did you hide your true nature?'

Torak did not reply.

She lowered the torch. 'Ah, but what does it matter now?'

A patch of darkness cut across the light, and dropped onto her shoulder. As Torak watched her stroke the soft bat fur, he wondered how she could caress her clan-creature, and yet stain her spirit with sin.

'The Opening of the Door is nearly upon us,' said Nef. 'You have work to do. Bring the offerings to the forest of stone.'

He stared at her. 'You mean – '

'We're going to kill them. We're going to kill them all!'

He swallowed. 'Where – where are you going?'

'Me?' barked Nef. 'I'm going to take care of the wolf.'

'What were you *thinking*?' whispered Renn after the Bat Mage had gone. 'Arguing with a Soul-Eater? With me right there, waiting to be discovered?'

'I thought I might be able to change her mind,' said Torak.

'Torak, she's a Soul-Eater!'

She was right; but he didn't want to admit it.

'Come on,' he said brusquely. 'When she finds Wolf gone, she'll raise the alarm. We've got to free the offerings and get out of here!'

Swiftly, straining their ears for footsteps, they worked

their way down the tunnel, heaving rocks aside and setting the captives free. The fox and the otter fled the moment there was a gap big enough to wriggle through. The eagle gave them an outraged glare, hitched its bedraggled wings, and swept off into the dark. The wolverine was a spitting bundle of rage, and would have attacked them both if Wolf hadn't emerged from the shadows and seen it off.

'Phew!' panted Renn. 'That's gratitude!'

'Do you think they'll find their way out?' said Torak.

She nodded. 'That gap between the slab and the cave mouth. They'll get through.'

'And Wolf?'

'It's big enough for him. But not for us. And I don't think we should count on being able to shift that slab.'

'You mean – we'll have to use the weasel hole.'

The blood drained from her face. 'If we get the chance.'

They fell silent. They hadn't been able to come up with a plan for stopping the Soul-Eaters, other than making their way to the forest of stone, and doing – something.

Wolf's claws clicked as he trotted to the end of the tunnel, then abruptly stopped. He stared into the pit of the ice bear.

With a sense of foreboding, Torak went to investigate. What he saw made his knees give. 'We'll have a better chance than these two,' he said.

'What do you mean?' said Renn.

He moved aside to let her see.

The Soul-Eaters had slaughtered the ice bear and skinned it, leaving the reeking, steaming carcass in the pit. They'd done the same to the lynx, then tossed its corpse onto the bear's.

Renn sagged against the cave wall. 'How *could* they? They've just left them to rot.'

This is evil, thought Torak. This is what evil looks like.

In death the ice bear seemed pathetically smaller. Torak's heart twisted with pity. 'May your souls find their way back to the ice,' he murmured. 'May they be at peace.'

'Torak . . .' Renn's voice seemed to come to him from a distance. 'It's time. We've got to go. We've got to stop them opening the Door!'

ᚴ

In the forest of stone, the rite of the Opening had already begun.

As Torak crouched in the shadows at the mouth of the cavern, his spirit faltered. Wolf trembled against him. Renn stood rigid.

The stone trees were spattered with scarlet. Acrid black smoke snaked from the altar, where the Soul-Eaters had made an offering of their hair. The Oak Mage and the Viper Mage prowled the shadows, jabbing at the dark with three-pronged forks, fending off the vengeful souls of the murdered hunters. Both were unrecognizable in their dead-eyed masks, their painted lips flecked with black foam. Both were stripped to the waist, clad only in a slimy, glistening hide.

The Viper Mage wore the lynx pelt: its gaping head set upon her own, its sleek hide rippling down her back as she brandished the Walker's strike-fire.

The Oak Mage had become the ice bear. With his hands thrust inside the forepaws, he wove between the stone saplings, hissing, slicing the air with his claws.

Only the Eagle Owl Mage was unchanged. Rooted to the stone, she faced the wall where the red handprints marked the Door. Her corpse hands covered the mace on which the fire-opal was set.

With a supreme effort, Torak shook himself free of the spell. Whatever they did, they had to act fast. Any moment now, and Nef would raise the alarm.

'The torches,' he breathed in Renn's ear. 'I can't see more than three. If we can put them out, then maybe . . . '

Renn didn't stir. She couldn't seem to take her eyes off the Soul-Eaters.

'*Renn!*' He shook her shoulder. 'The torches! We've got to do something!'

She dragged her gaze away. 'Here,' she whispered. 'Take my knife. I'll keep my axe.'

He nodded. 'The weasel hole. Where is it?'

'There, behind that greenish sapling. There's a big crack, you've got to climb up – '

'All right. We should be able to reach it, when the time comes.'

Suddenly he knelt, and pressed his face against Wolf's muzzle. Wolf gave a faint wag of his tail, and licked his ear.

'He'll find the other way out,' breathed Torak as he straightened up. 'He's got a better chance than we have.'

'And before then?' said Renn. 'How do we stop them?'

Torak stared at the circling, hissing Soul-Eaters. 'You see if you can douse the torches, while I keep them talking – '

'While you *what*?'

Before she could stop him, he'd risen to his feet, and stepped out into the light.

With startling speed the lynx and the ice bear spun round, and stared at him with dead gutskin eyes.

'The ninth hunter is come,' said the Oak Mage in a voice as deep as a bear's.

'But his hands are empty,' hissed the Viper Mage. 'He was to have brought the eagle, the wolverine, the otter, the fox.'

The talons of the Eagle Owl Mage tightened around the

head of the mace. 'Why has it failed?'

Torak opened his mouth to speak, but no sound came. What was Renn doing? Why were the torches still burning?

Desperately, he sought for some way of grabbing the fire-opal, and stopping them from opening the Door – of achieving the impossible.

A shout rang through the cavern – and Nef hobbled in. 'The wolf is gone!' she shouted. 'It's the boy, I know it is! He set the wolf free! He set them all free!'

Three masked heads turned towards Torak.

'Free?' said the Viper Mage with appalling gentleness.

Torak edged backwards.

The Bat Mage blocked his way.

The Oak Mage wiped the black froth from his painted lips and said, '"*The Wolf lives.*" That was the message from our brother across the Sea. What did it mean, we asked ourselves.'

'Then a boy came,' said the Viper Mage. 'A boy who wore the tattoos of the White Foxes, but didn't look like one. I felt souls in the air around me. What does this mean, I asked myself.'

Torak's hand tightened on his knife. And still the torches burned, and still the Soul-Eaters bore down on him.

'Who are you?' said the Oak Mage.

'*What* are you?' said the Viper Mage.

THIRTY

Tall Tailless was surrounded. Bravely he faced them, clutching the big claw; but against three full-grown taillesses, he didn't stand a chance.

Wolf lowered his head and crept forwards. The bad ones didn't hear him. They didn't know he was there.

Swivelling one ear, he heard the stealthy padding of the female, a few pounces away. A sizzling hiss, and that part of the Den went dark. Good. She was helping him. Wolf could see in the dark, but the bad ones couldn't.

Tall Tailless said something defiant in tailless talk, and the pale-pelt who stank of bear gave a cruel laugh. Then another part of the Den went dark. And another.

Suddenly, Stinkfur and Pale-Pelt leapt at Tall Tailless. He didn't dodge quickly enough – it didn't matter – Wolf was quicker than any of them. With a snarl he sprang at Pale-Pelt, knocking him to the ground and sinking his teeth into a forepaw. Pale-Pelt roared. Bones crunched. Wolf leapt away, gulping bloody flesh.

As he ran, his claws skittered on stone and he nearly went down, wobbling as he righted himself, because his newly shortened tail didn't give quite the balance it had before. He'd have to be careful, he thought as he raced through the dark to help his poor, blind pack-brother, who was still trying to get away from Stinkfur.

Not far off, the pack-sister held a glowing branch in one paw, narrowing her eyes as taillesses do when they cannot see.

Meanwhile, the Viper-Tongue had not been idle. She'd found her way through the silent trees, and past the Stone-Faced One to the end of the Den, where she was scraping a claw over the rock, hissing and whining in a way that made Wolf's pelt shrink with dread. He heard the clamour of demons. He didn't know what she meant to do, but he knew that he had to stop her.

And yet – Tall Tailless needed him! In his blindness, he was blundering towards Stinkfur!

Wolf faltered.

He decided in a snap – and leapt to the aid of his pack-brother, body-slamming him out of the path of the bad one. Tall Tailless slipped – steadied himself – and grabbed his pack-brother's scruff. Wolf led him to safety through the trees.

But it was too late to stop Viper-Tongue. Her whines rose to a hide-prickling scream as she spread her forepaws wide – and suddenly in the rock, a great mouth gaped.

Stone-Face gave a triumphant howl that pierced Wolf's ears like splintered bone. Then she lifted her forepaw high. The Den filled with the hard grey glare of the Bright Beast-that-Bites-Cold – *and the demons poured forth.*

Tall Tailless let go of Wolf's scruff and fell to his knees.

The pack-sister dropped the glowing branch and covered her ears with her forepaws. Wolf shrank trembling against Tall Tailless, as the terror of the demons blasted his fur.

He knew he had to attack them – it was what he was meant to do – but there were so many! Slithering, swooping, scrabbling over each other in their hunger for the cold grey light. Wolf saw their dripping fangs and their cruel, bright eyes. There were so *many* . . .

But suddenly, he smelt rage.

The female tailless had shaken off her fear, and was snarling with rage!

In amazement Wolf watched her snatch up the still-glowing branch, and hurl it at Viper-Tongue. It struck her full in the back – when she threw something, the female rarely missed – and Viper-Tongue howled with fury. Her forepaws lifted away from the rock, and the gaping Mouth crashed shut.

But even in so short a time, the demons had come pouring from it, and now the forest of stone thronged with them: swarming about the Bright Beast-that-Bites-Cold. And still Stone-Face held it high, forcing them to her will. And Wolf sensed that neither Tall Tailless nor the female – nor he himself – dared attack her, for they knew that she was the very evil of evils.

He was wrong.

The pack-sister's attack had roused Tall Tailless, and now he barked to her, and she turned and tossed him her great claw: the one that had bitten off part of Wolf's tail.

Tall Tailless caught it in one forepaw – then ran towards Stone-Face – towards the demons!

Terror dragged at Wolf's paws, but he loved his pack-brother too much to forsake him now. Together they ran through the fog of fear. Then Tall Tailless drew back his forepaw and swung the great claw – not at Stone-Face, not at the demons – but at a thin stone sapling towering overhead.

Clever Tall Tailless! The trunk cracked – teetered – and crashed down. The demons screeched and skittered away like ants from an auroch's hooves, and Stone-Face was brought down, and the Bright Beast flew from her forepaw, clattering across the floor – and its cold light was swallowed by the Dark.

As one, the demons howled. They were free! And now they were spreading through the Den like a great Fast Wet, and Wolf hid with Tall Tailless in the thicket of stone, his heart bursting with terror and despair as they swept past him.

Already he could hear the bad taillesses fighting among themselves, blaming each other for the loss of the Bright Beast-that-Bites-Cold. Only Wolf saw the pack-sister stumble upon it and snatch it up, and hide it in the scrap of swan's hide that hung about her neck.

Then she grabbed Tall Tailless by the forepaw, and dragged him by the dim glow of the branch towards a smaller Den high in the side of the main Den; a narrow Den like a weasel's tunnel, through which flowed the clean, cold smell of the Up.

With a pang, Wolf realized what they meant to do. They meant to go by a path he couldn't take. His tail drooped as he watched them peel off their overpelts and make ready to go.

Tall Tailless knelt. *Go!* He told Wolf. *Find the other way out! Meet us in the Up!* And Wolf wagged his tail to reassure him, because he sensed his pack-brother's worry, his unwillingness to leave him.

Then they were gone, and Wolf turned on one paw and

raced from the Den, following the clean, cold scent pouring in from the Up.

Torak was lost in an endless tunnel of crawling and gasping, and more crawling. This terrible, terrible hole. How had Renn managed it, not once, but three times?

It was night when they dropped exhausted into the snow. A windy night in the dark of the moon, with only the glow of stars on snow to light the way – and no sign of Wolf.

At least, not yet, Torak told himself. But he'll make it out. If anyone can, it's Wolf.

After the warmth of the caves, the cold was merciless, and their teeth chattered too hard for speech as they struggled to untie their bundled-up clothes and yank them on.

'The fire-opal,' panted Torak at last. 'I saw it fall – it touched rock. That means the demons are free!'

Renn gave a terse nod. In the starlight her face was pale, and her black hair made her look like someone else.

'Did you see where it fell?' said Torak. 'Did one of them pick it up?'

She opened her mouth – then shook her head. 'Come on,' she muttered, 'we've got to reach the skinboat before they get out!'

He didn't know if she meant the Soul-Eaters or the demons. He didn't ask.

Floundering through the snow, they made their way round the spur. The Eye of the Viper was shut, but as they reached it, Torak glimpsed a small, pale shape slip through a gap and race away. His heart leapt. The white fox had found the way out!

He turned to Renn, and saw that she was smiling. At least someone had escaped.

As they watched, they saw the scuttling darkness of the wolverine – who for once was more intent on getting away than on biting anyone. Then the eagle emerged: ungainly in the snow, until she spread her wings and lifted into the sky.

'Go safely, my friend,' Renn said softly. 'May your guardian fly with you!'

Then came the otter: pausing for a moment to dart Torak a penetrating glance before streaking off down the mountain. And finally – when Torak was turning sick with dread – Wolf.

He had a struggle to squeeze through the hole, but once he was out, he simply shook himself and came bounding down to them with his tongue hanging out, as casually as if he fled demon-haunted caves every night of his life.

When he reached Torak, he rose lightly on his hind legs, put his forepaws on Torak's shoulders, and covered his face in wet wolf kisses.

Heedless of the Soul-Eaters – heedless of demons – Torak snuffle-licked him back. Then together they raced down to the sleds, and Wolf bounded about in circles while they hurriedly retrieved their packs.

Down the mountain they ran, with Wolf pausing to let them catch up. At the head of the iced-in bay, he helped them find their skinboat, buried beneath a fresh fall of snow.

But when the skinboat was in the water, and hastily loaded with their gear, when Renn and Torak had taken their places – Wolf refused to jump in.

'Can't you make him?' cried Renn.

With a sinking feeling, Torak took in the set of Wolf's

ears, and the stubborn spread of his paws. 'No,' he said. He heaved a sigh. 'He hates skinboats. And he's better off going overland. They'll never catch him.'

'Are you sure?' said Renn.

'No!' he snapped. 'But it's what he means to do!' Of course he wasn't sure. Even in the Forest, a lone wolf's life is a short one – but out here, on the ice?

There wasn't even time to say goodbye. As Wolf stood looking down at him, their eyes met briefly – but before Torak could speak, Wolf had turned and sped away, a silver streak racing over the snow.

The sun was just cresting the mountain as they brought the boat about and headed south, slicing the water with their paddles. Luckily, the wind was behind them, so they made good speed.

When they were out of arrowshot, Torak turned.

'Look,' said Renn.

The mountainside was still in shadow, but stark against the grey snow, Torak saw a darker shadow pouring down the slope.

'Demons,' he said.

Renn met his gaze, and in the gloom her eyes were blacker than the Sea.

'We failed,' she said. 'The demons are loose upon the world.'

THIRTY-ONE

Far away on the northernmost edge of the Forest, the sun rose over the High Mountains. Around the Raven camp, birch trees stirred uneasily as they dreamed.

'Demons,' said Saeunn, crouching on a willow mat to read the embers. 'I see demons coming from the Far North. A black flood, drowning all who stand in its path.'

Only Fin-Kedinn heard her. The hunting had been good, and the rest of the clan was asleep, their bellies full of baked red deer, and rowanberry mash; but the Raven Leader and his Mage had sat up all night at the entrance to his shelter, while the stars faded and the sky turned grey, and around them the Forest slept on in the hushed radiance of a heavy snowfall.

'And there can be no doubt?' said Fin-Kedinn. 'It is the work of the Soul-Eaters?'

As the Raven Mage stared into the embers, the veins on

her bald pate throbbed like tiny snakes. 'The fire spirit never lies.'

An ember cracked. Snow pattered down from the spruce tree overhead. Fin-Kedinn glanced up – and went very still.

'We've come too far north,' said Saeunn. 'If we stay here, there'll be nothing between us and the demons!'

'What about Renn and Torak?' said Fin-Kedinn, his eyes fixed on the spruce.

'What about the clan?' retorted Saeunn. 'Fin-Kedinn, we must go south! We must head for the Widewater, take refuge at the Guardian Rock! There I can weave spells to protect us, set lines of power about the camp.'

When Fin-Kedinn did not reply, she said, 'This must be the end to what you've been thinking.'

The Raven Leader dragged his gaze back to the Mage. 'And what have I been thinking?' he said in a quiet voice that would have made any other clan member blanch.

Saeunn was undaunted. 'You cannot lead us into the Far North.'

'Oh, I wouldn't lead *you*, Mage. I'd make sure that you stayed here, in the Forest – '

'I'm not thinking of myself, but of the clan, as you well know!'

'And so am I.'

'But – '

'Enough!' With a slicing motion of his palm, he cut short their talk. 'When I tell you how to do Magecraft, you may tell me how to lead!'

Again he raised his head, and this time he spoke not to Saeunn, but to the creature who stared down at him from the spruce tree: the eagle owl with the feathered ears and the fierce orange glare, who sat watching. Listening.

'I won't lead the clan out of the Forest,' said Fin-Kedinn

without dropping his gaze. 'I swear it on my souls.'

The eagle owl spread its enormous wings and glided north.

THIRTY-TWO

Torak and Renn made good speed, and for a while, relief at having escaped the caves raised their spirits. It was good to be out in the brilliance of ice and Sea and sky; to hear Wolf's brief, reassuring howls drifting from the east – *I'm here! I'm here!* – and to howl back an answer.

'They'll never catch us now!' yelled Renn.

She told Torak how she'd slashed the Soul-Eaters' skinboats, and he laughed. Wolf was free, and they were heading back to the Forest. Soul-Eaters and demons seemed very far away.

Then, quite suddenly, the day turned. Flinty clouds darkened the sun. Fog crept in from the Sea. Torak's head ached with fatigue. His paddle was heavy in his hands.

'We've got to rest,' said Renn. 'If we don't, we'll capsize, or crash into an ice mountain.'

He nodded, too exhausted to speak.

It took all their strength to haul the skinboat out of the

water, and drag it across the sea ice to the shelter of an ice hill; to prop it up on shoresticks, and pack snow over it for a makeshift shelter.

As he worked, Torak remembered the sudden stillness that had come over the Viper Mage. 'What are you?' she had said. She had sensed his souls in the tunnel of the offerings, as they were making their way back to his body; maybe she had guessed that he was a spirit walker.

From far away came the deep 'oo-hu, oo-hu' of an eagle owl.

Renn paused with her mittens full of snow. Her face was taut. 'They're after us.'

'I know,' said Torak.

'Oo-hu, oo-hu.'

He searched the sky, but saw only fog.

Renn had already gone inside the shelter, and he was alone on the ice. Sounds came to him unnaturally loud: the moaning of the wind, the distant boom of crashing ice. His head ached, his eyes stung. Even the shelter and the hill were strangely blurred.

Out of the corner of his vision, he caught movement.

He spun round.

Something small and dark, flitting from ridge to ridge.

His mouth went dry. A demon?

He wished Wolf were here. But he hadn't heard a howl since mid-afternoon.

Drawing his father's knife, he went to investigate.

Nothing behind the ice hill. But he *had* seen it.

He sheathed his knife and crawled into the shelter. Renn was already huddled in her sleeping-sack. He didn't tell her what he'd seen.

They were too exhausted to pound blubber for the lamp, or to force down more than a few bites of frozen seal meat.

Renn fell asleep instantly, but Torak lay awake, thinking about that dark shape flitting from ridge to ridge.

The demons were out there. He could feel them sapping his spirits, quenching courage and hope.

And it's your fault, he thought. You failed, and now they're loose. It was all for nothing.

He woke feeling stiff and sore. His eyes felt as if someone had rubbed sand in them. He couldn't think of a single reason for getting up. The demons were loose. It was no use fighting back.

Outside, Renn was moving about in the snow. *Why* did she have to make so much noise? Surely she knew that every crunch of her boots was ramming another icicle into his head.

To put off going outside, he checked what remained of his gear. In the rush to get away, he'd left behind his axe and bow, but his waterskin was still around his neck, his tinder pouch and medicine pouch on his belt, and Fa's knife safe in its sheath.

The hilt felt curiously hot. Maybe it was an omen. He should probably ask Renn. But that would only give her a chance to boast about how much more she knew than him. The thought filled him with unreasonable rage.

When he couldn't put it off any longer, he crawled outside.

Overnight, the breath of the World Spirit had swallowed the world. The ice – the Sea – it had taken it all. The wind had gone. Without it, the cold wasn't so biting; but the boom of breaking ice was closer.

That's all we need, thought Torak. The thaw is coming.

'You look terrible,' snapped Renn. 'Your eyes – you should've worn your snow-visor.'

'I *know*,' growled Torak.

'Then why didn't you?'

Her voice was so grating. She was always telling him what to do. And *she*, of course, had worn her visor all day, because *she* never forgot anything.

In prickly silence they dismantled the shelter, and carried the skinboat to the edge of the ice; then went back to fetch their gear.

'Just as well I thought to slash their boats,' boasted Renn, 'or they'd have caught up with us by now.'

'Boats can be mended,' Torak said nastily. 'You won't have slowed them down for long.'

She put her hands on her hips. 'I suppose you think I should've made a better job of it? Well I didn't have time, I had to go and rescue you!'

'You didn't *rescue* me!' spat Torak.

She snorted.

To give her something to snort about, he told her why the Soul-Eaters were coming after them: about the spirit walking, and Seshru sensing his souls.

Her jaw dropped. 'You were *spirit walking*? And you never told me?'

'So? I'm telling you now.'

She was silent. 'Anyway, you're wrong,' she said. 'They're not following us because of that.'

'Oh no? What makes you so sure?'

'It's the fire-opal. I took it. That's why they're after us.'

'Why didn't you *tell* me?' cried Torak.

'I'm telling you now. There wasn't time before.'

'There was plenty of time!' he shouted.

'Don't shout at me!' shouted Renn.

He was shaking his head. 'So it's not only the Soul-Eaters who are after us, it's the demons as well!'

'I did mask it,' she said defensively. 'I've got herbs, and I put it in a swansfoot pouch that Tanugeak gave me.'

He threw up his arms. 'Oh, well that makes it all right! How could you be such a fool?'

'How could *you*? You were the one who spirit walked!'

Her voice rang out across the ice. The silence that followed was louder. They stood glaring at each other, chests heaving.

Torak passed his hand over his face, as if he'd just woken up. 'What are we *doing*?' he said.

Renn shook her head to clear it. 'It's the demons. They're making us fight.' She hesitated. 'I think they can smell the fire-opal. Or – sense it.'

He nodded. 'That must be it.'

'No, no, I mean, I *know* they can.' She caught her lower lip in her teeth. 'I heard noises in the night.'

'What kind of noises?'

She shuddered. 'I stayed awake to keep watch. Then I heard Wolf. He was howling, the way he does before he goes hunting. After that they were gone.'

He took a few paces, then turned back to her. 'We've got to get rid of it.'

'How? We'd have to bury it in earth or stone – and there isn't any out here, there's only ice!'

They stared bleakly at each other.

Renn opened her mouth to speak . . .

. . . and an ear-splitting crack split the air, as a fine black line zigzagged across the ice a hand's breadth from her boots.

She stared at her feet.

The sea ice gave a sudden heave, and she staggered back.

The black line was now a channel of water as wide as a paddle blade.

'A tide crack,' said Torak in disbelief.

Time seemed to slow. He saw that he stood on the landfast ice – the side that held the boat and their provisions – while Renn stood on the other side: the side that was breaking away.

'Jump,' he told her.

The floe lurched. She braced her legs to keep from falling.

'*Jump!*' he cried.

Her face was blank with shock. 'I can't. It's too late.'

She was right. The crack was already more than two paces wide.

'I'll get the boat,' he said. He raced over the ice towards the skinboat – stumbled – staggered upright again. Why couldn't he see properly? Why was everything taking so long?

He'd nearly reached the boat when it rocked – teetered – and slid gracefully off the ice, into the Sea. With a cry he lunged for it – but the waves sucked it just out of reach. He howled with rage – and the Sea Mother splashed saltwater in his eyes, laughing at him.

'Torak!' Renn's voice was muffled by the fog.

He got to his feet – and was horrified to see how far she'd drifted.

'*Torak!*'

He ran to the edge of the ice – but he was powerless, he could only watch as the Sea bore her away, and the breath of the World Spirit closed in around her.

Then there was nothing left but silence.

THIRTY-THREE

The ice gave another lurch, jolting Torak to his senses. He had to get away from the edge, or he'd be next.

The fog was so thick that he could hardly see; or were his eyes getting worse? Even this weak light felt like hot needles drilling into his skull.

In a blur he cast about for their remaining gear. Apart from what he had on him, there was a snow-knife, the sleeping-sacks, and no food. He *thought* he remembered seeing Renn stowing a food pouch in the skinboat, and hoped he was wrong, hoped she had it with her –

The sleeping-sacks? He had *both?*

Oh, Renn.

At least she had her bow with her, but . . .

He stopped short. She had the fire-opal. The demons would be after her.

As he recalled how he'd shouted at her, he burned with shame. Taking the fire-opal had been the bravest thing she could have done. Then she'd stayed awake all night, keeping watch. 'And all you could do was shout,' he said in disgust.

The fog whirled before his eyes, melting into a searing red blur. He squinted. Put his hand before his face. The red blur didn't change. He couldn't see.

'Snow-blind,' he said aloud – and the fog reached icy fingers down his throat. He'd never felt so vulnerable.

He did the only thing he could. He put his hands to his lips and howled.

Wolf didn't come. Nor did he send back an answering howl. Which must mean that he was out of earshot – and knowing Wolf's ears, that was a long way away off, indeed.

Again Torak howled. And again.

Silence. No wind. Just the insidious lapping of the Sea, and a horrible, waiting stillness. He pictured dark shapes flitting from ridge to ridge. He sensed that he was not alone.

'Get away from me,' he whispered to the demons.

He thought he heard laughter.

'Get away!' he shouted, waving his arms.

More laughter.

With a sob, he sank to his knees. Tears stung his eyes. Angrily he dashed them away.

If Renn were here, she'd be reaching for her medicine pouch.

That kindled a tiny spark of courage. Slipping off his mittens, he fumbled for his own pouch, found some elder leaves by their smell, and chewed them. They stung terribly when he pressed them to his eyes, but he told himself they were doing him good.

Then he had another idea. He found his mother's medicine horn, and shook a little powdered earthblood into his palm.

Suddenly, the air around him crackled with tension. Maybe the demons didn't like earthblood.

Mixing the red powder to a paste with spit, he daubed what he hoped was the sign of the hand on his forehead – remembering too late that he should have rubbed off the owl blood first. He didn't know if that would stop it working. He only knew that you made the sign of the hand to protect yourself, and he needed all the protection he could get.

He struggled to his feet – and this time he heard a hiss, and the scrabble of claws. Maybe they were shrinking back from the mark of power.

'Get away from me,' he told them shakily. 'I'm not dead yet. Neither is Renn.'

Silence. He didn't know if they were listening or mocking.

On hands and knees, he found the sleeping-sacks and strapped them on his back; then stuck the snow-knife in his belt. He forced himself to think. The thaw was coming, so he had to get further inland. Then head off and find Renn.

The day before, the current and the wind had carried them south. The ice floe, too, had carried Renn south.

'Head south,' he said out loud. And maybe the floe would get stuck in landfast ice, and she'd find her way ashore.

But where *was* south?

He took a few steps, but kept stumbling. The ice was so uneven, all these little ridges . . .

Ridges. The wind blowing the snow into ridges. Blowing mainly from the *north*!

'Thank you!' he shouted. He thanked Inuktiluk, too, for advising him to make an offering. The wind must have liked those boar tusks, or it wouldn't be helping him now.

Groping with his mittens, he felt the shape of the ridges.

Then he stood up, and squared his shoulders. 'Not dead yet,' he told the demons. 'Not dead yet!' he shouted.

He started south.

It was agonisingly slow going. At times he heard a juddering crunch, and the sea ice bucked beneath him. He probed the way ahead with the snow-knife. But if he did hit a patch of thin ice, it would probably be too late.

What had Inuktiluk said? *Grey ice is new ice, very dangerous . . . keep to the white ice.* Not much use when he couldn't see; when his next step might take him onto thin ice, or down a tide crack.

He struggled on. The cold sapped his strength, and he began to feel weak with hunger. How he was going to find food when he had neither harpoon, bow, nor sight, was beyond him.

After a while, he heard the sound of approaching wings. The sky was a pinkish blur, he couldn't even make out a darker blur flying towards him.

Owls fly silently, so it couldn't be the eagle owl; and these wingbeats had a strong, steady rustle that he recognized.

'Wsh, wsh, wsh.' The raven flew lower to inspect him. Then, with a short, deep caw, it flew away.

His belly tightened. That caw had sounded muffled, as if the raven had food in its beak. Maybe it had found a carcass, and was flying off to hide its cache. Maybe it would be back for more.

Not long afterwards, he heard it return. He strained to listen. He ran towards it.

Just when he was giving up hope, he heard the bark of a

white fox, and the sonorous caws of ravens at a kill-site. *Meat!* From the clamour, there were lots of them, so it must be a big carcass. Maybe a seal.

His foot struck something solid, and he fell. The ravens erupted into the sky in a wild clatter of wings, and the white fox uttered short barks that sounded suspiciously like laughter.

Torak groped for what had tripped him. It wasn't a wind ridge, but a smooth hummock of ice, twice the size of his head. Puzzled, he found another, a little further off. Then more of them, in a curving double line.

His heart began to thud. These weren't hummocks. They were tracks. The tracks of an ice bear. Inuktiluk had told him how the bear's weight packed the snow hard, then the wind blew away the surrounding snow, leaving perfect, raised paw-prints.

In his mind, Torak saw the seal basking in the sun beside its breathing-hole, oblivious of the ice bear stalking it downwind. Noiselessly the bear creeps closer, hiding behind every ridge and hummock. It is patient. It knows how to wait. At last the seal slips into a doze. The bear gathers itself for the silent charge . . . The seal is dead before it knows what struck.

At the carcass, the ravens had noisily resumed their feast, having apparently decided that Torak posed no threat.

They wouldn't be feeding if the bear was still close – would they? He was desperate to believe that. And by the sound of it, there were a great many ravens, as well as that fox, which must mean that the bear had left plenty of meat. Inuktiluk had said that when the hunting was good, ice bears take only the blubber, and leave the rest.

But what if it was hungry again? *What if it was stalking him right now?*

Suddenly the ravens burst skywards. Something had frightened them.

Torak's breath hammered in his chest. Reaching inside his parka, he drew his father's knife.

He pictured the great bear hunting him: placing its huge, furred paws soundlessly on the ice.

He got to his feet. The silence was deafening. He braced himself, and waited for the White Death to come for him.

Wolf knocked him backwards into the snow, and covered his face in snuffle-licks.

Wolf *loved* surprising his pack-brother. No matter how often he did it, Tall Tailless never knew he was coming, and Wolf never tired of it: the stalk – the pounce – the head-over-paws tumble.

Now, in an ecstasy of play-biting and tail-lashing – with his newly shortened tail, that he was fast getting used to – he clambered over his pack-brother. He was so happy he could howl! All thought of demons and bad taillesses and stranger wolves was chased away. After being crushed and cramped for so long, he was free to stretch and leap and lope! To feel the Bright Soft Cold beneath his pads, and clean wind in his fur! To play with his pack-brother!

As often happened when Wolf ambushed him, Tall Tailless was both cross and delighted. But Wolf sensed that this time, he was also in pain.

Where was the pack-sister? She'd been with Tall Tailless when they'd set off in the floating hide. Had she got lost on the Great Wet?

And Tall Tailless was being strangely clumsy. After his first joyful greeting, he'd made an awkward lunge at Wolf's muzzle, missed, and tried to lick his ear. Which was odd. Now his forepaw swung out and biffed Wolf hard on the nose. Wolf was startled. He hadn't done anything wrong.

Going down on his forelegs, he asked Tall Tailless to play.

Tall Tailless ignored him.

Wolf gave an aggrieved whine, and cast his pack-brother a questioning glance.

Tall Tailless stared – he actually *stared* – right past Wolf.

Wolf began to be worried. To stare like that must mean that Tall Tailless was extremely displeased. Perhaps Wolf had done something wrong without knowing it.

Then he had an idea. Loping over to the fish-dog kill and scattering the ravens, he bit off a scrap of hide, raced back with it, and tossed it at Tall Tailless' feet, looking at him expectantly. *There! Let's play toss-and-catch!*

Tall Tailless did nothing. He didn't even seem to know the hide was there.

Wolf padded closer.

Tall Tailless reached out a forepaw, and clumsily touched his muzzle.

Wolf studied the beloved, furless face. The beautiful wolf eyes were crumpled shut, and streaming wet. Delicately, Wolf sniffed them. They smelt wrong. He gave them a tentative lick.

Tall Tailless gulped, and buried his face in Wolf's scruff.

Suddenly, Wolf understood. Poor, poor Tall Tailless. He couldn't see.

To reassure him, Wolf rubbed himself against his shoulder, covering his overpelt in comforting Wolf smell. Then he nudged his head under Tall Tailless' furry forepaw.

Tailless rose unsteadily to his hind legs, and Wolf waited

until he was ready, then walked forwards as slowly as a newborn cub.

He would look after Tall Tailless. He would lead him to the fish-dog kill, and wait patiently while he ate – because he was still the lead wolf, so he got to eat first. Then, when Wolf had also eaten, he would lead Tall Taillesss in search of the pack-sister.

THIRTY-FOUR

In the Forest, the coming of spring is welcomed; in the Far North, it's feared. Now Renn understood why.

An ice mountain floated towards her out of the fog – tilted, and crashed into the Sea, sending out a wave that rocked the floe on which she huddled. She threw herself flat, and waited till the lurching eased.

Up ahead, two huge slabs smashed into each other: the larger grinding over the smaller, forcing it under.

That could have been me, thought Renn.

She had no idea where the Sea was taking her. She couldn't see any land. Only fog and looming ice in lethal black water. The din of the thaw was all around her. The trickle and gurgle of meltwater. The crunch and grind of ice.

Her floe was about twenty paces across, and she crouched in the middle, staring at the edge which the Sea Mother was gradually gnawing away. The wind moaned, and despite the White Fox visor, her eyes watered with cold. In the distance, but getting closer, she heard the thunderous voice of the ice river.

She wondered what she would do without a sleeping-sack, when night came. She remembered a story Tanugeak had told her of how her grandmother had survived a blizzard. 'She took off her mittens and sat on them, to stop the cold coming up from below; then she drew her arms inside her parka and hunched forward with her chin on her knees, so that if she fell asleep, she wouldn't topple over.'

Renn did as Tanugeak's grandmother had done, and felt warmer; but she was in no danger of falling asleep. She had to keep watch in case the fog cleared, and she got a glimpse of the shore. She had to stay on guard against Soul-Eaters in skinboats. And demons.

Hunger and thirst tormented her, but she was determined not to touch her provisions. Provisions! A morsel of frozen seal meat, and a bladder of water on a thong around her neck. She tried not to think of the food pouch she'd stowed in the skinboat, moments before it happened; just as she tried not to think about the demon.

It was here on the ice floe, she could feel it. But she only ever caught a flicker of darkness, a clatter of claws.

It would have come closer if she hadn't scrubbed off the Mountain Hare "tattoo" on her forehead, and daubed on the sign of the hand, remembering to add the lines of power emanating from the middle finger. She'd thought about adding Death Marks, too; but not yet.

In the swansfoot pouch, the fire-opal throbbed with cold fire against her breastbone. Casting it into the Sea would be the coward's way out. Who knew what evil it might do down there. And there was no earth or stone in which to bury it.

A sudden honking of geese overhead. Thrusting her arms into her sleeves, she drew her bow from its seal-hide carrier.

Too late. They were out of range.

'Stupid!' she berated herself. 'You should've been ready! You should always be *ready*!'

She sat and waited for more prey. She watched till her eyes hurt. At last, her head began to nod.

The demon was so close she could smell it. Its tongue flickered out to taste her breath. Its glare drew her down into seething black flame . . .

With a cry she jolted awake. 'Get away from me!' she shouted.

A flock of gulls lifted off from a nearby ice mountain. She fumbled for her bow – but the gulls were gone.

Somewhere behind her, the demon cackled.

'There will be more gulls,' she told it. There would have to be more gulls.

None came.

Her hand crept to her medicine pouch. Inside, nestling in her dwindling supply of herbs, lay the pebble on which Torak had painted his clan-tattoo last summer; she wondered if he even knew she'd kept it. And here was the grouse-bone whistle for calling Wolf. She longed to blow it. But even if he heard, he couldn't swim out this far. She'd only be endangering him.

Her thoughts drifted to the previous autumn, when Torak had tried to teach her to howl, in case she ever lost the whistle. She hadn't been able to keep a straight face, and he'd got cross and stalked off; but when she'd tried to summon him back with a howl, she'd sounded so odd that he'd laughed till he cried.

Now she attempted a wobbly howl. It wasn't loud

enough to summon Wolf, but it made her feel a bit better.

If any more gulls came, she ought to be ready. She checked the fletching on her best flint arrow, then took all the lengths of sinew thread from her sewing pouch, knotted them together, and tied the line to the arrowshaft. Next she oiled her bow and bowstring by rubbing them with the seal meat, resisting the temptation to gobble the lot. As she worked, she seemed to see Fin-Kedinn's rough hands overlaying her own. He'd made this bow for her, and it held not only the endurance of the yew from which it came, but some of his strength, too. It wouldn't let her down.

With the arrow nocked in readiness, she pushed up her visor, and settled down to wait.

Behind her the demon clawed the ice to distract her. Her lip curled. Let it try! Fin-Kedinn had taught her to concentrate. When she was hunting, nothing could distract her; like Torak when he was tracking.

In the distance, she heard the strange, neighing cries of guillemots. They were coming her way.

Doubts flooded her mind. *They're too far away, the line isn't long enough. Your hands are frozen, you can't shoot straight . . .* She ignored the demon, and concentrated on the prey.

They were flying low, as guillemots do, beating the air with their stubby black wings. Renn chose one, and fixed her eye on it, waiting out the gusts of wind.

The arrow flew straight, and the guillemot plopped into the Sea. With a shout of triumph, Renn hauled it in on the line.

Her shot had only caught the tail, and the bird was struggling. Murmuring thanks and praise, she slipped her hand beneath its wing and held its heart between her fingers, to still it. Then she cut off the wings, and gave one to the Sea Mother and one to the wind, to thank them for not killing her yet. The head she threw to the end of the floe for her clan-guardian, and she thanked her bow by smoothing on a little of the fat.

Finally, she slit the belly, drew out the warm purple breast, and crammed it in her mouth. It tasted oily and wonderful. The guillemot's strength became hers.

She plucked the carcass, keeping the feathers for fletching, and tied it to her belt. The demon had fled. She spat out a fleck of guillemot down, and grinned. Clearly it preferred her hungry and miserable to well-fed and defiant.

A raven swooped low, snatched the guillemot's head, and flew away. Renn felt a surge of pride. Ravens are one of the few birds tough enough to winter in the Far North. She was proud to be its descendant, a member of its clan.

Drawing back her hood, she rubbed snow on her hair to wipe away the last traces of Tanugeak's black stain. She was herself again. Renn of the Raven Clan.

She was trying so hard to spot the coast that she nearly missed it.

One moment the ice floe was slowly turning, and the next there was a crunch that nearly tipped her into the Sea, and it ground to a halt.

Back on her feet, she saw that she'd been looking the wrong way. Her floe had crashed into a jumble of pack ice. Then the fog parted – and the ice river towered above her.

The floe had become stuck at its northern edge. Before her stretched a glaring expanse of landfast ice, and beyond that, a swathe of jagged, shadowy hills which cowered beneath the vast blue cliffs of the ice river.

If she could get across the pack ice, if she could reach that landfast ice . . .

But what then? The ice river had only to twitch, and those cliffs would fall on her and crush her like a beetle.

She'd think about that later. Right now, she had to get ashore.

Shouldering her bow, she clambered off the floe and onto the pack ice. It rocked alarmingly, and she had to leap to the next bit, and the next, keeping always to the white ice, and never pausing, as Inuktiluk had taught her. The pack ice was riven with gaps – one misplaced step, and she'd be in the Sea. She was sweating by the time she reached what felt like landfast ice.

She bent double, too dazed to feel relief. It was hard to stay upright, as her legs still swayed to the rhythms of the Sea.

To the south, from deep within the ice river, she heard pounding. Eerie, grinding groans. She straightened up.

The wind hissed over the ice. The cold was so intense that her eyelashes stuck together. Her hand crept to her clan-creature feathers. This place didn't feel right. This dead cold. Those fanged hills at the foot of the cliffs, so sunk in gloom that they looked almost black.

With a start she realized that it wasn't shadow that was making them look black, it couldn't be, the cliffs faced west, and the low sun shone directly onto them. Those hills *were* black. And at their heart yawned a chasm. A chasm of black ice.

She felt strangely drawn to it.

Stumbling over the landfast ice, she made her way towards the black hills. As she got nearer, the ice beneath her boots turned black: brittle black ice that crackled at every step.

She stooped for a shard, and crushed it in her mitten. It melted, leaving nothing but black specks. She stared at her palm. Those black specks . . . they weren't ice, but *stone*. Stone from some buried mountain, crushed fine by the might of the ice river.

Her hand dropped to her side, and water dripped sadly from her mitten. Now she understood why the Sea had carried her here, to the dark underbelly of the ice river. She'd done the impossible. She'd found a way of burying the fire-opal in stone.

But the only life she could give it was her own.

THIRTY-FIVE

Beneath his mitten, Torak felt Wolf becoming restless. He hoped desperately that the scent trail Wolf had caught was Renn's, but he couldn't be sure. So much wolf talk isn't in the voice but in gestures: a glance, a tilt of the head, a flick of the ears. Being blind made it much harder to know what Wolf was saying. And although Torak's sight was slowly coming back, Wolf was still only a dark-grey blur.

The wind was restless too, moaning in his ears and tugging at his parka. High, thin voices reached him, just at the edge of hearing. Demons? Soul-Eater spies? Or Renn, calling for help?

Wolf stopped so abruptly that Torak nearly fell over him. He felt the tension in Wolf's shoulders; the dip of his head as he sniffed the ice. His heart sank. Another tide crack. They'd crossed three already, and it wasn't getting any easier.

Without further ado, Wolf wriggled out of Torak's grip – and leapt. Torak heard the whisper of paws landing on snow, then an encouraging bark. *Come!*

Torak unslung the sleeping-sacks and the side of seal ribs which he'd cut from the carcass, and threw them towards the shadow that was Wolf. He was reassured to hear a thud rather than a splash.

Now for the hardest part. He couldn't make out the crack, it could be anything from a hand's breadth to two paces wide. Too risky to kneel and feel its edge with his mittens; his weight might break it. He'd just have to jump, and trust that Wolf – who could leap three paces with ease – would remember that his pack-brother couldn't.

Another bark, and an impatient whine. *Come!*

Torak took a deep breath – and jumped.

He landed on solid ice, wobbling wildly. Wolf was there to steady him. He retrieved his gear, then put his hand on Wolf's scruff, and they headed off.

By mid-afternoon, and despite Wolf's impatient nudgings, he had to rest. While Wolf ran in anxious circles, he huddled on the ice, sawing meat from the seal ribs. His sight was improving all the time, and he could see the meat now. Well, he could make out a dark-red blur against the pinkish blur of the ice. He fumbled for his owl-eyed visor, and put it on.

To his surprise, Wolf gave a low growl.

Maybe he didn't like the visors.

'What's wrong?' mumbled Torak, too tired to speak wolf.

Another growl: not hostile, but uneasy. Maybe it wasn't the visor. Maybe he didn't like it that Torak had brought the meat: a draw for any ice bear within two daywalks. But he had no choice. Unlike Wolf, he couldn't devour half a seal, then go hungry for days.

An impatient nose-nudge. *Come on!*

Torak sighed, and heaved himself to his feet.

The day wore on, and he felt the cold deepening as the sun went down. Suddenly he couldn't take another step. He found a snow hill and hacked out a rough shelter, lined it with one of the sleeping-sacks, and crawled into the other.

Wolf crawled in too, and lay against him: heavy and beautifully warm. For the first time in days, Torak felt safe. With Wolf beside him, no demon or Soul-Eater or ice bear could get near. He fell asleep to the mothwing tickle of whiskers on his face.

He woke to darkness – and no Wolf.

He knew he hadn't slept long, and when he crawled outside, he saw a vast black sky glittering with stars.

He saw! The snow-blindness was gone!

He stood with upturned face, drinking in the stars.

As he watched, a great spear of green light streaked across the sky. Then a shower of arrows streamed upwards, and suddenly, rays of green light were rippling across the darkness: shimmering, melting, silently reappearing.

Torak smiled. At last. The First Tree. From the dark of the Beginning it had grown, bringing life to all things: river and rock, hunter and prey. Often in the deep of winter it returned, to lighten hearts and kindle courage. Torak thought of Fa, and wondered if he'd completed the Death Journey, and found his way safely into its boughs. Maybe even now, he was looking down on him.

Far in the distance, an eagle owl called.

Torak's skin prickled.

Then – much closer – he heard a slithering on the ice.

Crouching, he drew his knife.

'Drop it,' said Thiazzi.

4

'Where is the fire-opal?'

'I haven't got it.'

A blow to the head sent him flying. As he landed, his chest struck an ice ridge with winding force.

'Where is it?' bellowed the Oak Mage, yanking him upright.

'I haven't – got it!'

The huge fist drew back again – but Nef hobbled forwards and grabbed his arm. 'We need him alive, or we'll never find it!'

'I'll beat it out of him!' roared the Oak Mage.

'Thiazzi!' cried Seshru. 'You don't know your own strength! You'll kill him!'

The Oak Mage snarled at her – but lowered his fist, and let Torak fall.

He lay panting, trying to take in what was happening. With Wolf unaccountably gone, they must have crept up on him in the night. A few paces away, he saw two skinboats lying on the ice, their hulls patched with seal-hide. He couldn't see Eostra; but ten paces away, an eagle owl perched on a fang of ice, fixing him with fierce orange eyes.

As he stared at the murky forms of the three Soul-Eaters, he sensed the discord between them: threads of tension stretched between them like a spider's web.

Of course, he thought. They didn't complete the sacrifice, so they're not fully protected from the demons. He wondered if he could make use of that.

'Search him,' said the Viper Mage. 'It's got to be somewhere.'

Thiazzi and Nef seized Torak's parka and dragged it over his head, then ripped off his jerkin and the rest of his clothes, till he stood naked and shuddering on the ice.

The Oak Mage took malicious pleasure in making the search a slow one: shaking out mittens and boots, snapping the snow-knife in two, emptying Torak's medicine horn, so that its precious earthblood blew away on the wind.

'It isn't here,' said Nef in surprise.

'He's hidden it,' said Seshru. Drawing closer, she studied Torak's face, and her pointed tongue flickered out to moisten her lips. 'Those are Wolf Clan tattoos. *"The Wolf lives"*. Who *are* you?'

'I t-told you,' he stammered, 'I haven't got the fire-opal!'

Nef stooped for Fa's knife. 'Get dressed,' she told Torak without looking at him.

Clumsy with cold, he pulled on his clothes, then scrambled for what remained of his gear. His tinder pouch had been emptied, and his mother's medicine horn had lost its stopper; but in a corner of his medicine pouch, he found the remaining fragment of the Soul-Eaters' black root. He slipped it inside his mitten, closing his fist around it. He didn't know why, but he sensed that he might need it.

Just in time. Thiazzi seized his wrists and bound them behind him with a length of rawhide rope. The binding was cruelly tight, and Torak cried out. The Oak Mage laughed. Nef flinched, but made no move to stop him.

Torak noticed that Thiazzi's left hand was heavily bandaged in bloodstained buckskin, and missing two fingers. Good, he thought savagely. At least Wolf got his revenge.

'Where did you get this?' Nef said in an altered voice. She was standing very still, staring at the knife in her hands. Fa's knife.

Torak lifted his chin. 'It was my father's,' he said proudly.

A hush fell upon the Soul-Eaters. The eagle owl swivelled its head and stared.

'Your – father,' said Nef, aghast. 'He was – the Wolf Mage?'

'Yes,' said Torak. 'The man who saved your life.'

'The man who betrayed us!' spat Thiazzi.

Torak shot him a look of pure hatred. 'The man who discovered what you were! The man you murdered!'

'His *son*,' whispered Nef. Her brow creased. 'What – what's your name?'

'Torak.'

'Torak,' repeated the Bat Mage. Her eyes sought his, and Torak could tell that for the first time she was seeing him not merely as "boy", the ninth hunter in the sacrifice, but as Torak, the son of the Wolf Mage.

'"*The Wolf lives*"', the Viper Mage said again. Her lips curved in her sideways smile. 'So that's what it means. What a disappointment.'

The Oak Mage had reached the limits of his patience. Pushing past Seshru, he seized Torak by the hair and twisted back his head, pressing a blade against his throat. 'Tell us where you hid the fire-opal, or I'll slit your throat!'

Torak stared into the green eyes, and saw that he meant it. He thought fast. 'The girl has it,' he panted. 'The spirit walker.'

ᚃ

'What girl?' sneered Thiazzi.

'A *spirit walker*?' Nef said hoarsely.

Torak flicked Seshru a glance. 'She knows,' he said. 'She knows, and she hasn't told you!'

Thiazzi and Nef stared at the Viper Mage.

'You *knew*?' said Thiazzi accusingly, releasing Torak with such force that he fell to his knees.

'He's making it up,' said Seshru. 'Can't you see? He's trying to set us against each other.'

'I'm telling the truth!' cried Torak. Then to Nef and Thiazzi, 'You know there was a girl with me, you must have seen the tracks!'

They had. He could tell from their faces.

Nef turned to Seshru. 'There was a moment in the caves, when you sensed souls. But you never told us what.'

'She knew,' said Torak. 'She sensed the spirit walker, she sensed souls walking free, between bodies.' A plan was forming. A desperate, deadly plan that would put both him and Renn in danger. But he couldn't think of any other way.

Out loud he said, 'The girl is the spirit walker. She's got the fire-opal.'

'Take us to her,' said Nef.

'It's a trick!' cried Seshru. 'He's tricking us!'

'What can he do to us?' growled Thiazzi.

'If you let me live,' said Torak, 'I'll take you to the fire-opal. I swear it on my three souls.'

Silently, Seshru glided towards him, and brought her face close to his. Her breath heated his skin. He felt himself drowning in her peerless gaze.

Slowly she took off her mitten and raised her hand.

He flinched.

The perfect lips curved in a smile. Her chill fingers smoothed the sign of the hand from his forehead, 'You won't need that any more,' she murmured. One long forefinger caressed his cheek: gently, but letting him feel the edge of her nail.

'Your father tried to trick us,' she breathed, 'and we killed

221

him.' She leaned closer, and whispered in his ear. 'If you trick me, I shall make sure that you will never be free of me.'

Torak swallowed. 'I will take you to the fire-opal. I swear.'

Nef thrust Fa's knife into her belt, and stared at Torak with a strange, unreadable expression. 'How?'

'The wolf,' said Torak, jerking his head at the paw-prints that wound south across the ice. 'We must follow the tracks of the wolf.'

THIRTY-SIX

Wolf felt as if he was being torn in pieces.

He had to find the pack-sister. He had to save Tall Tailless from the bad ones. *And* he had to chase the demons back into the Underneath. But he couldn't do it alone, he needed help. He could think of only one way of finding it. That way would be dangerous: the most dangerous thing a lone wolf could attempt. But he had to try.

On and on he loped through the glittering Dark. In the Up, the Bright White Eye was hiding, but her many little cubs shed their light upon the land.

As Wolf ran, he thought of Tall Tailless, and felt a fresh snap of worry. Would his pack-brother understand why he'd gone? Would he wait for his return, or blunder off and fall prey to the Great Wet?

It was too terrible to think about, so Wolf tried to lose himself in the sounds and smells carried on the wind. The furtive scratchings of a white grouse snuggling deeper into

223

her burrow. The growls of the Great White Cold up ahead. The sharp, familiar scent of the pack-sister.

On Wolf went, following her scent. He knew that he had to find her *before* he went for help against the demons, although he didn't know why; he just felt it in his fur, with the sureness that came to him at times.

He raced up a long, sparkling slope, and paused at the top. Down there. She was sleeping down there in the dark.

A new scent assailed his nose, tightening his pelt and making his claws tingle. Demons. The urge to hunt them ran hot in his limbs. But not yet. And not alone.

Turning on one paw, he raced down the slope, the same way he'd come – then struck out to seek help.

The Dark wore on, and tirelessly he flew over the Bright Soft Cold. He came to a broken land where stunted willows rattled dry leaves in the wind. He slowed to a trot.

The scent-markings of the lead wolf were fresh, strong, and rich. This told Wolf that the stranger wolves had recently made a kill, and that the pack wasn't far away.

He kept close to the scent-markings, which would tell the stranger wolves that he'd entered their range on purpose, and was here because he wanted to be. He hoped this would make them curious rather than angry, but he didn't know. He didn't know what manner of wolves they were, or – most importantly – what kind of wolf their leader was. Wolves guard their ranges fiercely, seldom permitting a lone wolf to enter; and it's only rarely that a pack will allow a stranger to run with them, as Wolf had run with the pack on the Mountain, and Tall Tailless with the tailless pack that smelt of ravens.

The scent-markings were getting stronger, closer together. It wouldn't be long now.

It wasn't.

The white wolves came racing through the willows at a speed that took even Wolf by surprise. They were a big pack, and like Forest wolves, they ran in a line in the tracks of the leader; but they were slightly shorter than Forest wolves, and stockier. Wolf thought they looked very, very strong.

He stood absolutely still, waiting for them to approach. His heart tumbled in his chest, but he held his head and tail high. He must not look scared.

On they came over the Bright Soft Cold.

The leader glanced over his shoulder – and the pack spread out, forming a ring around Wolf.

In silence they halted. Their pelts glowed, their breath drifted like mist. Their eyes glinted silver.

Wolf stilled his own breathing, so that he would appear calm.

Stiffly the lead wolf walked towards him. His ears were pricked, his tail high, and his fur was fluffed out to the full.

Wolf dropped his own ears, but only slightly. His fur was fluffed up, but not as much as the leader's, and his tail was very slightly lower. Too high, and he'd seem disrespectful; too low, and he'd appear weak.

Sternly, the leader stared past him: too proud to meet his eyes.

Wolf turned his head a whisker to one side, and slid his gaze down and away.

The lead wolf moved closer, till he stood within pawing distance of Wolf's nose.

Hardly daring to breathe, Wolf stood his ground. He saw the scars on the leader's muzzle, and the bitten edge of one ear. This was a wolf who had fought many fights, and won.

The lead wolf took another step, and sniffed under

Wolf's tail, then at the bark binding the tip. He drew back sharply, twitching his ears in puzzlement. Then he brought his muzzle close to Wolf's. Close, but not touching, breathing in his scent.

Wolf, too, took deep breaths, tasting the strong, sweet scent of the leader, while around them the white wolves waited in silence.

The leader raised his forepaw – and touched Wolf's shoulder.

Wolf tensed.

The next moment would decide it. Either they would help him – or tear him to pieces.

THIRTY-SEVEN

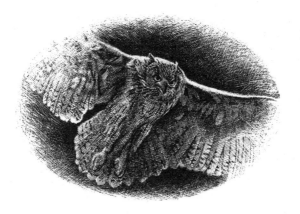

After a wretched night in a hastily hacked-out snow shelter, Renn sat waiting for dawn to come. Her last dawn. She kept saying it in her head, to make it real.

She knew she should have had the courage to end it last night, but she hadn't. She needed to see the sun one final time.

The night was quiet. Nothing but the restless wind, and an occasional rumble as the ice river shifted in its sleep. The stars had never looked so distant or so cold. She longed for voices. People, foxes, anyone. "Voice hunger" is what the clans of the north call it: when you're alone on the ice, and you crave voices more than warmth or meat; because you don't want to die alone.

It wasn't fair. Why *should* she go down into the ice with the demons? She wanted to see Torak again, and Fin-Kedinn, and Wolf.

'What you want doesn't matter,' she said out loud, 'this

is how it is.' Her voice sounded old and cracked, like Saeunn's.

Above the ice river, a slash of deep crimson appeared: a wound in the sky.

She watched the crimson melt to orange, then to a blazing yellow. No more excuses. She got to her feet. The Death Marks were stiff on her skin. The fire-opal was heavy on her breast. Shouldering her faithful bow, she started for the cliffs.

It began to snow. White flakes speckling black ice, an eerie reversal of how things should be. The ice was jagged. She had to fight her way over towering ridges and bottomless cracks. One slip, and she'd be swallowed, with no hope of getting out. And she had to get further in, to the black chasm right under the cliffs. That was where she would unmask the fire-opal, and summon the demons. That was where she would lead them down into the dark.

An ear-splitting groan – and to the south, part of the cliff-face collapsed. Billowing clouds of ice blasted her face. Nothing could withstand the might of the ice river. Not even demons.

She brushed off her parka, and pressed on.

It was noon by the time she neared the darkness under the cliffs. In the driving snow she stood on a ridge, staring down at the slash in the belly of the ice river.

There, she thought. In there it will be buried for good.

ᛢ

Torak had been walking all night, following Wolf's tracks by the glimmer of the Soul-Eaters' rushlight. Behind him Nef and Thiazzi trudged with the skinboats on their shoulders; in front went Seshru, the rushlight in one hand, the rope that bound his wrists in the other. At times, he sensed the sinister presence of Eostra, although he never saw her; but when he glanced up, there was the shadowy form of an eagle owl, wheeling against the stars.

His chest ached, his feet dragged. He forced himself to keep going. Nothing mattered, except finding Renn. Gritting his teeth against the pain, he twisted his wrists so that the rawhide bit into his flesh. He had to leave a blood trail. That was part of the plan.

Dawn came. In the ashen light, the land was humped and menacing. He sensed they were being followed. Either Wolf had come back, or his plan was working – but far too soon.

Seshru jerked at the rope, yanking him forwards.

Pretending to stumble, Torak fell to his knees, rubbing his bloody wrists in the snow.

'Up!' snapped Seshru, giving a tug that made him cry out.

'Listen to him whine,' sneered Thiazzi. 'Like that wolf when I stamped on his tail. Whining like a cub.'

You'll pay for that, thought Torak as he staggered to his feet. I don't know how, but you will pay.

Noon approached. It began to snow. Through the flying whiteness, Torak made out a long, low hill. Beyond it he heard the boom of the ice river; far to the south, on the very edge of hearing, the howling of wolves.

Seshru had reached the top of the hill. Her face was blank as a mask in its slit-eyed visor, and her black tongue flicked out to taste the air. She smiled. 'The demons are coming.'

Nef dropped the skinboat and hobbled up the slope. As she whipped off her visor, Torak was shocked to see how she'd aged in the course of one night. 'There,' said the Bat Mage. 'She's down there in the shadow of the cliffs.'

229

Renn halted twenty paces from the chasm, in the lee of a ridge of black ice.

Slipping her hands out of her mittens, she drew the swansfoot pouch from inside her parka. Her fingers were shaking so badly that it took several attempts to loosen the neck of the pouch, but at last she managed, and the fire-opal rolled onto her palm. It lay dull and lifeless, strangely heavier than when she'd carried it in the pouch, and so cold that it burned her skin.

You couldn't stop this now, she thought. Even if you wanted to.

Snow fell thickly, chilling her palm, but the fire-opal remained untouched.

Deep within the stone, a crimson spark flickered. The spark flared to a flame. Pure. Steady. Beautiful . . .

Shutting her eyes, Renn made a cage around it with her fingers. When she looked again, it was still glowing: crimson light bleeding through her flesh.

Snow swirled in her face. Beneath her boots the black ice shuddered. She raised her hand, and held up the fire-opal.

The ice river fell silent. The wind dropped to a whisper. Waiting to see what would come.

At first it was only a distant rustling: a murmur of hunger and hatred on the wind. Then it swelled to a raucous clamour that pierced her skull and beat at her spirit. The demons were coming.

An arrow shattered the ice a hand's breadth from her head.

'Don't move!' A man's voice shouted.

Torak scarcely recognized Renn.

Her red hair floated like flame in the whirling snow, and her white face was severely beautiful as she held up the fire-opal. She didn't look like his friend any more, she looked like the World Spirit in winter: a woman with bare red willow branches for hair, who walks the snow alone, striking terror in all she meets.

'Don't move!' bellowed the Oak Mage again.

'We will shoot!' warned the Bat Mage.

'You can't escape!' cried the Viper Mage, nocking another arrow to her bow.

'Get back!' shouted Renn – and took a step towards the edge of the chasm, ten paces behind her. 'There are cracks all around me, if you shoot, you'll lose it for ever!'

The Soul-Eaters froze. She was thirty paces away from them, well within arrowshot; but the risk was too great.

Desperately, Torak tugged at the rope that bound his wrists behind him, but he couldn't break free of the tether; Thiazzi had hammered the stake deep into the ice.

Thinking fast, he slipped his hand out of his mitten, opened his fist, and dropped the black root onto the ice, then twisted round to reach it with his teeth. He prayed that he hadn't left it too late, that his plan would work against the odds, and –

A shadow flew over him. 'Renn!' he shouted. 'Above you!'

She'd already seen it. As the eagle owl swooped towards her with talons outstretched, she lashed out with her knife, and sent it screeching skywards. 'Stay back!' she warned the Soul-Eaters sternly. 'You can't stop me!'

'Renn, don't do it!' yelled Torak. *'Don't jump!'*

She seemed to see him for the first time. Her face crumpled, and she was Renn again. 'Torak! I can't – '

Her eyes widened with horror as she stared at something

231

behind him – and he turned, and saw, through the whirling whiteness, a black tide racing like cloudshadow over the ice.

Demons.

For a moment he could only watch the darkness sweeping towards him. Then he bent his head, caught the root in his mouth, and chewed – gagging, forcing himself to swallow.

'Renn!' he shouted. *'Don't jump!'*

'Don't jump!' shouted Torak – and Renn hesitated.

Through the snow she saw him kneeling on the black ice: tied to a stake, his hood thrown back from his bruised face. The Soul-Eaters stood on either side of him, he didn't stand a chance – and yet for a moment, hope made her falter. He sounded so certain.

But the demons were sweeping closer, and the Soul-Eaters were moving forwards, bearing down on her.

She saw Torak sway – and watched in horror as the blood left his face, his eyes rolled up into his head, and he pitched forwards onto the ice.

Get up! she told him silently. Do something, anything, just let me know you're still alive!

He lay still.

It's over, she thought in disbelief. I'm the only one left.

Her fingers tightened about the fire-opal, and she edged backwards, closer to the chasm.

THIRTY-EIGHT

The bile was bitter in Torak's mouth as he lay face down in the snow.

With the last of his strength he turned his head, and saw Renn backing towards the chasm, and the Soul-Eaters advancing on her. Then the demons came roaring over him. He sensed their hunger for the fire-opal, and their terror of the wolves who hunted them: the white wolves of the north and the grey wolf of the Forest, who'd sought them tirelessly through the snow, and now came streaking across the ice, driving all before them.

'Wolf . . . ' Torak tried to say, but his lips wouldn't move. Cramps twisted his guts. The sickness came at him in waves.

Just before he slid into darkness, he saw the Viper Mage turn, her mouth slack with horror. There, at the edge of the pack-ice: a great white bear exploded from the Sea . . .

. . . and now he was surging onto the ice, shaking the

water from his fur. He was leaping towards the evil ones, and they quailed before him, their terror rank on the wind.

The Viper Mage faltered with an arrow nocked to her bow. She glanced from the bear to Torak's slumped body, and her face contorted with fury. 'The boy! The *boy* is the spirit walker!'

With one sweep of his paw, the bear sent her screaming through the air, to land in a limp huddle on the ice. Over the crackling blackness he bounded, drinking in the scents streaming towards him on the wind. The fury of the Oak Mage, the terror of Renn. Before him the Bat Mage fled, the demons parted like a river. His growl filled the sky, his roar shattered ice. He was invincible!

Torak felt the fury of the ice bear as his own; he felt its blood-urge drowning him in a crimson flood. He fought to conquer it . . .

He lost.

The killing hunger roared through him, the hunger which had led him as he'd followed the blood trail over the snow. He would slaughter this prey: the evil ones who dared invade his ice, the girl with the flaming hair! He would feast on their hot, tender hearts, he would kill them *all*!

Before him the evil one with the pale hair brandished a feeble weapon. Scornfully he swatted it aside, delighting in the anguished howl of the fallen.

The prey whimpered and squirmed. He moved in for the kill . . .

. . . and a great grey wolf leapt in front of him. It stood facing him, its lips drawn back from its fangs in a snarl.

The bear bellowed his rage. He reared and pounded the ice with his forepaws, twisting his head, roaring at the wolf.

The wolf stood its ground, unafraid. Its amber eyes were fixed on the bear's: steady and strong as the sun. They pierced the darkness of the bear's souls, and found Torak. They saw his souls, they called to him. With an agonising jolt he shook himself free of the blood-urge – he knew Wolf, and he knew himself again. He wrenched the souls of the ice bear to his will.

Thiazzi still cowered before him: his arm broken, his weapons lost.

Torak faltered. Here was a Soul-Eater at his mercy: to be killed with a single shake of his terrible jaws. But now it wasn't the blood-urge of the bear which drove him, it was his own. *He* would do the killing – with the might of the greatest of hunters at his command. And he *wanted* to kill. The Oak Mage had tortured Wolf, and tried to kill Renn, and hunted his father to death. Oh, how he wanted to kill!

But Wolf's amber eyes were fixed on him; and suddenly he knew that if he killed the Soul-Eater now, then, truly, he would become as one of them.

With a deafening roar he rose once more on his hind legs, looming over the Oak Mage. With a roar he crashed down, pounding the ice so that black shards flew. He – would – not – kill!

In the instant that he turned from killing, he saw Renn stagger to the chasm, poised to jump. He saw the Bat Mage hobble after her, snatch the fire-opal from her hand, and push her away from the edge with such force that she went flying.

Then the Bat Mage turned with a look of bitter triumph, and called to Torak's body lying on the ice: 'The debt is repaid! Tell your father when you meet him! *The debt is repaid!*'

She threw herself in – and the demons gave a rending

howl, and leapt after her. The ice river groaned, the black ice collapsed, shutting the chasm for ever – and the light of the fire-opal was quenched.

THIRTY-NINE

Torak awoke on the ice, lying on his back.

His head was spinning, and he felt sick. But the last snowflakes were drifting gently onto his face, and the sky had a lightness to it that told him the demons were gone.

Renn sat beside him, her head on her knees. She was shaking.

'You all right?' he mumbled.

She straightened up. She was very pale, and there was a Death Mark on her forehead that he hadn't noticed before. 'Mm,' she said. 'What about you?'

'Mm,' he lied. He shut his eyes, and visions whirled in his head. The Bat Mage on the brink of the chasm. The Oak Mage cowering before him: *him*, the ice bear, bent on killing . . .

'The Soul-Eaters are gone,' said Renn. 'They took the skinboats and fled. At least, I think they did.' She told him how she'd scrambled to safety just before the ice crashed down, and how, when the snow clouds had cleared, the Viper Mage and the Oak Mage were gone. So was the eagle owl, and the white wolves.

Torak opened his eyes. 'Where's Wolf?'

'He hasn't gone far.' She plucked at the fur of her mitten. 'He helped me find you. I couldn't see for the snow, then I heard him howling. It was horrible. I thought he was mourning you.'

'Sorry,' muttered Torak.

'The Viper Mage,' she said with a catch in her voice. 'She knows you're a spirit walker.'

'Yes.'

'So now they all know.'

'Yes.'

She stared across the ice and shivered. 'What did the Bat Mage mean, "The debt is repaid"?'

He told her how his father had once stopped the Bat Mage from killing herself.

'Ah,' said Renn. Then she put something heavy into his hand. 'Here. This is for you.'

It was Fa's blue slate knife.

'When she pushed me aside,' said Renn, 'she must have stuck it in my belt. I didn't find it till afterwards.'

Torak's fingers closed over the hilt. 'She wasn't wholly bad,' he murmured. 'Not all the way through.'

Renn stared at him. 'She was a Soul-Eater!'

'But she did her best to repair what she'd done.'

He thought about the souls of the Bat Mage, trapped in the black ice with the demons. And he thought about the small dark shadow he'd seen lifting off from Nef's shoulder just before she jumped. She'd sent her beloved bat away so that it wouldn't perish with her.

'It was you, wasn't it,' said Renn in a low voice. 'The ice

bear. You spirit walked in the ice bear.'

He met her eyes, but didn't say anything.

'Torak, you might never have got out! You might have been trapped in it for good!'

Painfully he raised himself on one elbow. 'There was nothing else I could do.'

'But – '

'You were the one who risked everything, who was prepared to give your life to keep the fire-opal buried. That was so brave . . . I can't imagine doing that.'

She scowled, and plucked more fur off her mitten. Then she shrugged. 'There was nothing else I could do.'

Silence between them. Renn took a handful of snow and scrubbed the Death Mark off her forehead. Then she set about cleaning the wounds on Torak's wrists.

'What if no ice bear had come?' she said. 'What would you have done then?'

'I'd have spirit walked in Thiazzi,' he said without hesitation, 'or Seshru. I wasn't going to let you die.'

She blinked. 'You saved my life. If you hadn't – '

'Wolf saved us,' said Torak. 'He hunted down the demons. He stopped me killing Thiazzi. He saved us all.'

As if they'd summoned him, Wolf came loping over the ice, slipped, righted himself with a deft twirl of his shortened tail, and skittered to a halt in a shower of snow. Then he pounced on Torak and gave him a thorough face-licking.

Suddenly Torak wanted to bury his head in Wolf's scruff and cry till his heart broke: for the Bat Mage, for himself, and in a tangled way, for his father.

'Here,' said Renn, holding out a scrap of seal meat.

He sniffed, took the meat, and tried to sit up, but the pain in his chest made him wince.

'Are you hurt?' said Renn.

'No, I just fell. Bruised my chest.'

'Do you want me to take a look?'

'No,' he said quickly, 'I'm fine.'

She looked puzzled. Then she gave another shrug, and went off to leave a piece of meat for the clan guardian. When she came back, she gave another piece to Wolf, keeping the last for herself.

They ate in silence, watching the sun sink towards the Sea. The wind had gone, and the ice river was asleep. The afternoon was still. Torak watched a solitary raven rowing across the vast white sky – and was suddenly sharply aware of how far they were from the Forest.

He glanced at Renn, and saw that she'd had the same thought.

She said, 'We've got no food, no blubber, and no skinboat. How in the name of the Spirit are we going to get home?'

That was how Fin-Kedinn and Inuktiluk found them when they came up from the south in their skinboats: Torak and Renn huddled together on the ice, with Wolf standing guard beside them.

FORTY

After that first stunned moment, Renn had given a strangled sob and thrown herself at her uncle. He'd stood on the ice and held her, and she'd breathed in his smell of reindeer hide and Forest.

He'd borrowed a skin-boat from the Sea-eagle Clan, he told her, and kept to the leads between the skerries and the coast until he'd reached the camp of his old friends, the White Foxes.

'And the rest of the clan?' she said, wiping her nose on her sleeve.

'Back in the Forest.'

'In the Forest? So you –'

'– came alone. I thought you needed me more.'

Now she lay curled in his skinboat, wonderfully warm beneath a sleeping-sack of white winter reindeer hide. Torak was in Inuktiluk's boat, and Wolf was keeping level with them on the ice.

After a while, she said to Fin-Kedinn's back, 'I still don't understand. The Soul-Eaters. Torak says they want to make all the clans the same; but we *are* the same. We all live by the same laws.'

Fin-Kedinn turned his head. 'Do we? Tell me. Since you've been in the Far North, what have you lived on? Seal?'

She nodded.

'And what do seals eat?'

She gasped. 'Fish! They're hunters. I never thought.'

Fin-Kedinn swerved to avoid a chunk of black ice. 'The Ice clans live as the ice bear does. They have to, or they wouldn't survive. Some Sea clans do too. In the Forest, it's different. That's what the Soul-Eaters want to change.'

Renn was thoughtful. 'They told Torak that they speak for the World Spirit. But –'

'Nobody speaks for the World Spirit,' said Fin-Kedinn.

After that, they didn't talk again.

It was an overcast day, and the sky was heavy with snow. Gulls wheeled overhead. A fox trotted over the ice, scented Wolf, and fled. Renn watched Fin-Kedinn's paddle slicing the water, and began to feel drowsy.

The spirit bees were back. She reached out to touch them, laughing as they brushed her fingers. Then they were gone, and she was alone on a high mountain, and red eyes were coming at her from the dark . . .

She cried out.

'Renn,' Fin-Kedinn said softly. 'Wake up.'

She screwed up her eyes against the light. 'I had a dream.'

The Raven Leader steadied the boat by sticking one end of his paddle in a cross-strap, then twisted round to look at her. 'The Soul-Eaters,' he said quietly. 'You got close to them, didn't you?'

She caught her breath. 'Before, they were just shadows, but now I've seen them. Thiazzi. Eostra. The Bat Mage . . . Seshru.'

They exchanged glances. Then Fin-Kedinn said, 'When we reach the Forest, tell me everything. Not here.'

She nodded, comforted. She didn't want to talk about it yet. She didn't want to bring it back.

Fin-Kedinn took up his paddle, and they moved off again.

Inuktiluk steered his boat alongside them. Torak sat behind him, and Renn tried to catch his eye, but he didn't see her. With his short hair and fringe he looked disturbingly unfamiliar.

He'd been very subdued since the battle on the ice. At first she'd thought it was because of what he must have witnessed in the caves. Now she wondered if there was something more; something he wasn't telling her.

A little later, she said to Fin-Kedinn, 'It isn't over, is it?'

Again, the Raven Leader turned to look at her. 'It's never over,' he said.

Wolf was troubled because Tall Tailless was troubled. So now, in the deep of the Dark, Wolf decided to brave the great white Den of the taillesses who smelt like foxes, and make sure that his pack-brother was safe.

Luckily, all the dogs had been taken off to hunt, and Wolf was able to crawl into the Den un-smelt. A tangle of scents hit his nose: reindeer, fish-dog, tailless, fox, lingonberry; but it wasn't hard to find his pack-brother among them.

Tall Tailless slept curled in his reindeer hide, back to

back with his pack-sister. He was frowning and twitching; Wolf sensed the depth of his trouble. Tall Tailless was trying to make a choice about something. He was frightened. He didn't know what to do. More than that, Wolf didn't understand.

For the present, though, his pack-brother seemed safe with the other taillesses, so Wolf turned his attention to the interesting smells in the Den. The bladder of a fish-dog was intriguing – until he bit it, and it spurted him with wet. Then he found a hanging ball of hide, and patted it with his paw. It gurgled. Looking inside, he was startled to see a small tailless cub gazing up at him. Wolf licked its nose, and it gave a happy squeal.

Next, Wolf went to sniff the fish-dog meat that hung from a branch in the middle of the Den. Around him the taillesses were whiffling in their sleeps. Stretching his neck, he took the meat delicately in his jaws, and lifted it down. He was just about to leave when he caught a gleam of eyes.

Of all the taillesses, the lead wolf of the raven pack was the one Wolf respected the most. Only this tailless slept as lightly and woke as often as a normal wolf. He was awake now.

Wolf dropped his ears and wagged his tail, hoping the lead wolf hadn't noticed the meat in his jaws.

The lead wolf had. He didn't growl. He didn't need to. He simply crossed his forepaws on his chest, and regarded Wolf.

Wolf understood, put down the meat, and left the Den.

Out in the Dark again, he found himself a place in the Bright Soft Cold, and curled up. Now he was sure that Tall Tailless was safe, at least for the moment, because the leader of the raven pack was watching over him.

The clearing in the Forest was aglow with firelight, and heady with the smells of woodsmoke and roasting meat. Fat sizzled on the fire – 'The first real fire,' said Renn, 'that we've had in half a moon!'

After the dim flicker of the White Fox blubber lamps, it was wonderful to be able to scorch themselves before a proper Raven long-fire. An entire pine tree lay ablaze in the middle of the clearing, its flames leaping higher than a man could jump, its embers hot enough to singe your eyebrows if you got too close.

Many people from other clans had joined the Ravens on the banks of the Axehandle, to celebrate the return of the travellers from the Far North, and the vanquishing of the demons. All had brought food. The Boars had brought a whole side of forest horse, which they'd baked in a pit, to much good-natured argument about whether spruce boughs or pine gave a better flavour. The Otters brought delicious sticky cakes of cranberry and reed flour, as well as a strange-tasting stew of dried bog-mushrooms and frogs' legs, which nobody much liked, except them. The Willows brought piles of salted herring, and several skins of their famously potent rowanberry brew; and the Ravens provided great coils of auroch-gut sausage stuffed with a delicious mix of blood, marrowfat, and pounded hazelnuts.

As the night wore on, everyone became flushed and voluble. Dogs raced about excitedly, and those trees that remained awake leaned closer to the fire, warming their branches and listening to the talk.

Torak hadn't drunk as much as the others, because he didn't want his souls to wander. He'd done his best to take part in the jokes and the hunting stories, but he knew he wasn't very good at it. Even before the Far North, he hadn't really belonged, and now it was harder. People kept looking at him and whispering.

'They say he was with the Soul-Eaters for *days*,' breathed a Boar girl to her mother.

'Sh!' hissed the mother. 'He'll hear!'

Torak pretended he hadn't. He sat on a log by the fire, watching Fin-Kedinn cutting chunks of horse and putting them in bowls; Renn wrinkling her nose as she fished a frog's leg from her bowl, and surreptitiously fed it to a waiting dog. He felt cut off from them. They didn't know what he was concealing; and he didn't know how to tell them.

Of everyone, only Inuktiluk had seemed to have some idea of what was tormenting him. As they'd stood together on the ice on their last morning in the Far North, the White Fox hunter had turned to him and said, 'You have good friends among the Ravens. Don't be in a hurry to leave them when you're back in the Forest.'

Torak had been startled. How much did Inuktiluk know, or guess?

The round face had creased in a smile tinged with sadness. 'It seems to me that you're like the black ice bear, who comes once in a thousand winters. You may never find peace. But you will make friends along the way. And many lands will know your name.' Then he'd put both fists to his chest and bowed. 'Hunt well, Torak. And may your guardian run with you.'

In the clearing, food had given way to singing and story-telling. Suddenly, Torak couldn't bear it any longer. When no-one was looking, he slipped off to his shelter.

Throwing himself onto the willow mat, he stared into

the fire at the mouth of the shelter, wondering what to do.

'What's the matter?' said Renn, making him jump.

She stood on the other side of the fire. He thought she looked as frightened as he felt. 'You're not thinking of leaving?' she said.

He hesitated. 'If I did, I'd tell you first.'

Picking up a stick, she poked the fire. 'What is it you're afraid of?'

'What do you mean?'

'There is something, I can feel it.'

He didn't reply.

'All right,' she said, throwing away the stick, 'I'll guess. In the caves, you had blood on your forehead. You said it was tainted. Was it – did they make you take part in the sacrifice?'

It was a good guess, though not the right one. But he decided to go along with it. 'Yes,' he said. 'The owl. The first of the nine hunters. I killed it.'

Renn's face drained of colour.

Torak's heart sank. How would she feel if she knew the rest?

But she recovered fast, and forced a shrug. 'After all, I fletch my arrows with owl feathers. Though I don't actually kill for them, I wait till I find a dead one, or someone brings me one.' She realized she was talking too fast, and sucked in her lips. 'We can make this right, Torak. There are ways of purifying you.'

'Renn –'

'You don't have to leave,' she said urgently. 'That won't solve anything.'

When he didn't answer, she persisted. 'At least wait till you've talked to Fin-Kedinn. Swear you won't leave till you've talked to Fin-Kedinn.'

Her face was so open and hopeful. He swore.

When she'd gone, he bowed his head to his knees. Suddenly he was back on ice, with his hands tied behind his back. Seshru was running her finger down his cheek. 'You will never be free of me,' she whispered in his ear. Then he felt Thiazzi's strong grip on his shoulders, holding him down, and Seshru was pricking his chest with a bone needle, rubbing in the stinking black stain made from the bones of murdered hunters and the blood of the Soul-Eaters.

'This mark,' she breathed, 'will be like the harpoon head beneath the skin of the seal. One twitch, and it will draw you, no matter how hard you struggle . . . '

Opening the neck of his jerkin, Torak put his finger to the crusted scab on his breastbone. He wondered if he could ever bring himself to show the Ravens – the Ravens who trusted him – this mark on his chest. The three-pronged fork for snaring souls.

The mark of the Soul-Eater.

FORTY-ONE

Fin-Kedinn woke Torak before dawn, and told him to come and help check the fishing-lines. When Torak emerged from the shelter, he found Renn waiting with her uncle. He knew from their faces that she'd told the Raven Leader of their talk the night before.

Nothing was said as they made their way through the sleeping Forest. Fog lay thick in the valley; along the riverbank, the bare branches of the alders made a delicate purple haze. Torak glimpsed Wolf, weaving between the trees. The only sound was the Axehandle, which was bubbling noisily under the ice that still crusted its banks.

They reached the flat, boggy part of the valley where the river broadened into pools. It was across these pools that wovenbark ropes had been strung, with baited lines trailing in the water.

The catch was good, and soon they had small piles of perch and bream. Fin-Kedinn thanked the spirits of the prey, then stuck a fish head in the fork of a spruce for the clan guardian. After that they woke up a fire beneath a battered old oak, and began the finger-numbing work of gutting, and scraping off the scales. As each fish was cleaned, they threaded it by the gills on a line which they hung from the oak, well out of Wolf's reach.

A breeze sprang up. The oak was slumbering too deeply to feel it, but the beech trees sighed, and the alders rattled their tiny black cones, chattering even in their sleep.

A weasel in its white winter coat rose on its hind legs to snuff the wind. Wolf pricked his ears, and shot off in pursuit.

Fin-Kedinn watched him go. Then he turned to Torak and said, 'I told you once of the great fire that broke up the Soul-Eaters.'

Renn froze with a fish in one hand.

Torak stiffened. 'I remember,' he said carefully.

Scrape, scrape, scrape went Fin-Kedinn's antler knife, scattering fish-scales. 'Your father caused it,' he said.

Torak's mouth went dry.

'The fire-opal,' said the Raven Leader, 'was the heart of Soul-Eater power. Your father took it. He shattered it into pieces.'

Renn put down the fish. 'He *shattered* the fire-opal?'

'Then he started the great fire,' said Fin-Kedinn. He paused. 'One Soul-Eater was killed in that fire. Killed trying to reach a fragment of the fire-opal.'

'The seventh Soul-Eater,' murmured Renn. 'I wondered about that.'

Torak stared into the red heart of the embers, and thought of his father. His father, who had started the great fire. 'So he didn't just run away,' he said.

'Oh, he was no coward,' said the Raven Leader. 'He was

clever, too. He made it appear that he and his mate had also perished in the fire. Then they fled to the Deep Forest.'

'The Deep Forest,' said Torak. The previous summer, he'd reached its borders. He remembered the dense shadows beneath the secretive, watchful trees. 'They should have stayed there. They would have been safe.'

With his knife, Fin-Kedinn woke up the fire. In the flaring light, his features seemed carved in granite. 'They should have stayed with your mother's people, yes. Leaving was their undoing.' He looked at Torak. 'But they were betrayed. Your father's brother learned that they still lived. From then on, they were hunted. And your mother – ,' he drew a sharp breath, 'your mother wouldn't endanger her people by staying. So they left.' Again he stirred the embers. 'The following summer, you were born.'

'And she died,' said Torak.

The Raven Leader did not reply. He was gazing into the past, his blue eyes bright with pain.

Torak turned his head and stared at the birch trees that stretched their naked branches to the cold sky.

Wolf returned, with a hare's front leg dangling from his jaws. He splashed into the shallows, tossed the hare's leg high, then made a spectacular leap and caught it in mid-air.

'The fire-opal,' said Renn. 'You said it was broken into pieces.'

Fin-Kedinn fed more wood to the fire. 'Tell me, Renn. When you held it in your hand, how big was it?'

Torak twitched in irritation. What did that matter now?

'About the size of a duck's egg,' said Renn. She caught her breath. 'It was only a fragment!'

The Raven Leader nodded. 'That from which it came was almost the size of your fist.'

There was a silence. Wolf lay on the bank, quietly

demolishing the hare's leg. Even the alders had stopped talking.

Torak said, 'So the stone that went down with the Bat Mage was only one piece. There may be more?'

'There are more,' said the Raven Leader. 'Think, Torak. There was at least one other that we know of. The Soul-Eater across the Sea must have had one, to have made the demon bear that killed your father.'

Torak struggled to take it in. 'How many in all?'

'I don't know,' said Fin-Kedinn.

'Three,' said Renn in a low voice. 'There were three.'

They stared at her.

'Three red eyes in the dark. I saw them in my dream. One taken by the Sea. One by the Bat Mage. And one . . . ' she broke off. 'Where's the third?'

Fin-Kedinn spread his hands. 'We don't know.'

Torak raised his head and stared into the gnarled branches above him. High up – so high that he hadn't spotted it till now – he saw a ball of mistletoe. The oak wasn't asleep after all, he realized. There above him was its small, green, ever-wakeful heart. He wondered what secrets it knew. Did it know about him? Did it see the mark on his chest?

Slipping his hand inside his parka, he touched the scab. This mark by itself endangered those around him, just as Renn's lightning tattoos protected her. And somewhere in the Forest, or in the Far North, or beyond the Sea, the three remaining Soul-Eaters were plotting: to find the final fragment of the fire-opal; to find him, Torak the spirit walker . . .

'Renn,' said Fin-Kedinn, making him start. 'Go back to camp, and tell Saeunn about the fire-opal.'

'But I want to stay here,' protested Renn.

'Go. I need to talk to Torak alone.'

Renn sighed, and got to her feet.

Suddenly, Torak felt that it was terribly important to speak to her before she left. 'Renn,' he said, drawing her aside and talking under his breath so that Fin-Kedinn wouldn't hear, 'I need you to know something.'

'What?' she said crossly.

'There are things I haven't told you yet. But I will.'

To his surprise, she didn't roll her eyes impatiently. She fiddled with her quiver-strap and scowled. 'Oh well,' she muttered, 'everybody has secrets. Even me.' Then she brightened up. 'Does this mean you're staying?'

'I don't know.'

'You should stay. Stay with us.'

'I don't fit in.'

She snorted. 'I know that! But you don't fit in anywhere else either, do you?' Then she flashed him her sharp-toothed grin, hoisted her bow on her shoulder, and walked off through the trees.

For a while after she'd gone, neither Torak nor Fin-Kedinn spoke. The Raven Leader skewered a big bream on a stick, and set it to roast in the embers, while Torak sat brooding.

'Eat,' said Fin-Kedinn at last.

'I'm not hungry.'

'Eat.'

Torak ate – and discovered that he was ravenous. He'd finished off most of the bream before he realized that the Raven Leader had eaten little.

It was the first time they'd been alone together since Fin-Kedinn had rescued them on the ice. Torak wiped his mouth on his sleeve, and said, 'Are you angry with me?'

Fin-Kedinn cleaned his knife in the snow. 'Why should I be angry?'

'Because I went off to seek Wolf without your leave.'

'You don't need my leave. You're nearly a man.' He paused, then added drily, 'You'd better start acting like one.'

That stung. 'What was I supposed to do, let the Soul-Eaters sacrifice Wolf? Let them overrun the Forest with demons?'

'You should have come back and sought my help.'

Torak opened his mouth to protest, but the Raven Leader silenced him with a glance. 'You survived by luck, Torak. And because the World Spirit wanted you to. But luck runs out. The World Spirit turns its favour elsewhere. You need to stay with the clan.'

Torak remained stubbornly silent.

'Tell me,' said Fin-Kedinn. 'What tracks can you see around you?'

Torak stared at him. 'What?'

'You heard me.'

Puzzled, Torak told him. The deep, dragging hoof-prints of an auroch. A few raggedly bitten-off twigs left by a red deer. A cluster of barely visible hollows, each with a tiny pile of frozen droppings at the bottom, where some willow grouse had huddled together for company.

Fin-Kedinn nodded. 'Your father taught you well. He taught you tracking because it teaches you to listen: to stay open to what the Forest is telling you. But when he was a young man, he never listened to anyone. He was convinced he was right. Tracking, listening – that was your mother's gift.' He paused. 'Maybe by teaching you tracking, your father was trying to prevent you making the same mistakes he did.'

Torak thought about that.

'If you left now,' Fin-Kedinn went on, 'it would be you against three Mages of enormous power. You wouldn't stand a chance.'

On the riverbank, Wolf had finished the hare's leg, and now stood wagging his tail at his name-soul in the water.

Fin-Kedinn watched him. 'A young wolf,' he said, 'can be foolhardy. He may think he can bring down an elk on his own, but he forgets that it only takes one kick to kill him. And yet if he has the sense to wait, he'll live to bring down many.' He turned to Torak. 'I'm not telling you to stay. I'm asking you.'

Torak swallowed. Fin-Kedinn had never asked him anything before.

Leaning towards him, the Raven Leader spoke with unaccustomed gentleness. 'Something's troubling you. Tell me what it is.'

Torak wanted to. But he couldn't. At last he mumbled, 'The knife that you made for me. I lost it. I'm sorry.'

Fin-Kedinn read the evasion in his face, and sighed. 'I'll make you another,' he said. With the aid of his staff, he rose to his feet. 'Watch the catch. I'm going up the hill to check the snares. And Torak . . . Whatever it is that's wrong, you're better off here, with people who – with your friends.'

When he'd gone, Torak remained by the fire. He could feel the Soul-Eater tattoo burning through his parka. *You will never be free of us . . .*

In the shallows, Wolf had found fresh prey: the battered carcass of a roe buck which had drowned further upstream, and was now drifting slowly past. He pounced on it, and it sank beneath his weight, taking him with it. He surfaced, scrambled onto the bank, shook the water from his fur, and tried again. Again the buck sank. After the third attempt,

Wolf sat down, whining softly. A raven alighted on the carcass, and laughed at him.

Maybe the Viper Mage was right, thought Torak. Maybe I will never be free of her.

He sat up straighter. But *she* will never be free of *me*.

You know who I am now, he told the Soul-Eaters silently, but *I* know *you*, too. I know who I'm fighting. And I'm not alone. I can tell the Ravens what's happened. I will tell them. Not today, but soon. I can trust them. Fin-Kedinn will know what to do.

The breeze loosed a flurry of snow from the branches overhead, and at the same moment, the sun came out, and turned the falling flakes to tiny slivers of rainbow.

Wolf came loping up the bank, bringing the fresh, cold smell of the river. They touched muzzles. On impulse, Torak pulled down the neck of his parka, and showed Wolf the Soul-Eater tattoo. Wolf gave it a sniff and a lick, then wandered off to snuffle up the fish-scales around the fire.

He doesn't mind, thought Torak in surprise.

With a new sense of hope, he glanced about him. Signs of spring were everywhere. Fluffy silver catkins bursting out on the willow trees. Sunlight gleaming on the sharp buds of beechlings pushing through the snow around their parents.

He remembered the offering he'd made on the night that Wolf was taken. He'd asked the Forest to watch over Wolf. It had heard him. Maybe now it would watch over him, too.

Around mid-afternoon, Fin-Kedinn returned, carrying three woodgrouse and a hare. He didn't look at Torak, but Torak could see the tension in his face as he went to the oak tree and began untying the lines of fish.

Torak stood up and started to help. 'I want to stay,' he said.

Fin-Kedinn's blue eyes glinted. He pressed his lips together in a smile. 'Good,' he said. 'That's good.' Then he put his hand on Torak's shoulder and gave it a shake, and together they started back for camp.

Soul Eater is the third book in the *Chronicles of Ancient Darkness*, which tell the story of Torak's adventures in the Forest and beyond, and of his quest to vanquish the Soul-Eaters. *Wolf Brother* is the first book, and *Spirit Walker* is the second. The fourth book, *Outcast*, will be published in 2007. There will be six books in all.

A WORD ABOUT WOLF

At the start of *Wolf Brother*, Wolf was three moons old. By the beginning of *Soul Eater*, he's twenty moons old, and he looks like a full-grown wolf – but he isn't, not in terms of experience.

When he ran with the pack on the Mountain of the World Spirit, he picked up some of the hunting skills he'll need if he's to survive, but he's still got a lot to learn.

And although he'll soon be physically capable of fathering cubs, he won't be doing that for a while. Many wolves are three years old or more before they find a mate and start a family. Until then, they often act as baby-sitters for their younger brothers and sisters, looking after them while the rest of the pack is out hunting.

Because Wolf's chest is narrow, and his legs are long and slender, he can plough through deep snow quickly and easily. His big paws act like snowshoes, letting him run over the top of crusted snow, where the sharp hooves of deer might sink right in.

Because it's winter, Wolf's fur is much thicker than it was in *Spirit Walker*, which makes him look even bigger. His pelt has two layers: the short, fluffy **underfur**, which traps air to insulate him from the cold; and the long, coarse **guard hairs** which protect him from rain, snow, and scratchy juniper bushes. It's because of his superb winter pelt that Wolf can brave the Far North without feeling the cold like Torak and Renn.

Unlike them, Wolf has incredible endurance. Even his walk is twice as fast as Torak's (unless he's deliberately slowing down to let Torak keep up), but most of the time he prefers to trot: a beautiful, fluid, floating gait which he can keep up for hours. And his run, of course, is *much* faster than Torak's.

Some of Wolf's senses are much better than Torak's, while others are about the same. We don't know very much about a wolf's sense of **taste**, although we know that their tongues can sense the same kinds of taste as us: salty, sweet, bitter and sour. But we don't know how meat tastes to Wolf; or water, or blood.

It's thought that wolves' **eyesight** is roughly similar to ours, although they're better at distinguishing shades of grey, and seeing in the dark. They also seem to be better at spotting movement – which is useful for hunting in the Forest – and it's thought that they don't see in colour, at least, not as well as we do.

Wolf's sense of **hearing** is better than Torak's. He can

hear sounds that are too high for Torak to catch, and his large ears help him pick up very faint sounds. This partly explains why not even Torak will ever be able to grasp all the subtleties of wolf talk, or express himself as well as a real wolf: because he can't make or hear the highest yips and whines, as Wolf can.

Wolf's sense of **smell** is *much* more sensitive than Torak's. It's not known for sure exactly *how* much, but judging from the number of smell receptors in his long nose, it's been estimated at between a thousand to a million times better.

Like all wolves, Wolf communicates by means of **wolf talk**: a highly complex combination of sounds, movements, and smells. Torak knows more about this than we do, but wolf scientists and observers are learning more all the time.

When Wolf uses his **voice**, he doesn't only howl. He can make all sorts of other noises, including yips, grunts, wheezes, whines, growls, and snarls.

He also uses **movement**: from big gestures like body-slamming or waggling his paws, to more subtle twitches of his eyes, muzzle, ears, hackles, paws, body, tail, and fur.

He uses his **scent** to communicate, too, by spilling it, or rubbing against a marking-point (or Torak) – in ways which not even Torak fully understands.

And of course, when Wolf wants to say something, he may not use only *one* such sound, movement or smell, but a complex **combination** of several, which changes depending on who he's

talking to, and the mood he's in. Thus if he wants to smile at Torak, he might bow his head and flatten his ears, wrinkling his muzzle and wagging his tail, while whining, nose-pushing, and giving Torak's face and hands tickly little nibbles. All just to say hello!

Michelle Paver
2006

AUTHOR'S NOTE

Torak's world is the world of six thousand years ago: after the Ice Age, but before the spread of farming to his part of the world, when north-west Europe was one vast Forest.

The people of Torak's world looked just like you or me, but their way of life was very different. They didn't have writing, metals or the wheel, but they didn't need them. They were superb survivors. They knew all about the animals, trees, plants and rocks of the Forest. When they wanted something, they knew where to find it, or how to make it.

They lived in small clans, and many of them moved around a lot: some staying in camp for just a few days, like the Wolf Clan; others staying for a whole moon or a season, like the Raven and Willow Clans; while others stayed put all year round, like the Seal Clan. Thus some of the clans have moved since the events in *Spirit Walker*, as you'll see from the amended map.

When I was researching *Soul Eater*, I spent time in a snowy forest in the foothills of the Carpathian mountains in Romania. I was lucky enough to see the tracks of wolves, boar, deer, lynx, badger and many more (although rather to my relief, the bears were still hibernating). I also observed ravens at a carcass, and from my guide I learned how to fake a kill in order to attract these most intelligent of birds.

To learn about husky-sledding, I met some huskies in Finland, and then again in Greenland, where they took me on several exhilarating (and freezing) races across the ice.

For insights into the lives of the Ice clans, I studied the traditional skills of the Inuit of Greenland and northern Canada: their hunting, their snow-houses, and their superb hide clothes. It was in Greenland that I experienced at first hand the might of wind and ice, and – on one memorable solo hike – the terror of glimpsing a polar bear in the distance.

To get closer to polar bears, I went to Churchill in northern Canada, where I watched them at rest and at play, by day and night. It's a privilege to come face to face with a wild polar bear, and to meet the gaze of the creature whom the Inuit of north-west Greenland call *pisugtooq*, the Great Wanderer. I think I'll always be haunted by the look in those fearsome, yet strangely innocent, dark eyes.

I want to thank Christoph Promberger of the Carpathian Large Carnivore Project in Transylvania for sharing some of his knowledge of tracking, wolves, and ravens; the people of Churchill, Manitoba, for helping me get closer to wild polar bears; the people of east Greenland for their hospitality, openness and good humour; the UK Wolf Conservation Trust for some amazing times with some wonderful wolves; and Mr Derrick Coyle, the Yeoman Ravenmaster of the Tower of London, for sharing his extensive knowledge of some very special ravens. As always, I want to thank my agent, Peter Cox, for his unfailing enthusiasm and support; and my wonderful editor and publisher, Fiona Kennedy, for her imagination, commitment and understanding.

Michelle Paver
2006

Here is a preview of the first chapter of *Outcast*,
book four of *Chronicles of Ancient Darkness*.

oNE

The viper glided down the riverbank and placed its sleek head on the water, and Torak stopped a few paces away to let it drink.

His arms ached from carrying the red deer antlers, so he set them aside and crouched in the bracken to watch. Snakes are wise, and know many secrets. Maybe this one would help him deal with his.

The viper drank with unhurried sips. Raising its head, it regarded Torak, flicking out its tongue to taste his scent. Then it coiled neatly back on itself and vanished into the ferns.

It had given him no sign.

But you don't *need* a sign, he told himself wearily. You know what to do. Just tell them. Soon as you get back to camp. Just say, 'Renn. Fin-Kedinn. Two moons ago, something happened. They held me down, they put a mark on my chest. And now . . .'

No. That wasn't any good. He could picture Renn's face. 'I'm your best friend – and you've been lying to me for *two whole moons!*'

He put his head in his hands.

After a while he heard rustling, and glanced up to see a reindeer on the opposite bank. It was standing on three legs, furiously scratching its budding antlers with one hind hoof. Sensing that Torak wasn't hunting, it went on scratching. The antlers were bleeding: the itch must be so bad that the only relief was to make them hurt.

That's what I should do, thought Torak. Cut it out. Make it hurt. In secret. Then no-one need ever know.

The trouble was, even if he could bring himself to do it, it wouldn't work. To get rid of the tattoo, he'd have to perform the proper rite. He'd learnt that from Renn, whom he'd approached in a roundabout way, using the zigzag tattoos on her wrists as an excuse.

'If you don't do the rite,' she'd told him, 'the marks just come back.'

'*They come back?*' Torak had been horrified.

'Of course. You can't see them, they're deep in the marrow. But they're still there.'

So that was the end of that, unless he could get her to tell him about the rite without revealing why he needed to know.

The reindeer gave an irritable shake and trotted off into the Forest; and Torak picked up the antlers and started back for camp. They were a lucky find, big enough for everyone in the clan to get a piece, and perfect for making fish-hooks and hammers for knapping flint. Fin-Kedinn would be pleased. Torak tried to fix his mind on that.

It didn't work. Until now, he hadn't understood how much a secret can set you apart. He thought about it all the time, even when he was hunting with Renn and Wolf.

It was early in the Moon of the Salmon Run, and a sharp east wind carried a strong smell of fish. As Torak made his way beneath the pines, his boots crunched on flakes of bark scattered by woodpeckers. To his left, the Green River chattered after its long imprisonment under the ice, while to his right, a rockface rose towards Broken Ridge. In places it was scarred, where the clans had hacked out the red slate which brings hunting luck. He heard the clink of stone on stone. Someone was quarrying.

That should be me, Torak told himself. I should be making a new axe. I should be doing things. 'This can't go on,' he said out loud.

'You're right,' said a voice. 'It can't.'

They were crouching on a ledge ten paces above him: four boys and two girls, glaring down. The Boar Clan wore their brown hair cut to shoulder length, with a fringe; tusks at their necks, stiff hide mantles across their shoulders. The Willows had wovenbark strips sewn in spirals on their jerkins, and three black leaves tattooed on their brows in a permanent frown. All were older than Torak. The boys had wispy beards, and beneath the girls' clan-tattoos, a short red bar showed that they'd had their first moon bleed.

They'd been quarrying: Torak saw stone dust on their buckskins. Just ahead of him, he spotted a tree-trunk ladder notched with footholds, which they'd propped against the rockface, to climb up to the ledge. But they were no longer interested in slate.

Torak stared back, hoping he didn't look scared. 'What do you want?'

Aki, the Boar Clan Leader's son, jerked his head at the antlers. 'Those are mine. Put them down.'

'No they're not,' said Torak. 'I found them.' To remind them he had weapons, he hoisted his bow on his shoulder and touched the blue slate knife at his hip.

Aki wasn't impressed. 'They're mine.'

'Which means *you* stole them,' said a Willow girl.

'If that was true,' Torak told Aki, 'you'd have put your mark on them and I'd have left them alone.'

'I did. On the base. You rubbed it off.'

'Of course I didn't,' said Torak in disgust.

Then he saw what he should have seen before: a smudge

of earthblood at the base of one antler, where a boar tusk had been drawn on. His ears burned. 'I didn't see it. And I didn't rub it off.'

'Then put them down and get out of here,' said a boy called Raut, who'd always struck Torak as fairer than most. Unlike Aki, who was spoiling for a fight.

Torak didn't feel like giving him one. 'All right,' he said briskly, 'I made a mistake. Didn't see the mark. They're yours.'

'What makes you think it's that easy?' said Aki.

Torak sighed. He'd come across Aki before. A bully: unsure if he was a leader, and desperate to prove it with his fists.

'You think you're special,' sneered Aki. 'Because Fin-Kedinn took you in, and you can talk to wolves and you're a spirit walker.' He raked his fingernails over the scant hairs on his chin, as if checking they were still there. 'Truth is, you only live with the Ravens because your own clan's never come near you. And Fin-Kedinn doesn't trust you enough to make you his foster-son.'

Torak set his teeth.

Covertly, he looked about. The river was too cold to swim; besides, they had dugouts on the bank. That meant there was no point running upriver, either – or back the way he'd come, he'd be trapped in the fork where the Green River merged with the Axehandle. And no help within reach. Renn was at the Raven camp on the north bank, half a daywalk to the east; and Wolf had gone hunting in the night.

He set down the antlers. 'I said you can have them,' he told Aki. He started up the trail.

'Coward,' taunted Aki.

Torak ignored him.

A stone struck his temple. He turned on them. 'Now who's the coward? What's brave about six against one?'

Beneath his fringe, Aki's square face darkened. 'Then let's make it even: just you and me.' He whipped off his jerkin to reveal a meaty chest covered in reddish fuzz.

Torak froze.

'What's the matter?' sniggered a Boar girl. 'Scared?'

'No,' said Torak. But he was. He'd forgotten the Boar Clan custom of stripping to the waist for a fight. He couldn't do that, or they'd see the mark.

'Get ready to fight,' snarled Aki, making his way down the ladder.

'No,' said Torak.

Another stone whistled towards him. He caught it and threw it back, and the Boar girl yelped and clutched a bleeding shin.

Aki had nearly reached the bottom of the ladder, his friends swarming after him like ants on a honey trail.

Grabbing one of the antlers, Torak ducked behind a pine, hooked the tines in the nearest branch, and swung into the tree.

'We've got him!' shouted Aki.

No you haven't, thought Torak. He'd chosen this tree because it grew nearest the rockface, and now he crawled along a branch and onto the ledge they'd just left. It was littered with quartz saws and grindstones, a small fire, and an elkhide pail of pine-pitch, planted in hot ash to keep it runny. Above him the slope was less steep, with enough juniper scrub to make it climbable.

Throwing stones and dodging theirs, he raced to the ladder and gave it a push. It didn't budge. It was lashed to the ledge with rawhide ropes, no time to cut it free. He did the only thing he could to stop them coming after him. He seized the pail and emptied it down the tree-trunk.

There was an outraged roar – and Torak dropped the pail in astonishment. Aki was faster than he looked, he'd nearly reached the ledge. Without meaning to, Torak had just dumped hot pine-pitch all over him.

Bellowing like a stuck boar, Aki slid down the ladder.

Torak clawed at juniper bushes and hauled himself towards the ridge.

He ran north-east through the trees, and their cries faded. He *hated* running away. But better be called a coward than get found out.

After a while the slope became gentler, and he was able to skitter down it and make his way to the river again, keeping off the clan trail and sticking to the wolf trails which he could find almost without thinking. Once he reached the ford, he could get across and double back to the Raven camp. There'd be trouble, but Fin-Kedinn would be on his side.

In a willow thicket on the bank, he came to a halt, the breath sawing in his chest. Around him the trees were still waking from their long winter sleep. Bees bumped about among the catkins, and a squirrel dozed in a patch of sunlight, its tail wrapped around the branch. In the shallows, a jay was taking a bath. No-one was coming. The Forest would have warned him.

Shaky with relief, he leaned against a tree-trunk.

His hand moved to the neck of his jerkin and touched the tattoo on his breastbone. The Viper Mage hissed in his mind. *'This mark will be like the harpoon head beneath the skin of the seal. One twitch, and it will draw you, no matter how hard you struggle. For now you are one of us . . .'*

'I'm not one of you,' muttered Torak. 'I'm *not!*'

But as he'd lain awake through the storm-tossed nights of winter, he'd felt the mark burning his skin. He dreaded to think what evil it might do. What evil it might make *him* do.

Somewhere to the south, Wolf howled. He'd caught a hare, and was singing his happiness to the Forest, his pack-brother and anyone else who was listening.

Hearing Wolf's voice lightened Torak's spirits. Wolf didn't seem to mind his tattoo. Nor did the Forest. It knew, but it hadn't cast him out.

The jay flew up, scattering droplets, and for a moment, Torak followed its flight. Then he pushed himself off the tree and began to run. He left the thicket – and Aki head-butted him in the chest and sent him sprawling.

The Boar Clan boy was almost unrecognisable. His reddened eyes glared from a skull that was black and slimy with pitch, and he stank of pine-blood and rage. 'You made a fool of me!' he shouted. 'In front of everyone, you made a fool of me!'

Struggling to his feet, Torak scrambled backwards. 'I didn't do it on purpose! I didn't know you were there!'

'Liar!' Aki swung his axe at Torak's shins.

Torak jumped out of the way, then side-stepped and kicked Aki's axe-hand. Aki dropped the axe. He drew his knife. Torak drew his too, and they circled one another.

Torak's heart hammered against his ribs as he tried to remember every fighting trick Fa and Fin-Kedinn had taught him.

Without warning, Aki lunged. He mistimed it by a heartbeat. Torak kicked him in the belly, then punched him hard in the throat. Choking, Aki went down, grabbing at

Torak's jerkin. The throat-lacing ripped – and Aki saw it. The mark on Torak's chest.

Time stretched.

Aki released him and staggered back.

Torak's legs wouldn't move.

Aki glanced from the mark to Torak's face. Beneath the pine-pitch, his features were blank with shock.

He recovered fast. He pointed one finger at Torak, aiming straight between the eyes. He made a sideways cut of the hand: a sign Torak had never seen before.

Then he turned and ran.

丰丰

Aki must have regained his dugout and paddled faster than a leaping salmon, because when Torak finally reached the Raven camp by mid-afternoon, the Boar Clan boy had got there first. Torak knew at once from the stillness of the Ravens as he ran into the clearing.

The only sounds were the creak of the drying racks and the murmur of the river. Thull and his mate Luta, whose shelter Torak shared, stared at him as if he were a stranger. Only their son Dari, seven summers old and Torak's devoted follower, rushed to greet him. He was yanked back by his father.

Renn burst from a reindeer-hide shelter, her dark-red hair flying, her face flushed with indignation. 'Torak, at last! It's all a mistake! I've told them it isn't true!'

Behind her, Aki emerged with his father, the Boar Clan Leader, and Fin-Kedinn. The Raven Leader's face was grim, and he leaned on his staff as he crossed the clearing; but when he spoke it was in the same quiet voice as always. 'I've vouched for you, Torak. I've told them this can't be so.'

They had such such faith in him. He couldn't bear it.

The Boar Clan Leader glared at Fin-Kedinn. 'Are you calling my son a liar?' He was a bigger version of Aki: the same square face and ready fists.

'Not a liar,' replied Fin-Kedinn. 'Simply mistaken.'

The Boar Clan Leader bridled.

'I've told you,' said Fin-Kedinn, 'the boy is no Soul-Eater. And he can prove it. Torak, take off your jerkin.'

'What?' Renn turned on her uncle. 'But you can't even *think –* '

Fin-Kedinn silenced her with a glance. Then to Torak, 'Quickly now, let's clear this up.'

Torak looked at the faces around him. These people had taken him in when his father was killed. He'd lived with them for nearly two summers. They had begun to accept him. Now he was going to end that.

Slowly he took off his quiver and bow and laid them on the ground. He untied his belt. There was a ringing in his ears. His fingers belonged to someone else.

He said a prayer to the Forest – and pulled his jerkin over his head.

Renn's mouth opened, but no sound came.

Fin-Kedinn's hand tightened on his staff.

'I told you,' cried Aki. 'The three-pronged fork, I *told* you! He's a Soul-Eater!'

CHRONICLES OF ANCIENT DARKNESS

Six adventures. One quest.

There are six books in the Chronicles of Ancient Darkness, and all feature Torak, Renn and Wolf.

In *Wolf Brother*, Torak finds himself alone in the Forest, when his father is killed by a demon-haunted bear. In his attempts to vanquish the bear, Torak makes two friends who will change his life: Renn, the girl from the Raven Clan, and Wolf, the orphaned wolf cub who will soon become Torak's beloved pack-brother.

In *Spirit Walker*, a horrible sickness attacks the clans, and Torak has to find the cure. His search takes him across the Sea to the islands of the Seal Clan, where he encounters demons and killer whales, and gets closer to uncovering the truth behind his father's death, as well as learning of his own undreamed-of powers.

In *Soul Eater* Wolf is taken by the enemy. To rescue him, Torak and Renn must journey to the Far North in the depths of winter, where they brave blizzards and ice bears, and venture into the very stronghold of the Soul-Eaters.

Outcast takes place on and around Lake Axehead. Torak is cast out of the clans, and has to survive on his own, separated from Renn, and even from Wolf.

In *Oath Breaker* one of Torak's closest friends is killed, and he tracks the murderer into the mysterious heart of the Deep Forest. Here the clans are at war, and punish any outsider venturing in. In the Deep Forest, Torak learns more about his mother, and about just why he is the spirit walker.

A legend for all time.

E FAR NORTH ↑

FOX, NARWAL
AN, WALRUS CLANS

RAVINE

MOUNTAIN OF
THE WORLD
SPIRIT

ICE
VER

ICE
CLIFFS

SCREE SLOPES
CAVE

MOUNTAIN
HARE CLAN

ER'S
EY

ICE
RIVER

AKE
HEAD
AN

SWAN
CLAN

THE HIGH MOUNTAINS

THE
DEEP
FOREST

AUROCH, LYNX,
FOREST HORSE,
RED DEER,
BAT CLANS

LS

DEN

CH ROCK

TWATER

ROWAN
CLAN

MOORS